THE TOWER AND
THE EMERALD

Books by Moyra Caldecott

FICTION
Guardians of the Tall Stones:
The Tall Stones
The Temple of the Sun
Shadow on the Stones
The Silver Vortex

Weapons of the Wolfhound
The Eye of Callanish
The Lily and the Bull
The Tower and the Emerald
Etheldreda
Child of the Dark Star
Hatshepsut: Daughter of Amun
Akhenaten: Son of the Sun
Tutankhamun and the Daughter of Ra
The Ghost of Akhenaten
The Winged Man
The Waters of Sul
The Green Lady and the King of Shadows

NON-FICTION/MYTHS AND LEGENDS
Crystal Legends
Three Celtic Tales
Women in Celtic Myth
Myths of the Sacred Tree
Mythical Journeys: Legendary Quests

CHILDREN'S STORIES
Adventures by Leaflight

THE TOWER AND THE EMERALD

a novel by

Moyra Caldecott

Published by
Bladud Books

First published in Great Britain in 1985 by Hamlyn Paperbacks

Published in digital formats in 2000 by Mushroom eBooks
www.mushroom-ebooks.com

This edition published in 2005 by
Bladud Books, an imprint of
Mushroom Publishing, Bath, UK

www.mushroompublishing.com

ISBN 1-84319-271-3

Printed and Bound by
Lightning Source

Contents

1

An old spell undone

The hunting party of Prince Caradawc, son of Goreu, drew together at the sound of the calling horn. What had gone wrong? Princess Viviane, far to the rear, her mind only half on the hunt, heard the thin horn-silver sound like bird call through the thick green of the forest. It was not the sound of victory, the long low note of the kill, it was a brief agitated trill.

'The hounds must have lost the scent,' she thought. What would the Lord Goreu say from his great furred chair, looking at his slender son. 'Are you fit for a woman if you can't provide her meat?' Caradawc would flush, always a shade too timid when outfaced by his mighty father, and she would have to endure the old man's arm about her, the smell of his breath on her face, and the innuendoes that if young men were not ready for their responsibilities, older men would have to take them on. She dreaded being alone with her future father-in-law, Goreu the Great, Goreu the Mighty Lecher. How beautiful his son was in comparison: hair nut-brown touched with sun-gold: eyes sea-blue and clear as the sky, and in form – the finest of any young man she had ever seen. She thought she loved him, though in fact she knew nothing of him but his beauty.

The horn called again and she followed it, her white mare stepping unhurriedly through the bracken, the rider stooping gracefully under the overhanging branches of oak, ash and thorn. Sparkles of sunlight flickered like emeralds in the crown of the forest, half dazzling her. She felt warm, relaxed, happy. Her own home was far away but for the first time since she left it she felt no homesickness. This would be her new home, this forest of shimmering gold and green.

She heard voices calling her and increased her pace. She

came upon the others gathered in a clearing, Caradawc standing on his stirrups to look back along the way they had ridden, his face anxious. It lightened at once when he saw her, but he said nothing. She joined the circle around him quietly and waited with the rest for what he would say.

The hounds were behaving strangely. It was as though when they had lost the scent, they also lost interest in the hunt. Many of them lay sleeping – only Cuall, Caradawc's favourite, was still alert and he sat on his haunches, his ears cocked, his eyes searching the undergrowth surrounding them. From time to time he gave a low growl or a faint but unmistakable whine. Viviane, too, could sense something, but she could not define it. She shivered slightly though she was not cold, and drew instinctively closer to Caradawc. He explained that they would rest awhile and then fan out to try to start up some more game.

'The dogs are tired,' he added calmly, but she noticed a puzzled frown. He had never known them behave in quite this way. He sprang down from his chestnut and reached up his arms to her – and she slid from her silver-white mare into his arms. He held her lightly – like a stranger. When would he take her as his woman with confidence and strength? Her body stirred to his, but always there was this barrier, this hesitation on his part . . . this uncertainty. Was it the giant shadow of his father that inhibited him . . . the knowledge that his father's way with women was wrong yet he himself had not yet found a way of his own?

He let her go almost at once and moved away. The servants served barley bread and ale and the hunters sat on fallen logs and lichen-covered rocks, hungry and glad of the rest. A stream as clear and cold as melted ice fell over mossy boulders and she stooped to drink, parting the fern fronds. It seemed to her that as she did so she heard fine voices and faint music, but when she lifted her head she could hear nothing but the sound of water falling over the rocks and the murmur of her friends as they talked quietly of the day's adventures.

Caradawc sat alone, hitting the toe of his boot with a switch of young beech, deep in thought, a stiff leather mug of ale forgotten beside him.

Suddenly she heard a sound over to the left of the clearing, and she stood up to see more clearly. Surely . . . surely it was a hart? He stood in shadow, but she could see his eyes – and they were looking into her own. She turned at once to her companions but none of them seemed to have noticed, though the hart had moved again with a sharp crackle of twigs. She could now see him distinctly, a red gleam to his velvet flanks, his tall antlers branching proudly. Surely the dogs would sense him? But they were all asleep – even Cuall, at his master's side, lying as still as death.

She moved very slowly and carefully towards Hunydd, her mare, thinking to signal to the others as soon as she could catch their attention. She did not dare to take her eyes off the hart lest he should disappear. She whispered Caradawc's name, but he did not look up. There was no doubt that the hart was aware of her. His eyes never left her own and his whole body was poised for flight.

When she reached the mare she hesitated, and a sly thought came to her. How beautiful it would be to bring him down herself: to show Caradawc – no, Goreu – that she was no simpering maiden to be put upon, but a strong and independent woman who could provide for herself if need be. She would bring the carcase to the betrothal feast as gift to her beloved – as proof that she would bring worthy blood into the family.

Silently she mounted Hunydd, the lovely creature responding at once to her mistress's firm but gentle guidance. Carefully she checked the arrows in her quiver, and the bow of red yew resting on her saddle. Around her, as though frozen, the scene remained the same, her companions talking and eating, the dogs sleeping, the prince staring at his boot, his thoughts far, far away . . .

But the hart waited no longer. He turned his handsome head and slipped away into the shadows. Hunydd and Viviane followed. Always in sight, but just out of range, the creature moved so gracefully that hardly a twig snapped, barely a branch was pushed aside. She knew he could have moved more swiftly, but it seemed as though he was playing with her. Time and again he looked back as if to be sure she was following. Each time their eyes met she fancied she detected challenge and mockery. She forgot the hunting party; she forgot Caradawc. There was only one thing in her life and that was to bring down this arrogant animal.

At last he paused within range, and she lifted her bow and let fly the slender feathered arrows, one after the other. But each fell short, or to the left or right. She could not believe it! She was justly proud of her skill with the bow and the target seemed an easy one. How could she have missed? The hart stared at her calmly, unafraid.

She urged Hunydd to go faster, but the hart sensed the change of pace and fled even more fleetly from her. The forest became thicker, darker, wilder. Branches nearly knocked her from the saddle, gouged a shallow cut along the flank of the mare. Normally Viviane would have stopped at this injury, but now she could think of nothing but the creature ahead of her, and how much she wanted . . . no, how much she needed to bring it down. More than once it paused within range, and more than once an arrow that left her bow true turned falsely aside before it reached its mark.

It was Hunydd who first sensed enchantment – and refused to go further no matter how hard her mistress drove her on.

Impatiently Viviane slid from her back and pursued the creature on foot, caring nothing that the forest was full of wild boars, and that the hart itself was fiercely antlered.

The forest grew darker and so thick that the young woman could scarcely force her way through. Brambles scratched her bare ankles and arms, and tore at her hunting tunic. The thick coil of copper-red hair, once so neatly piled that it resembled a crown, was now loosened by a passing branch and tumbled round her shoulders and down her back. She pushed it from her face, scarcely aware of what was happening to her. The animal was out of sight but she was following the sound of it. All that she could think of was that she must see it again . . . that she must face it . . . that she must look into its eyes . . .

Suddenly she was alone in a terrible silence. She stood still, like an animal herself, her head tilted, listening, her nostrils sniffing the air. But her prey had vanished as mysteriously as it had come.

For a long while she stood there, catching her breath, trembling with the strain of the pursuit, at first not even considering her plight, so far from her companions, so deep inside the forest. But gradually as she rested, she became more aware of her predicament. She put an ear to the ground, hoping to catch the vibrations of the other horses, or perhaps of her faithful Hunydd coming to look for her. But there was no sound – except occasionally the soft rustle of a leaf falling from a tree.

What a fool she had been! Anger with herself temporarily kept her from fear. Hunydd had showed more sense than she had. Reflecting on everything that had happened she now knew without any doubt that she had been *spell-led*. But by whom, and why? She knew no one apart from her betrothed, his family and friends in this alien country. She had made no enemies, crossed no witches. Tears began to prick behind her eyes and a lump rose in her throat. She swallowed angrily and jumped to her feet, wiping the tears away with the dusty back of her hand. This morning all had seemed so fair: her future settled and not unpleasant. Why, why had she allowed herself to be so misled? If she did not regain control of her life soon she knew that she could die in this forest.

Resolutely she turned about and started back the way she had come, following the broken strands of bramble and bracken, the crushed fern, the scuffed moss.

She had been walking a long time and was on the verge of despair when it suddenly seemed the trees were less dense, the shadows less dark over to the right. When she saw a shaft of bright sunlight she began to run, calling to Caradawc, convinced she had at last found the clearing where she had left him.

But there was no clearing, no familiar faces.

Instead she found herself at the edge of the forest, overlooking a gently sloping valley with a low, flat hill beyond. It was a relief to see open space and sky at last, and she hoped she had come full circle in the forest and was back to Goreu's grazing lands.

But the landscape was not familiar. There was no path or track in sight; no herdboy with his docile lumbering charges; no village women drawing water from the stream that ran at the foot of the hill.

Viviane's eyes kept returning to the hill across the valley. She felt a strong urge to climb it – to stand upon that strange, blunt summit – to feel the wind in her face and to rejoice at last in vast open spaces and unencumbered vistas . . .

She began to wade downwards through the tall grass, falling to her knees at the valley stream and drinking deeply. She washed her face and hands, her scratched and bleeding arms and legs, and then began to climb the slope beyond. It was steep, but even so she was surprised at the effort it cost her to move upwards. Surely it was not weariness alone that made her limbs feel so heavy? It was almost as though there was some force dragging her down to prevent her reaching the top. She fought it, knowing that it had become as important to her to climb the hill as it had been before to hunt the enchanted deer.

At last she reached the rim of the hill, the hair on her forehead clinging damply with sweat. Involuntarily she gripped the knife at her belt, not knowing what she might encounter there.

She now stood on a ridge beside a deep ditch. Facing her was the flat summit of the hill. It was occupied by a circle of huge slabs of stone – of the kind it was thought a race of giants used to erect to their gods. These were not standing upright and tall, but each one lay flat as though blown down by some dread force at the centre.

She gazed around her in wonder. Although it was late in the afternoon, the summer sunlight still fell sweetly on the green grass and the flowers that grew amongst it. Behind her the same forest that had seemed so dark and dangerous when she was lost in it now, from this distance and from above, glowed richly with every pleasant shade of green. To the north, over clear grassland, she could see a thin plume of smoke and knew that there she might find people to take her in against the night.

She should have set off at once to seek them, but found herself loath to leave this strange place. She had heard of such mounds and such stones before, always as places haunted by demons, to be avoided at all costs. She was frightened and yet fascinated, and told herself that a few moments longer here would do no harm. In the sunlight all seemed innocent. The crystals in the stone occasionally flashed and sparkled, and buttercups, daisies and celandine glowed in the green grass. She climbed down into the ditch and up the other side – standing on the grassy edge to look at the giant monoliths that lay spread out around the circular summit. She felt her life was on the verge of a great change – and not just because of her impending marriage to Prince Caradawc. Whatever it was, she both dreaded and longed for it. She had been brought to this place for some purpose, and could not leave without knowing what that purpose was. She touched one of the stones nervously, but quickly withdrew her hand. Did she imagine vibration?

She took one step forward . . . and then another. She knew she wanted to move towards the centre. And she did not notice at first that with step after tentative step she was walking a spiral. She watched her feet press the grass and flowers down. She heard her voice humming a tune, but did not notice that the tune was unfamiliar to her – nor that she was beginning to sing phrases in a language that was strange to her . . .

Finally at the centre she lifted her head and looked around her. She suddenly sensed that no one had entered this circle since that ancient time when the huge stones were blown down – nor had any sound broken the silence until her song.

She was alone.

No, she was not alone.

Quickly, apprehensively she turned around, glancing over her shoulder. She could see no one.

'Fool,' she told herself.

She decided she must leave this place at once, her heart now beating fast, like a small bird's caught in a trap. Finding that they were sweating, she wiped her hands against her tunic.

Then she tried to move – but she could not.

Fragments of thought that seemed not her own began to tease her mind. At first they were strange disconnected phrases in an alien tongue, and then – growing more coherent – what appeared to be sentences. At first she fought them, thinking that fear was driving her insane . . . but then she began to recognize the words . . . began to understand their meaning.

It seemed a voice was speaking to her, pleading with her . . . whispering: *'Unwind the spiral . . . unwind . . . unwind.'* She shut her eyes, listening to the shadows of sounds that were not sounds crowding into that vast dark hollow which had been her mind.

'Who are you?' Her own thought-voice like thin smoke curled around the other . . . touched and dissolved. 'Who? Where are you?'

'I am at your feet . . . the earth holds me . . . ai aaii the earth holds me!'

She felt the other-pain, the other-loneliness, the long, long years, the centuries, the millennia of darkness, of waiting . . .

Pity became her heart . . . sorrow her breath.

She reached out her hands . . . they moved . . . they floated on the air . . . but her feet were still rooted . . . deep as a tree . . . to the earth . . .

'The earth holds me . . .' The other-suffering was her suffering.

'I cannot move . . .' Was it her own voice cried out or his?

'I will help you,' she breathed. 'Help me to help you.'

'Unwind . . . unwind the spiral!' His words were unmistakable.

She swayed like a tree in the wind striving to uproot herself.

'I cannot,' she sighed.

Words came . . . other words . . . strange words she did not understand.

'Say the words,' he whispered. *'Say them aloud with your earth-voice . . . your voice of throat and mouth . . . your voice of flesh . . . of life . . .'*

It seemed to her the words were all around her and she reached up and plucked them, making them her own . . . singing them as she had sung walking the spiral into the centre.

Her limbs moved. She staggered and almost fell – and then found herself, step by step, unwinding the spiral . . . still in darkness . . . aware only of his voice.

As she walked, her step strengthened, the turning of the spiral easing, quickening at every moment.

Half done, her whole body shook with exultation.

'At last! At last!! At la-ast . . .!'

She forced herself to stop moving. There was something in the voice that screamed within her – that made her shiver.

What was she doing? What was she, Viviane, allowing herself to do?

Who was this man? Why was he here . . . imprisoned?

'Go on! Go on!' he shrieked, but the violence in his voice made her even more hesitant.

She felt something was very wrong. What if . . .?

'Pity me . . .' he whispered. 'Pity me!'

She felt his pain, but forced herself to open her eyes.

'I must think clearly,' she said aloud, and aloud she said: 'Who are you and why are you imprisoned?'

A cold wind shook the grass at her feet, and then she experienced such a feeling of suffering and longing and pain that she could scarcely bear it.

'I must know,' she insisted. 'I *must.*'

'*I was falsely accused . . .*'

His words were everywhere. She looked from side to side and they were everywhere . . . invisible . . . inaudible . . . but louder than the thunder of a waterfall.

'Pity me,' he wept. '*I was innocent. They pinned my soul to this place for eternity . . . They caged my soul that I might never live again . . .*'

Pity filled her heart. She began to move again, eager to put his suffering at an end, knowing now why she had been drawn to this place.

She stepped lightly – as though moving along spiral lines, invisible, yet marked.

And then again she paused. The exultation she had just been feeling was somehow not the exultation of pure joy. There was something else . . . a sense of triumph.

She frowned. Behind words lay always other words . . . And these were the ones one should strive to hear.

What if those who had imprisoned him had reason for what they did?

'Ask yourself . . .' His voice was soft again – silence within silence. '*Ask yourself who would be the innocent and who the guilty. He who lies here denied what rightfully belongs to every living being . . . or they who deny it?*'

It seemed to her she saw the circle of tall stones standing erect, each transmitting the energy of sky to earth and earth to sky. Between them the force flowed from one to other, completing the ring. Within this ring, four priests and one priestess in cloaks of wolfskin and eagle feather, with golden torques about their arms and around their necks, stepped slowly and deliberately to the rhythm of the fatal chant-spell, gradually, inexorably, closing the spiral. Each face was masked: the mask of Judgement: set and hard and impersonal: but through the eyeholes the eyes glittered: some with triumph: some with fear: all with hate.

In the centre lay a man with both legs ritually broken: his handsome face the face of an angel . . . pleading with them for mercy . . . protesting innocence with words so persuasive that surely no one with a heart could remain unmoved. How many times had the powerful and the corrupt destroyed those who threatened them, she thought.

She started to move again, resolved to unwind the spiral, finding the strange words she had spoken before now coming easily to her mind. But this time there were changes in the sequence. She was trembling, almost dizzy with the turning. But now she was determined to make haste.

Stumbling, she finally completed the last steps and fell panting on to the grass. She was drained – exhausted – but well pleased with what she had done.

A cloud must have passed over the sun, for a sudden chill made her shiver. As she looked up, the icy cold that a moment before had touched her flesh now reached her heart. In shock she clambered to her feet. There was no cloud – but a dark and shapeless miasma over the land. The buttercups at her feet seemed dead . . . the grass scorched as though a fire had passed swiftly over it. The sky was clear and black as night – but without moon or stars!

Horrified she stared around her, her hands up to cover her mouth . . .

What had she done? *Oh God! What had she done?*

Then she heard a cruel and mocking laugh. She spun round, but the circle was empty . . . truly empty now. She knew that she had broken the ancient spell, and the prisoner was set free.

Suddenly she remembered.

She knew that she had not always been Viviane, daughter of Garwys, betrothed of Caradawc – but once was Fiann, priestess, and lover of Idoc, a priest turned sorcerer.

How sweet her adolescent love had been . . . the touch of him . . . his eyes . . . the turn of his head . . . Everything about him had made her heart beat faster. There had been a time when the whole of her life hung on a word, a glance, from him. She had even entered the priesthood to be near him.

When Idoc first lay with her the ecstasy had shut out all other thoughts, all other dreams. As his flesh entered hers, her experience of him had been total. But those early years had passed, and the handsome young man changed, becoming ever more remote and secretive, lying with her only rarely, and each time more selfishly and violently than the last, until her love and her body were so bruised and shamed that she swore never to let him touch her again.

Yet his colleagues honoured him increasingly as he passed with brilliance each trial and test devised for him. At last he stood so high among the adepts that he was named as successor to the High Priest.

She could see him now standing in the Holy Place, bowing his head as each ceremonial robe was placed over him: the white, the blue, the purple; and with each robe an ancient mighty Name, each Name a Power. She saw the marking as each Name was given: on the soles of the feet, on the palms of the hands, and finally on the forehead. She saw his eyes as the crystal and the rod of silver were placed in his hands, the circlet of silver and hawk feather on his brow. How many times had she run her fingers through that long, thick black hair, kissed that severe but handsome face, traced those winged eyebrows to the strong, straight nose? Ah, but he was handsome – magnificent in his robes. Surely now that he had so much, he would not demand more? Surely now that the long and gruelling training and initiation were over, he would relax and be as loving with her as he used to be?

But this was not to be. His very first act was to rid himself of the three priests who had not been wholehearted in his choosing. Two died suddenly, mysteriously and horribly, and the third fled for his life. They all realized, too late, that they had given power to someone who was either a madman or a demon. From that time on no one was safe – nothing was sacred. The High Priest found himself no more than a figurehead, powerless to interfere. The ancient laws were now twisted round to suit Idoc's whim. Anyone who dared to cross him was cruelly destroyed.

At last, in desperation, realizing that his genius for destruction was not limited to their own community, but that his ambitions reached out across the whole country, the priesthood secretly planned to use a binding spell, the last resort of the desperate, a spell so fearful that whoever pronounced it risked his own life.

The spell was cast. With their last act of knowledge the priests pulled down the Stones upon themselves and closed the circle forever. She could hear the sound of their falling now, the roar, the rushing wind, the thud that struck her heart into darkness.

And then . . . the long silence.

Now, standing in another life, in another body, Viviane – who had been Fiann – remembered the look in Idoc's eyes when he realized that she had betrayed him.

She began to shake. 'O God,' she sobbed. 'O God . . . O God . . .' Should she call on the Christ? On the Holy Spirit? Or on the ancient gods of her people?

Stumbling, she fled . . . fell and rose and ran . . . and fell again . . . Where should she go? Where was there to hide? She could not believe that she had been foolish enough to fall victim to his cunning and his charm once again.

Viviane crouched by the stream in the valley, weeping, fingering her knife . . . wondering if she should kill herself . . . but she knew that the death of the body would be no escape . . .

And then she heard a sound, faint at first, but steadily increasing. Puzzled, she held her breath and listened. She was so distraught with fear that at first she did not recognize it. It was the distant sound of a hunting horn, the calling note of a party searching in the forest.

She leapt up, frantic with fear that they might pass her by, and began to run towards the forest, calling their names.

'Caradawc!' she screamed as she ran. 'Caradawc!'

The dark shadow had lifted from the land, the forest was in leaf again, the grass springy beneath her feet. Overhead a lark sang in the clear air. Tears streamed down her cheeks, her breath coming short with the effort of running. Surely she had imagined the whole thing?

The horn blew loud and clear, and when its notes died away she could hear voices shouting her name amid the thunder of hooves.

Suddenly the party broke out of the cover of the forest.

Caradawc waved and galloped ahead to meet her, full tilt down the slope of the hill. How beautiful he looked! How she loved him! She could see the relief on his face, the white flash of his smile . . . Then suddenly his horse lost its footing on the uneven ground and Caradawc was sent flying over his head. The others laughed. The young prince's horsemanship was unquestioned, and spirits were high now that they had found her.

But then a strange thing happened. Caradawc's chestnut reared up on its hind legs, whinnying with fear, and then galloped off towards the west. Caradawc himself lay still, his body buckled awkwardly in the grass. Viviane reached his side at the same moment as his great friend, Gerin. Together they turned him over and straightened him out.

'He must have hit his head on that stone,' Gerin said, allowing her to cradle her lover in her arms. Caradawc was very pale and still, and there was a thin trickle of blood from beside his temple.

Viviane looked anxiously into Gerin's eyes.

'He'll be all right,' he said soothingly. 'He's taken worse falls than this in battle.'

The others were now dismounting and crowding round them, but Cuall, Caradawc's dog, howled disconsolately and backed away from his master as though he did not recognize him.

Gerin arranged for Caradawc to be lifted up on to his steed in front of him, while his friend Rheged galloped off to bring back the prince's horse. Cai, another close friend, rode on ahead to warn Goreu of his son's accident.

Gerin had said that Caradawc would be all right, but would he? He looked so pale . . . so dead. Seeing him slumped against Gerin, his legs flopping against the flanks of the horse, Viviane found it difficult to imagine him conscious again. She shuddered. Could Caradawc's fall have anything to do with what had occurred in the ancient circle? Impatiently she dismissed the idea. 'That way madness lies,' she thought, and she stroked her mare's silky mane as she rode, taking comfort from the animal's companionship.

Goreu's dogs came streaming through the gates and over the fields to meet them, barking with excitement. The sun had set while they were still in the forest, and the long twilight had almost faded. Some of Goreu's people with torches were standing anxiously in the quarter-light, peering at the party of dark shapes picking its way carefully down the last hill slope. The hunting dogs joined in the din, excited as they were to smell home at last, and the horn blower, carried away by the occasion, blew continually on his horn. Every man, woman and child who lived around Castle Goreu – serving its master, sheltering under his protection – was out, milling about them, asking what had happened. The cries of alarm when Caradawc was lowered down gently in the arms of his friends brought the huge bulk of Goreu himself into the courtyard, growling like a bear. But when he saw the young prince he was shocked into silence, and as the flickering torch flames lit up his face, Viviane saw no trace of the contempt he usually showed towards his son.

They carried Caradawc to his room and laid him on his bed, Goreu calling for Kicva, the healing woman, part Druid trained, whom he trusted more than the Christian priest with his cedar box of herbs and ointments.

Viviane washed the prince herself, stripping off his dusty clothes one by one.

Goreu strode about the room, glowering and grumbling, more irritated now than worried, complaining that they had returned without meat from a forest teeming with deer and boar, sneering at his son for not being able to stay on his horse . . .

Kicva came at last and pushed Viviane aside with her bony hands.

'My lord,' the young woman turned, outraged, to Goreu. 'Surely the priest has been called? You are not trusting your eldest son to this . . . this . . .'

Words failed her as she stared at the evil-smelling crone. The great age of the Druids was long past . . . the Romans had seen to that . . . but still the Celtic people clung to threads of the old knowledge, ragged as they were, often meaningless and dangerous for being misunderstood. Viviane, whose own father still held to the old religion, knew something of the Druid faith, and looked on Kicva as a sorry representative of the ancient line of bard-masters and shaman-priests that lay behind her.

At Viviane's words Kicva turned on her a look of such malevolence that the young woman shrank away from her – but then, remembering Caradawc's plight, she stood her ground, meeting the woman's eyes stare for stare.

'The Christian will be called,' Goreu said. 'There will be time enough for his mumblings. But first Kicva will tend him, for she nursed me as a child and saw my father through all his battle wounds. Stand back, girl! Give her room,' he commanded.

Viviane moved out of the woman's way but still kept close to Caradawc, taking his limp hand in hers.

'I can't work with all these people here,' the old hag snarled, looking at Goreu. 'Send them away.'

'You heard her,' he snapped. 'Everyone leave the room!'

'I will not!' Viviane said defiantly, as the others moved to leave. Gerin paused at the door, anxiously meeting her eyes, asking her silently if she wanted him to stay. She shook her head and he reluctantly left. She settled down upon the edge of Caradawc's bed, clutching his hand as though she believed no force on earth could prise her fingers from his.

Goreu took her roughly by the arm and jerked her away. If she had not let go her lover's hand, he would have been hauled off the bed with her.

'Go to your room, girl,' he snapped. 'I am in no mood for this!' And he pushed her angrily towards the door. She looked back, her arm bruised from his rough handling . . . Already the old woman was stooping over the young prince, Goreu standing beside him, holding up the lamp. It was as though she were already forgotten: a stranger who had briefly intruded and then passed on. There was something disturbing in the scene: something sinister in the flickering light that held the three figures together against the surrounding darkness.

But she was too tired to worry about it. She found that she could barely drag herself to her own chamber. She hardly felt the servant undress her and bathe her face. Dimly she knew that she pushed her hands away when she started the combing . . . and then she sank into the merciful oblivion of a dreamless sleep . . .

Caradawc remained unconscious for three days. The life of the castle was subdued as its young prince, heir to his father's kingdom, lay silent, locked in a shell of darkness that no one could penetrate.

For some reason Goreu and Kicva would not allow the Christian priest near Caradawc. Viviane brought him to the door several times, but Kicva had locked herself in with her charge and would let no one enter. In vain Viviane alternately pleaded with Goreu and railed against him, furious that she also was barred from the chamber. But Goreu was morose and sulky and unmoved by anything she could say. He had put his faith in Kicva and was determined to follow her instructions minutely.

'The Christian can pray in his chapel,' he said gruffly. 'Kicva knows what she is doing.'

'What does she say? How does she explain it?' Viviane begged to know.

'His soul is on a journey. It will return,' Goreu said briefly.

'If it is his soul that is affected, surely the Christian . . .'

'The Christian knows nothing about the soul,' he growled.

Viviane bit her lip. There were many things she would have liked to say to him – but how could she speak to such a stubborn old man, holding like a dog to an old bone?

She turned away and sought the comfort of Hunydd in the stables. 'If only I'd listened to you,' she sighed, stroking the soft muzzle, 'none of this would have happened.' But she knew that we can never unravel Time and what has been, is, and always will be.

During that night, the third of Caradawc's 'journey', Goreu came to her chamber.

She did not at first know that he was there. Deep in sleep she began to dream that Caradawc's fingers were exploring her body. She stirred and groaned with the pleasure of it . . . and then a sound woke her and she found it was not the prince but his gross father who floundered in her bed, heaving himself upon her, his hand where she had dreamed her lover's was. She pulled away in horror, crying out and beating her fists on his grey head. He clasped her tightly and forced his face into her breasts. What had seemed so delicate and beautiful a moment before was now an outrage.

'Viviane, girl . . .' the old man ground out in a hoarse whisper as he wrestled with her. 'Don't fight me. I'll show you what a real man feels like . . . not a boy. My son is no use to you. He'll never wake up. You need me just as I need you!'

'I'll never need you!' she screamed, fighting like a wildcat for her freedom, spitting and biting and tearing with her nails. 'Get out of here!'

As she frantically turned her face to escape his kiss she saw a figure at the door.

'Help me!' she screamed. But the figure did not move.

Then Goreu lunged his bearded face at hers again. She bit his nose and as he screamed and momentarily withdrew she saw the figure again.

It was Caradawc. He was standing quite still watching them, a small terracotta Roman lamp held high in his hand, its flame lighting the whole shameful scene with extraordinary brilliance while their monstrous shadows played across the wall.

She called his name, and Goreu loosened his grip and looked round, shocked.

She wrenched herself away from the man and he fell off the bed, landing heavily on the flagstones, swearing and muttering. She staggered upright, naked before the prince, scratched and bleeding, her long red-gold hair floating around her like fire in the lamplight.

Suddenly he moved, and it seemed to her the scene remained totally static except for that movement. Afterwards she could not remember if it all happened between one breath and the next, or whether it took longer. At any rate she watched as though in a dream as he crossed the room, picked up the dagger from her little wooden table, and plunged it between the shoulders of his crouching father. She had never seen him move more decisively. Goreu had been partly right when he had accused his son of being 'a boy' – but he had changed. It was no boy who strode across the room.

She heard the gasp of her own breath, part horrified, part exultant. Her hate for the old man was so bitter at this moment that she felt no pity as he slumped and lolled, blood spurting from the wound.

'Caradawc,' she whispered and reached out her arms to him, thinking that he would need comfort when he realized what he had just done. When he would begin to feel remorse.

But he ignored her and stood looking down on his handiwork for what seemed a long time. Her arms dropped to her sides. He did not need her.

Then, without looking at her, he strode towards the door. When he reached it he turned. The lamp, which he had put down when he seized the dagger, shone on his face. For the first time he looked into her eyes. For the first time she saw clearly into his. *They were not the eyes of Caradawc – but of Idoc.*

Horrified, she stood and stared at the open doorway, even when he was no longer there. And then sheer, mindless terror took her over.

She rushed to the door and shut it with trembling hands, leaning heavily against it, her heart pounding. She saw the body of Goreu . . . she saw the eyes of Idoc . . . All she could think about was getting away, as far away as possible. Darting across the room, she seized her long blue cloak and flung it over herself. She seized the little oil lamp and dashed it at the furs on her bed . . .

She climbed out of the window . . . She rushed to the stables . . .

Now, looking back, she saw the blaze of flames leaping from her bedchamber and hoped that all would think that she had perished there.

Moonlight and shadow wove a cocoon around her, soon distancing her from Castle Goreu. But where could she go to be safe from Idoc? Where hide? She thought of her distant home, her father's castle with the green ocean rolling at its foot, but between her and it lay many leagues of dangerous travel. Besides, would not the man she dreaded also look for her there?

'Christ of All the Worlds! Angels of Light!'

The prayer in her heart was wordless, but the cry for help was unmistakable.

In all the Realms of Being beyond our own the impact of her cry was felt. Angels, Spirits of Light, who had never known the weight of a physical body, nor the limitations of Time and Space, chose to take on form to give her aid, while those human souls who were already on their way to the higher Realms chose to stay behind to help her in her time of trial. Cave spirits and mountain spirits . . . nereids of the sea and river nymphs . . . tree elementals and the keepers of Springs . . . all saw her riding on her white mare, her long hair streaming out behind her like flame, her body naked beneath the long blue cloak.

But the beings of Light were not the only ones who saw her. Idoc had now left Caradawc and – a dark presence in a dark tower – stood brooding before his tall obsidian scrying mirror, seeing all that he chose to see, whether it be past, present or future; whether it be one league distant or a thousand.

2

The challenge of the black knight

Caradawc was acknowledged as Lord of Castle Goreu, king of all the territory conquered and held by his father. He mourned Viviane whom he supposed had perished in the fire, as he mourned for the days that were past when he had been carefree and happy. His father had made many enemies in his lifetime, but his formidable strength had kept them all at bay. Now that he was dead, and a young untried man stood in his place, it seemed that some landholders were ready to challenge his right to hold what he had inherited.

At night, the dream he had had in those 'lost' days still haunted him. He wandered through a darkness where there were no stars . . . He was aware of searching for something or someone and that a nameless passion drove him on . . . but for what or for whom he could not tell. Sometimes he found himself mounting a narrow spiral staircase, a flickering torch throwing a huge shadow both ahead of him and behind him. Sometimes he stood in a chamber at the top of a tower and stared into a black mirror. The reflections that stared back at him chilled his blood.

It was himself in every physical detail – handsome, tall, slender – but in the eyes he saw such brooding evil, such bitterness and lust for vengeance that he woke trembling and groaning, Cuall growling at his side.

It was not long before Huandaw, son of Neved, arrived at the castle, claiming that he had come to attend the funeral of his old friend and to pay respects to the new king. Caradawc knew very well that there had existed no friendship for ten years or more between the two old warriors. But as the man put on such a show of sorrow, and as they had been companions in youth before Goreu had forcefully taken half his lands, he was allowed to camp nearby. It was only when Gerin observed that there were more armed men in Huandaw's camp than mourners that a consultation was called in the Great Hall, and a herald was sent out to request the presence of Huandaw.

When the herald did not return, Caradawc and his friends knew that the moment for confrontation had come. Rheged and Cai were sent out under cover of darkness to seek help; the gates were locked, and guards mounted at every possible vantage point.

As Caradawc waited through the night, wondering if the dawn would bring his death, he thought of Viviane. She had come into his life unsought, presented by her father to his father to cement an alliance. Their wedding was to have been a political matter, and until they had met he had no interest in it. Indeed he had strongly resented it. But within days of her arrival at his father's court he had begun to love her. She was not simpering and docile, as the women around his father had always been, but full of life and spirit. When he feared that he had lost her in the forest he had been desolate, and now that he *had* lost her, he thought he would not be sorry to lose his life on the morrow. He had officially mourned his father's death because it was expected of him, but the real loss he suffered was his lovely princess.

He searched and searched his mind for memories of those missing days. Perhaps in there, somewhere, lay some knowledge of importance – something that might give him Viviane back. Her body had not been found – nor her mare. Was it possible that she had murdered his father and then fled, for his charred bones were found in her chamber and her knife was nearby? If this was so, his duty was to hunt her down and avenge his father. But he had known his father well enough to assume that whatever he had received was probably deserved. No, it were better to believe her dead so that the question of vengeance need never arise. But how could he endure the years ahead without her? The long night seemed cruelly drawn out by his desperate longing for her.

Just before dawn, when he should have been most alert, he finally fell asleep. Clearly he saw her standing in a forest glade, clad in a simple white dress. With her was a tall woman, luminously beautiful, a sheen of silver-green on her skin, a crown woven of willow wands from which ivy trailed to mingle with the shimmering leaf-light silk of her robes, and the fine flow of her green hair. She was tying a cord of green silk around Viviane's waist. He saw Viviane turn her head as though listening for a moment, as though she sensed that he was near, but as he reached out for her he was woken by the whine of an arrow past his ear and the smash as it hit an earthenware water jar standing on the table. Cursing, he staggered to his feet, seized his weapons and ran down the corridor, shouting for Gerin.

But Gerin and the others were already at their posts and the battle was raging. There was no sign of Rheged or Cai or their reinforcements.

As the hours passed and Huandaw's men attacked time after time, Caradawc began to doubt if his men could hold out. There was a well of fresh water in the courtyard but the food supplies would not last long. However, the walls were strong and high and his archers nimble and accurate. If it came to hand-to-hand fighting he and his companions would give a good account of themselves.

Just before noon a shout of joy drew all eyes to the east. Cai and Rheged were returning with every man they could muster, and among the ragged crowd of peasants and labourers there were some real fighting men.

Suddenly the battle was turned about, and Caradawc led his men out of the castle to attack Huandaw on the field. Arrows were no longer feasible with the two sides so closely interlocked and the fighting now was hand-to-hand with swords and axes. Rheged swung his axe fiercely and mercilessly. He had lost count of the men he had slain and was beginning to think it would not be long before Huandaw led his men into retreat. But suddenly he was confronted by a huge man in black armour, an iron visor over his face: nothing to be seen of him but a dangerous gleam through the eye slits. Rheged's boisterous confidence was shaken – but he was no blustering coward and faced up to the stranger boldly. Long and savagely they fought, Rheged at last falling to a blow from the blunt end of his opponent's axe. As he fell he thought it odd that the man did not slice him in half with that swing, but then pain and darkness overwhelmed him and he lay as though dead.

It seemed to him that he and the black knight were alone in an extraordinary place – the sky pitch-black but with no stars, yet the ground on which they stood was in bright light. Neither they, nor the bare, bleached trunks of the dead trees cast any shadows. He was standing upright again with his axe in his hand, delighted that he would have another chance at his assailant. To Rheged war had always been glorious: peace was the grey and boring period between battles. He swung at the black knight, and the knight parried. Soon they were locked in a contest every bit as fierce as before. Blow and counter-blow, neat feint, swift footwork . . . the two men were formidable warriors and well matched. Rheged at last gained the advantage and the other staggered and fell. He pressed home another blow, and another, until the knight could rise no more. Sweating and triumphant Rheged made sure his opponent was dead by driving his sword through the chinks in his armour. His whole body tingled with exhilaration, and his heart pounded with the excitement of victory, the relief of danger well met and conquered. And then, consumed with curiosity, Rheged stooped over the body and raised the vizor. He stared into a face hideous with plague sores. He backed away, shivering and terrified, already feeling the fatal disease crawling over his skin.

'No!' he screamed, and started to run, his weapon dropping from his hand. A voice seemed to whisper in his head, in the air around him, in the black sky.

'This is war,' the whisper was telling him. *'Stay! Look! Do you not see the glory of it? Do you not feel the pride?'*

Night was falling on the battlefield and Huandaw's warriors were retreating, carrying their wounded, before Rheged was found. Those who looked after the dead were harvesting their bitter crop in baskets drawn on sleds. Women who no longer had the protection and comfort of husbands wept, very much afraid of the future. Mothers stared into the gathering dark, remembering their sons' first faltering steps . . . the years of growth and effort now brought to nothing . . .

Caradawc, Gerin and Cai were standing beside Rheged's bed

when he became conscious again. He stirred and opened his eyes slowly, looking around himself calmly, even smiling faintly to see their anxious faces . . . and then it was as though he remembered something. His face distorted with appalling disgust and fear. He looked at his hands, his arms. He tore aside the bed covers and looked with terror at his limbs. Beginning to scream, he seized a cloth and began to rub his body, shuddering.

'Get away!' he cried out to his friends. 'Leave me! You'll catch it too. There's no hope for me . . .'

They stared at him in amazement. There were no marks on his body. They had washed the dirt of battle off him, yet here he was scrubbing his skin as though it was covered with the most unutterable filth.

Gerin grasped him by the shoulders and shook him. Caradawc sat on the edge of his bed and firmly held his wrists. Together they forced him to lie down. They looked into his eyes and assured him that there was nothing to fear – he was home and safe among friends.

Gradually he became calmer, and accepted that there was no blemish on his skin. Then he began to laugh and told them the whole story as though it had been nothing more than a bad dream.

'I wonder who that black knight was,' Rheged said at last, sobering.

The three friends had been listening with growing seriousness for each of them had encountered the same mysterious knight, and each had his own memories.

Young Cai, who boasted so much of the women he had lain with that he was often called 'The Goat', was actually a virgin and very much afraid of committing himself to the act. His encounter with the black knight had taken the form of a hand-to-hand battle ending in his own defeat, the huge man standing over him with his feet on either side. Cai shivered as he remembered the scene, but dared not tell his companions. He had lain there looking up, expecting the death blow at any moment, the man's legs like mighty columns of polished black basalt stretching for ever above him, the man's crotch like a huge arch and beyond it against the sky the foreshortened shape of the head. He could barely see the visor, but he would never forget the gleam of the eyes through those iron slits as the man bent forward to look at him. Although he could not see the face, he had an overwhelming conviction that the black knight was enjoying the fear he could see in Cai's eyes. Unlike Rheged, Cai did not enjoy battle. He hated it, but the code of honour among his companions being what it was, he would rather die than admit it. He kept to himself the thought that they would not be risking their lives now if Goreu hadn't stolen land from Huandaw in the first place.

He shut his eyes and waited for death, hoping the knight would be merciful, and make it swift and clean. But no blow came, and after a time Cai opened his eyes. In the place of the black knight there was a giant snake . . . rearing up against the sky, its malevolent yellow eyes staring into his . . . its venomous forked tongue flickering in and out of its huge jaws. The scales of its body shimmered and glittered like jet and emerald. It was the most magnificently beautiful creature he had ever seen, and in his heart he could not have then distinguished between the fascination and the fear. He stared back into its eyes, unable to move . . . paralysed. Suddenly it struck – and the scream he gave seemed to shatter it into a million glittering pieces that fell around him like rain. Doubling up in agony, Cai writhed and groaned.

He must have passed out, for suddenly he was lying in a grassy slope far from the battlefield . . . and a woman so beautiful she could have been a goddess was tending his wound. From the ivy in her hair down to her sandals, she was all in green. He lay naked, her gentle hands administering herbal ointments . . .

Now – remembering – his cheeks burned.

On hearing Rheged's story Gerin moved to the window and stood looking out. His own encounter with the black knight had been equally strange, but he was not prepared to talk about it.

He, too, had been challenged on the battlefield, and had fought long and hard. In the end it had been he who had felled the other and, standing above him, had felt, as Rheged had felt, an uncontrollable urge to discover who his opponent was. With one foot on his opponent's chest, Gerin had roughly hauled off the black helmet with its high, dark plume. As he did so, quantities of brilliant red-gold hair had fallen out of it like a stream of molten lava. Shocked, he stared down into the pale, dead face of Viviane.

The Lady Viviane! The memory of her made him tremble. He could see the long dark eyelashes against her cheek, the sad curve of her mouth, the contrast of her softness against the harsh metal of the armour. Without pausing to think how it could possibly be her, he had unlashed the metal plates from her and lifted her in his arms, his heart aching, calling on her name . . .

He bit his lip now lest he should cry out and his friend Caradawc would know how he had kissed her limp body, held her close . . .

But Caradawc would not have heard him, even if he had spoken, for he had a memory of his own. He had put up a good fight against the stranger – but had to yield at last. Backed against a tree, sword pointed at his throat, he had waited for his death. Why did the man not strike? The waiting was more painful than he could imagine the fatal cut would be. The waiting was prolonged, limitless . . . Caradawc's acceptance of his fate gave way to hope that he might yet live – and with the hope came fear. He realized just how badly he wanted to live; he realized just how much he feared death.

'Strike!' he cried, sweating and trembling with the strain of waiting. 'For God's sake, strike!'

'Strike?' mocked the knight.

'Or let me go!' The words were wrung out of the young warrior – words which he had been taught were shameful for a knight to speak. He pleaded, he wept, he grovelled . . . suddenly desperate for life at all costs.

The black knight laughed, and his laughter rolled hollowly across the land like thunder. He laughed and laughed, but his sword point never left the young man's throat.

And then with his left hand he had lifted off his helmet, and Caradawc could see who his tormentor was.

It was Goreu, his own father, dead and buried – yet here before him, laughing, as he always laughed . . .

The four young men in the room drew together silently – and silently took each other's hands. All forming the circle knew that from that moment there would not be peace for any of them if the black knight was not faced again – and faced this time with full awareness of what the challenge meant.

Idoc watching, smiled, and stroked the cold black surface of his mirror, the images fading as he did so. There had been four men and one woman who had brought about his downfall in that ancient life – and all were now ready for his vengeance.

Over Goreu's fields the night-owl swooped, and one more small rodent ceased to breathe.

3

The green chapel and the river horse

The Green Lady had found Viviane exhausted and sobbing, having ridden all the night and most of the day. Gently she lifted her from Hunydd's back and carried her to a place where she could rest, touching her eyelids with sleep and laying her down on a grassy bank so comfortable that a swan's-down pillow would have seemed lumpy in comparison.

When the young woman awoke and stood up, she found herself clothed in white with a green silk girdle swinging at her side. Wonderingly she touched the fabric, the weave so fine she could believe magic had been in the spinning and the weaving of it. She was alone, but beside her she found bread and wine which she fell upon hungrily. It was not until she had satisfied her hunger and her thirst that she looked around and pondered where she was. She was certainly deep in the forest, in a clearing – the trees crowding thick and tall around the edges. But this was no natural clearing. She stood inside a ruined building, open to the sky, the forest already reclaiming what it could. She moved about and tentatively explored, thoughtfully touching the lichen-covered stones that remained in place where once the walls had been. At the eastern end she found a table of stone, the huge slab cracked across but not yet fallen. Behind it the ruined walls formed a semicircle, and from them grew a huge beech tree, its silver-grey branches spreading wide, shimmering with light. Awed, she stood and gazed up at it, drinking in its force and beauty, its energy, its power.

She put out a hand to touch what she thought was a low-lying branch but found that it was a root, the blocks of the ancient wall and the roots of the tree so intertwined that it was impossible to decide whether the building was turning into a tree, or the tree into a building. She found that her heart was beating hard, almost aching, knowing that she was in a sacred place. It seemed to her that the huge branches reached out like arms to protect the space between. She felt compelled to kneel – overwhelmed by the feeling that she was in the presence of the Divine – and as she knelt it seemed to her that she was no longer alone.

Viviane opened her eyes, and light suddenly blazed in, dispelling the darkness behind her lids. Every leaf in the towering tree seemed individually lit. She could see the fine hairs around the young leaves like rays of silver. Between her and the tree the Green Lady stood in an aura of light, her eyes infinitely wise and kind. She held out her hand and helped the young woman back on to her feet. She was trembling, but the lady smiled and murmured that she should not be afraid: that she was among friends. Viviane turned her head and looked back along the ruined nave. The place was crowded now with joyful beings.

A young boy lifted his arm to wave to her and she saw that his fingers were supple twigs with leaves growing from all the joints, his hair a crown of living shoots. She waved back at him, finding nothing strange in such a combination of human and plant form. A girl smiled at her, folding a fine gold mist around her like a cloak. Another being was winged. Another transparent, shining like a crystal. Tree spirits were everywhere, green and brown and muscular. There were water nymphs whose liquid forms seemed continually to flow away and yet never leave . . . She saw a mountain-hermit standing separate from the rest, a gnarled stick in his gnarled hand, the oldest man she had ever seen . . . And she knew that he, and she – and all who were present – were more than a million years old, and had seen God in many forms but not yet – no, not yet in the form beyond all forms . . .

All this while beings had been coming and going at the altar, laying down gifts and taking up others. Nuts and leaves and flowers, baskets woven of river reeds, pottery vessels, wine jars, wool and flax both woven and unwoven, bread and fruit . . . Each brought something and each took something away. She heard the chattering, the laughing, and an occasional spontaneous burst of singing. She wondered what she should offer.

She felt so loving, so part of all these beings. She longed to give. What did she have that they needed?

An old, old crone tottered up to the altar and laid down something she could not see. She was clad in rags and Viviane could see goose pimples of cold standing out on her thin arms. She suddenly remembered the only thing she had brought with her – her blue cloak, her mother's cloak, the soft warmth of which had seen her through many a fierce northern winter. Her mother was dead and she would hate to part with it – but it was the only thing she now possessed . . . the only thing of her own to give . . .

She looked around to see what had happened to it, and found the Green Lady standing beside her holding the cloak folded in her outstretched hands as though she knew it would be needed. With a lump in her throat Viviane laid it on the altar. With it she felt she gave up her childhood and her childhood home. There would be no turning back now to the carefree days, the caring arms, the loving breast to weep on . . .

The ancient woman's rheumy eyes lit up at the sight of it. She was so old, so doddering, she could not lift it, and Viviane had to put it over her bony shoulders. It looked incongruous on the stooped, skeletal figure, and trailed on the ground behind her. Momentarily Viviane felt such a pang of pain at parting with it that she almost seized it back – but stopped herself. The old woman looked gratefully into her eyes and pointed with her shaking, withered hand at what she herself had laid on the altar. Viviane stared uncomprehendingly for a moment, then reached out and picked up the small, ragged bundle, trying to hide the disappointment that this was all she was to receive in exchange for her valuable royal cloak.

'Open it,' the Green Lady said to her quietly, knowing her thoughts, yet not condemning them.

Unwillingly Viviane peeled off the filthy wrappings. She gasped. Inside she found an exquisite sphere of crystal, shining softly with light the colour of pink rose petals. She gazed into its depths. She turned it from side to side. She trembled at its beauty. Suddenly she thought she saw a star in its depths; but as soon as she held it still the star vanished. She turned it round again. *Nothing.* And then, suddenly, it was there! It seemed to hover above the surface, yet when she tried to touch it, to pick it off, she found it was deep inside the crystal ball, an ephemeral shadow of light, lighter than light . . . the spirit of light . . . there and not there . . .

There was a pouch of soft doeskin at her waist. She slipped the rose-crystal sphere into it for safe keeping, now content beyond belief at this exchange of gifts. When she looked around to thank the old woman, there was no sign of her. The ruined chapel was deserted, the altar empty.

Viviane took a deep breath and turned from the altar and the mighty tree that grew behind it. She hated to leave this place, but she knew that she had to, as surely as she had needed to part with her childhood and her mother's cloak. Here she might learn to understand things she had never understood, but she could only learn 'out there' in the world, how to put that understanding into practice.

Slowly she retraced her steps along the path to the gaping hole that had once been the west door. On the threshold she hesitated, looking out into the forest. Already memories of what she had been fleeing from were crowding back.

Hunydd was cropping quietly in a patch of sunlight – but where was she to go? She really did not feel at all ready for what she had to face.

She took a step back into the chapel. But then she realized that she might never be ready. The readiness would come with the doing of whatever had to be done, not in the fearing of it.

Resolutely she stepped forward again, and whistled for Hunydd. The mare tossed her mane and came at once to her mistress. Viviane mounted and set her course for the north. There was a monastery she knew, called the Community of the Fish, ruled by a remarkable Irish abbot, Father Brendan, tucked away in a steep-sided valley, where she had spent some time as a child during the dangerous period before her father secured his kingdom. If she was to be safe anywhere she felt she would be safe there.

But what she did not know was that the dark tower lay between her and the sanctuary she sought.

An hour of riding took her out of the forest into open countryside. She came upon a village and was given food and drink and a warm cloak by the smith's wife.

'It is no bad thing for a young lady to become a nun,' the smith's wife thought, on hearing that Viviane was on her way to a monastery. Praying and singing all day seemed a preferable way of life to the one of heavy work she herself had in bringing up seven sons and five daughters. She looked down at her own rough hands and misshapen figure, remembering when she, too, had been a beautiful girl. She patted Viviane's shoulder. 'Say a prayer for us, my dear,' she said. 'Think of us.' She, like most ordinary people, thought herself too busy to pray, and relied on others to do it for her.

The smith offered some village men as escort, but Viviane refused, not wanting to involve others in her problems. She said she did not have far to go, and if she could perhaps be given a knife and a flint for making fire she was sure she would be all right.

The smith hesitated: bread and an old unwanted cloak were one thing, but an expensive knife was another. He would have refused had he not realized that she was from a noble family and thought about the rewards that might come his way from a grateful father. He chose the best knife he had and honed it carefully. He gave her a broad leather belt and a sheath in which to house it.

'You don't want to ride about looking like a grand lady,' his wife said, fussing around Viviane as she prepared to leave. She pulled the hood up over the young woman's shining hair and arranged the long cloak over the fine white weave of her dress. 'There now,' she said proudly. 'You look almost like a peasant.'

Almost. But not quite.

The road that led out of the village was deeply rutted, red valerian and foxglove flowering profusely in the ditches on either side, while at ground level blue speedwell and wild strawberry spilled over with the grass to the very edge of the cart tracks. The woodland had mostly been cleared for farming, but there were still clusters of trees holding out against the axe.

It was late afternoon before Viviane decided that she must have taken a wrong turning. The instructions she had received from the smith had been simple. She was aiming for the local monastery, where she hoped she would be able to obtain proper directions to Father Brendan's more remote Community of the Fish. Yet there was no sign of the river, or the ferry she must use before she could reach it.

She slipped from Hunydd's back and tethered her lightly to a young birch sapling. They were both tired, and a rest might help her to think more clearly and recall the details of the directions she had received. Wearily she lowered herself on to a log and sat hunched up with her elbows on her knees and her head buried in her arms. The courage she had brought with her from the chapel of the Green Lady was now rapidly leaking away, and she wondered what would become of her if she did not find shelter before nightfall.

Perhaps she dozed off. At any rate her thoughts were so self-absorbed that she was suddenly startled, as though from sleep, by the feeling that she was being watched. She leapt up at once, her hand on the knife at her belt. A few yards from her a man was standing – a tall man dressed in black, his arms crossed on his breast, a sword at his side. The intent stare he was giving her came from beneath lowered brows. His mouth was set in a hard line.

Idoc! She would know him anywhere, any time! How long had he been watching her?

She turned at once and ran to Hunydd, hauling up her skirts and leaping on the mare's back as easily as if she were in hunting gear. Hunydd's tether must have worked loose because nothing delayed the smooth, swift flight. As she leaped a small ditch she looked back over her shoulder and saw him standing there still, gazing after her impassively, making no attempt to pursue her.

At first she could think of nothing but of leaving Idoc as far behind her as possible, but once she felt this was achieved, she sought for some kind of track that might lead her to a farmhouse or village. Eventually she saw a fairly well-worn road to the left and pulled gently on the reins to guide Hunydd towards it. But the mare, who usually responded to the slightest touch from her mistress, seemed not to notice and continued in the direction they had been going. A firmer tug on the reins was equally ineffectual, and Viviane spoke sharply, pulling in the leather firmly to bring them to a halt. The mare shook her head to relieve the pressure of the bit, and galloped on.

'Hunydd!' shouted Viviane, pulling with all her strength, astonished at the creature's disobedience. Shadows were gathering and the sun was near to setting. She experienced a twinge of fear. Why would the mare not respond?

The mare increased her pace, flying over obstacles, her hooves cracking and thundering on the earth, small pebbles spinning from her hooves. Viviane noticed foam at the sides of her mouth and on her flanks and tugged less firmly on the reins so as not to hurt her.

'Whoa! Hush! Hush!' she called. 'Hunydd! Friend!'

But still the mare galloped on, faster . . . wilder . . . A jerk of her head caused Viviane to lose the reins. She clung to the animal's neck, knitting her fingers in the long matted mane.

Long matted mane? Suddenly Viviane realized her steed was not Hunydd! White it was – but in her haste to get away from Idoc she had not noticed the substitution.

As she leaned over the fearsome neck she saw that its eyes were glowing red, and she knew that she was lost. Such demon horses she had heard about luring people on to their backs and riding off with them. These creatures were deep-water fiends. They rose from the watery depths and they returned to them . . . their hapless victims with them.

Viviane loosed her feet from the stirrups, thinking to fling herself off the creature's back – preferring the bruising she would receive to the drowning. But although her feet were now free, she found a force held her to the beast's back and she could not leave it.

So this was why Idoc had not pursued her!

They were galloping beside the river now, the very river she had been seeking: but now she would rather they had not found it. It was wide and deep, and the rays of the setting sun stained the water the colour of blood. The fiend she sat on was making the most horrible noises . . . shrieking and howling and wailing like no earthly horse. Perhaps it was calling to its fearful mate

. . . or perhaps rejoicing that it was nearly home. The current was running swiftly beside them – the water grey and muddy where it was not red. She had never seen water so dark and sombre before. No bright water sprites would live here, only dark and harmful things: savage and cruel beings.

The creature rose on its hind legs and gave one last fearful bellow before it plunged. She was pulled down with it, feeling the icy water coursing over her skin, thundering in her ears. Frantically she held her breath, hoping against hope that once in its natural habitat the creature would release her and there might be a chance of escape.

Greasy bubbles were surging past her, and her chest ached with the effort of holding her breath. Her steed's hairy sides were growing slimy and slippery, its tail like rotten leather that had lain long in a stagnant pool . . .

'O God in Heaven . . .' her heart sighed as she slipped into darkness, giving up the struggle . . .

Caradawc and his three friends, Gerin, Rheged and Cai, rode out together from Castle Goreu, determined to find the black knight and solve the mystery of the attention he was paying them. They had each confessed that he had confronted them, though the story each told his companions and the true story of what had happened were not necessarily the same.

As they set out in the early-morning mist they rode close, talking and laughing, four young men embarking on an adventure, full of hope.

He had appeared to them during their battle with Huandaw, and so it was towards Huandaw's lands that they headed first.

In mid-afternoon it was Caradawc's decision that they should separate so as to be less conspicuous. In his mind was the thought that when he met the black knight he would rather the others were not there to witness what happened. A recurrent nightmare had greatly disturbed him since the battle. In his dream he killed his father – not once, but many times. Wherever he turned his father seemed to be there – laughing at him. Time and again he saw himself plunging a dagger into Goreu's back, only to find that his father was still standing unharmed, still laughing.

It was thus that Caradawc found himself alone at sunset,

riding along the bank of a wide river, his chin sunk on his chest, brooding about his father. There must have been a time when he had loved him, but he could not remember it. His first memory was of the fear in his mother's face when he failed to bring down the bird his father expected him to kill with the bow he had just given him. He remembered even today the pity he had felt for the creature as it beat against the bars of its cage and the joy with which it flew to the heavens at its release. He remembered how he had deliberately missed the target. It was his mother's face that alerted him to his father's wrath; the way she gathered him hastily to her side, to protect him with her slender arms.

'He is very young,' she had pleaded. 'Must you take him now?'

But taken he had been 'to be made a man,' and he himself had become the bird in the cage, longing for his freedom.

A breeze sprang up and the sudden chill of evening brought Caradawc back to the present. Clouds had gathered low on the horizon, but not yet closely enough to shut out the huge orb of the setting sun. A flight of geese passed over, honking forlornly, the water dark as the grave beneath them, the sky as red as fire.

A movement, a flash of white, in the distance caught his eye. He reined in and strained to see what it could be. The light now was deceptive and the object, whatever it was, seemed to billow and change like a sail before the wind.

At length he discerned it was a rider on a white horse that was galloping towards him, though still too far away for him to distinguish details. He waited where he was, preparing for the encounter, but suddenly the steed seemed to rear on its hind legs and plunge into the river, taking its rider with it. Caradawc stared astonished at the swirl of water, tinted red by the setting sun, which closed over their heads. A moment of shock . . . but when he realized that they were not rising to the surface again, he drove his heels into his chestnut and galloped forward.

It was difficult to be sure where they had gone in; the river's face was a blank. But he thought he remembered a particular tree at the spot, and took a chance, leaping from his horse, and plunging in. The water was cold and murky and he came up for air twice before the third dive gave him what he was looking for. A woman's body was floating, held back from the tow of the strong current by the waterweeds that had entangled her. There was no sign of the horse at all.

Frantically he cut at the weed and pulled and tugged, his lungs aching with the effort; and he himself was almost dead before he had her free. Together they burst through the surface of the water, he taking great gulps of air, while she still lay inert. He dragged her to the bank and hauled her out, pummelling her roughly till she choked and coughed and vomited water and the vile river slime.

'Live!' he shouted as he worked, his heart breaking to see the state she was in, though as yet he had not recognized her through the mud and weed that clung to her.

At last she was breathing, though not yet conscious, and he fell back to recover his own breath. It was then he saw it was Viviane. Joy leapt in his heart like a flame in dry kindling, and it was all he could do not to fall on her and smother her with kisses.

He sat back on his haunches, gazing at her, her long hair matted and dark and interwoven with slime-weed, her gown torn and soaked in mud.

There were runnels of blood where her skin had been torn, but she was alive and he had found her! He was both shivering and smiling, feeling this was perhaps the happiest moment of his life . . . asking no questions . . . seeking no answers . . .

But moments break like waves and cannot be held back.

He heard a sound behind him and turned quickly. It was nearly dark now and the figure that stood beside him was almost indistinguishable from the shadows. He sensed the malevolence rather than saw it. He had dropped his knife in the water when he had finally freed the girl from the weeds; his other weapons were on his horse a few paces to the left. The stranger was watching him intently. Whether he was armed or not was difficult to tell, but Caradawc did not feel like taking a chance. Cautiously he rose and stepped towards his chestnut, keeping his eyes warily on the dark figure. The man did not stir.

'Who are you, sir?' Caradawc challenged.

'You know me well,' came a voice as dry as dead leaves blown by the wind.

'You are mistaken, sir,' the young man said, but his voice faltered. How many more paces to his horse?

'You know me as well as you know yourself,' the other said and took a step forward.

Caradawc turned swiftly and leapt across the remaining distance between himself and his horse. The chestnut trampled nervously, and Caradawc found that he could not get a firm grip on the weapons fastened to the saddle.

'Whoa,' he said softly. 'Gently, friend.' But the horse suddenly bolted, as he had done once before, apparently terrified. Caradawc swung round, determined to face the stranger with his fists if need be. The huge dark figure was very close now, shutting out what feeble light there remained from the day.

'Hold, sir!' Caradawc said warningly, raising his hands to ward him off. But the stranger continued forward until Caradawc could bear it no more, and lunged out.

To his astonishment his arm met no resistance. Although the stranger appeared as solid as he was, his flesh had no substance. He came still closer, undeterred by the blow, and Caradawc felt an icy shadow touch him, then spread over him. Suddenly the figure was gone, and Caradawc was shaking with cold. It felt as though an iron fist had seized his heart and was squeezing it. He sensed himself sinking into a bottomless pit . . . falling . . . spinning . . . his voice crying out as though from a great distance . . .

When Viviane opened her eyes she found Caradawc bending over her.

'Ah, my love,' she murmured softly, seeing how handsome he looked, how gently he lifted her in his arms. The full moon poured its light upon them, the river was like a sheet of silver. He kissed her, stroked her hair.

'It has been so long,' he whispered and his touch became rougher, more intimate. At first she did not resist, still half dazed by her experience. But then she remembered the eyes that had stared from Caradawc's face in her chamber, the knife brutally plunged into Goreu's back.

'Idoc!' she cried – but the sound was smothered as he kissed her. And, though a doubt still lingered, she let herself be taken.

At the end, with her lover resting beside her, she rose on her elbow and looked down on his face in the moonlight. The features were those of Caradawc, but was there something about the expression – a hardness of line that belonged to an older man – a slight curl to the lip as though he was savouring a victory, not an act of love?

The fear that had become her unwelcome companion since that ill-fated hunting expedition now returned. He was heavily asleep, and if she were very, very careful she might just be able to slip away. With tiny, imperceptible movements she eased herself away from him, rolling finally out of reach. She stood up silently, trembling with fear lest he should wake. But luckily he did not.

She had no means of knowing which way would be the safest for her to take, but she thought it best to try to retrace her steps in search of Hunydd. To be a woman alone was bad enough, but without a mount her plight was really desperate. She began walking quietly, trying not to make a sound, but as soon as she felt she was out of earshot she began to run, stumbling occasionally on the uneven ground. She felt at her belt and was relieved to find that she still had the smith's knife and the Green Lady's little pouch containing the precious rose-crystal sphere.

It was nearly dawn before she dared stop for rest. She had left the river and worked her way back as best she could in the direction she hoped would bring her to Hunydd. Exhausted, she could go no further. She found a sheltered place on a soft bank among bushes and fell asleep.

When she woke she felt much refreshed. The morning sun was well up and everything sparkled – buttercups shining everywhere and birds busy about their business as though nothing untoward had happened. Cautiously she examined her immediate environment. In such a pleasant spot it seemed inconceivable that just a few hours before she had been fighting for her life against enchantment.

After smoothing her dress as best she could, she followed the sound of trickling water and found a spring from which she drank thirstily before washing herself. Her hair soon began to dry in the sun, all its brilliant flame-like lights returning. Then she found a wild apple tree and ate heartily, though the apples were very sour.

But where would she find Hunydd?

As though in answer to this thought, she heard a sudden whinny, and a party of children came out of the wood, leading Hunydd amidst them and chattering excitedly at their find. Upon her back a slender green figure was riding. It waved cheerfully at Viviane, then seemed to dissolve into light and disappear. She stood amazed for a moment, wondering if she had imagined the figure, for the children did not seem to have noticed its presence, nor its disappearance. Then, as the party seemed about to pass her by without a glance, she pulled herself together and rushed forward to tell them that the mare was hers.

They laughed. 'Such a ragged peasant woman could not own such a fine horse.'

Surprised, she looked down at herself. Certainly her fine white gown was no longer so fine or so white, and the cloak from the smith's wife had been ragged to begin with and was worse now. Luckily, at this moment Hunydd pulled away from the children and came up to her mistress.

Then they were curious, wanting to know why a lady like her was wandering about the countryside looking like a peasant. She told them she was escaping from a very wicked man, and asked them to direct her to the monastery she sought. One of the older boys said he knew the place she meant. It lay on the other side of the river. Her heart sank. She did not relish facing those murky depths again, but she followed where the children led, through meadows of tall grass, musk mallow and clover, through copse and barley field and, finally, to the river. From time to time she glanced uneasily over her shoulder, fearing that Idoc would find her again before she reached sanctuary. She could not shake off the feeling that he was even now watching her.

When Caradawc awoke, both Viviane and Idoc had left him. The sun shone warmly on his skin and his chestnut horse, Osla, was not far away, cropping contentedly. He remembered nothing clearly after the dark hand had touched him, except the sensation of falling, and . . . but this he could not be sure of . . . a terrible yearning.

He stood up and took his bearings. The river that had seemed so cruel and fearsome at sunset was placid and golden now in the daylight, willows growing along its banks. He must have lain there all night, because his limbs were stiff and painful. For a while he paced up and down, stamping and clasping his sides with his arms, trying to get rid of the cramps and the lingering night cold. He wondered if anything he remembered had really happened. Had he indeed found Viviane, only to lose her again?

He whistled and Osla came running, apparently unrepentant for having deserted him.

'That's a fine thing to do,' he chided. 'Run off when I need you most.' But he did not scold him too hard, for he too had felt the icy clutch of fear. Neither he nor his steed would ever run from battle, but what they had faced the evening before was not natural – a grim wight sent from the dark regions to destroy them.

He climbed on Osla's back and set off along the riverbank, not knowing where to go or what to do next.

4

The ferry and the rose-crystal sphere

The children chose a different route to the river, much shorter than the one Viviane had already used, and their cheerful voices lifted her spirits. When they reached the ferry station the raft was over the other side, so they sat on the small jetty to wait, their legs dangling over the edge. From time to time there was a soft ripple, a curved flash of silver, and then a splash as a trout leapt into the air for a dragonfly and then fell back into its own element.

At last they could see the raft returning across the water and the children pushed and jostled each other at the end of the jetty to have the privilege of catching the mooring rope. Viviane stood behind them, looking over their heads at the sturdy craft, more punt than raft, and the ferryman who stood wielding a long punt pole as he neared the bank. She noticed a large, flat oar lying at his feet, no doubt for use when in deeper water.

She stroked Hunydd and murmured soothing things to her, more to comfort herself than the mare. Knowing now what lurked beneath the surface made her fearful of the crossing, though she had been on many a ferry before.

To her surprise the ferryman was an old man, but, watching the way he manoeuvred his ungainly craft to the jetty, threw the rope and leapt after it on to the planks, she knew he was as fit and strong as need be for his work.

'This lady has to cross the river,' the children chorused, 'but she has no coin. You'll take her, won't you?' they cried. 'Good old ferryman – you'll take her, won't you?'

The man looked at her sharply, his expression clouding.

'I take no one without payment,' he said sourly. 'I have a family to feed. If I let one go free, all will expect it.'

'Just this once, old man – just this once!' pleaded the children. 'No one will see.'

'Not even this once,' he said firmly. 'No payment. No crossing.'

Viviane joined her pleas to theirs. 'I swear I'll return and pay you as soon as I have reached my friends,' she said. She thought that surely the holy brothers and sisters at the monastery would help her when they knew her plight.

'No payment. No crossing!' he repeated sternly, standing with his arms crossed on his chest, glaring stubbornly at her.

She looked round helplessly. She had nothing with which to barter. She could not and would not part with Hunydd's saddle, nor the smith's knife.

Watching her closely and seeing what she was thinking the old man suddenly pointed at her waist.

'I'll have that green girdle,' he said.

Involuntarily she put her hand to the fine, strong, silk cord. It had been given her by the Green Lady and was surely some form of magical protection.

'I cannot part with this,' she said, thinking fast. Perhaps it would be better to give up the knife. It had come from no faery source. 'You can have my knife.' And she started to undo the belt to give him the knife and its sheath.

'No,' he said. 'I have a knife. I want the green girdle.'

'You can have the leather belt *and* the knife,' she said.

But he was not interested, for it seemed he had set his heart on the girdle and nothing would direct his attention away from it. Viviane's every instinct told her not to part with the girdle, yet she had heard that evil spirits hated crossing water, and apart from her determination to seek sanctuary with the Community of the Fish, she hoped by crossing the river to leave Idoc well behind her.

Even as she hesitated a horseman was sighted by the children, and they shouted out that the ferryman would soon have another customer. Viviane looked back over her shoulder and, although the rider was still a fair distance away, she was sure it was Caradawc.

'If only it *was* Caradawc,' she thought desperately. But Caradawc inhabited by the soul of Idoc was more than she could bear.

44

'You can have the green girdle,' she cried hastily to the ferryman, 'but only if you cast off now before that horseman arrives.'

'He's the wicked man she's running away from!' the children cried in delight, crowding off the jetty on to the bank to get a better view.

'Please!' she begged, her fingers trembling as she untied the knot the Green Lady had fastened so lovingly.

The ferryman glanced speculatively from her to the rider and back again.

'I'll have the girdle *and* the knife,' he said.

'But, you said . . .' she cried.

'And the leather belt,' he added.

'All right!' she almost screamed. 'You'll get them – but *please* cast off now.'

He gave her a last amused look and released the rope from the post. He seemed to be moving deliberately slowly as he picked up the punt pole and put it in place to start. He looked at the rider rapidly approaching and then he looked at her – still hesitating to push the craft off.

The horseman was obviously heading for the ferry, because he was galloping now and shouting for them to wait. He was near enough for Viviane to see without a doubt that it was Caradawc. She finally managed to undo the knot, and almost flung the precious green silk at the ferryman. He caught it deftly and, with a smile she hated, he swung it round until it fastened around his forearm like a snake.

She looked back at Caradawc, tears streaming down her face . . .

He was calling her name.

Oh God . . . if only she knew! She would give anything for it truly to be Caradawc. But she could not be sure. Would she ever be sure again?

'Go!' she shrieked at the ferryman. 'You've got what you wanted – now *go!'*

He pushed off the craft at last.

Caradawc reined up at the jetty, shouting after them. The children milled around him pummelling him and trying to pull him from his horse. Her anguished emotions were torn between wanting him by her side and dreading that she might discover he was once again inhabited by Idoc's fell spirit.

The young king, like a giant among dwarfs, managed to fling the children aside. Frantic to reach her, he dived into the water and started to swim towards her. It seemed to her the ferryboat was scarcely moving and the ferryman was delaying deliberately. Caradawc was gaining on them. She looked round angrily at the ferryman. He had a sly, unpleasant face, and his eyes were shining like beads. She could see the silk cord on his arm, and there was something horrible about the way it now seemed that the veined and knotted forearm was wound round the green cord, rather than the cord around the arm – almost as though he was absorbing the silk into his body.

Caradawc had now reached the boat and was stretching up his hand to seize the side. He looked into her eyes, and she gasped. They were the sea-blue eyes of Caradawc, untroubled by anything but his love and concern for her.

Then she rushed forward to help him, wild with joy – but the ferryman tripped her so that she fell sprawling on the deck. Then he struck the man in the water full in the chest with the punt pole. Her face almost on a level with Caradawc's, she saw the agony that flushed across it . . . saw him gasp and flounder . . . saw him sink . . .

'No!' she cried, struggling to her feet. 'Help him! Get him out!'

'Make up your mind, lady,' the ferryman mocked her. 'One moment you want to escape him, and the next you want him for your bed.'

'How dare you!' she screamed. She tried to wrench the pole from him but he held it firmly. She saw his yellow teeth as he grinned. '*Help* him,' she demanded. 'I made a mistake. It's not the man I thought it was.'

'It's too late now,' the ferryman said callously. 'The current will have taken him away.'

Distraught, Viviane peered downriver. A dark shape that could have been a man or merely a log was being carried rapidly downstream, a scum of waterweeds and debris floating with it.

The ferryman returned to his task. He set down the pole and

pulled on the rudder rope with his bare foot, one toe very much longer than the others. With his hands he worked the paddle-oar to prevent the ferry drifting too far with the current.

In despair Viviane stared at the river, too exhausted by the conflict of her emotions to think clearly. Then suddenly she remembered that she had received *two* gifts at the Green Lady's chapel: there was also the rose-crystal sphere in the little leather pouch she had worn on the green cord around her waist. Terrified that she might have lost this too she turned to the place she had been standing when she had ripped off the girdle. The man presumably had not noticed the pouch, or he would most certainly have been interested in its contents. She searched discreetly and spotted it at last, lying where it had rolled against a coil of rope. The ferryman was still looking back in her direction and she could not make a move without his seeing her. If only he would turn . . . But he did not.

Viviane stood up and, pretending to peer over the side towards their destination, she moved until her skirt covered the pouch. Then she staggered slightly and sat down on the coil of rope. Carefully, under the cover of her skirt, she retrieved the pouch and prised it open until she held the small rose-crystal sphere naked in her hand. She did not know how it could help her – only that it would.

Gripping it tightly, she looked up at the ferryman.

She caught her breath.

Behind him stood a mighty being of bronze and yet of flesh, of darkness and yet of light. Upon the one skull he had two faces, one looking forward, one backward. Past and future seemed to flash through him like lightning, his eyes seeing what was not to be seen.

Terrified, she drew back, and then remembered what she clutched in her hand. She raised it up. She watched the sunlight flash through it, the star riding just above the surface . . .

Suddenly the Janus-god was gone.

The ferryman seemed confused. He rushed forward, but appeared not to be able to see her. He searched the water on either side of the boat . . . he looked frantically towards the bank.

Like the star in the rose-crystal sphere, she was momentarily invisible!

She slipped over the side and swam and waded the short distance to the bank, the water hardly moving under the lee of a bend in the river.

It was Hunydd who gave her away, scrambling beside her up the steep bank, breaking off great chunks of loose earth as she did so. She heard the ferryman shout, and breathlessly hauled herself up by clutching roots where the lapping water had undercut the bank. With a foot in the loop of one, she grabbed Hunydd's bridle, and used the mare's strength to swing her up on to the riverside path.

She guided the mare downstream, hoping that they would come upon Caradawc, but there was no sign of him – only the river flowing hard and strong to the distant sea; the willows crowding thickly, leaning well over the water as though to drink; the occasional heron watching for fish. She looked frequently over her shoulder to check if she was being followed.

She saw no one. But in the scramble to mount Hunydd she had dropped the precious rose quartz sphere, and the dark river mud had sucked it down into its depths.

Eventually Viviane gave up searching for Caradawc and turned to the north, away from the river, hoping to find the monastery the smith's wife had described. She headed into woods of oak and ash and alder, Hunydd's hooves muted on the thick carpet of leaves and ground ivy. Out in the sunshine on the other side she found peasants working the strip fields, women and children beside the men, bent double, pulling weeds, hoeing and trimming. They straightened up when they saw her and stared at her silently. She asked a woman with a child on her hip for directions, and was given them, briefly, unsmilingly. She supposed she must appear strange to them, a ragged woman on a mare fit for a princess.

Following instructions she climbed towards the long rocky ridge beyond the fields. She could feel the peasants' eyes still upon her back.

Near the top Hunydd began to sniff the air nervously and sidestep a little. But Viviane urged her on firmly until they could look down on to the plain on the other side; and there she saw the reason. The monastery, which a few hours previously must have consisted of a collection of sturdily built wooden houses gathered around a central chapel, was now a smouldering and blackened ruin. Viviane shivered, the thought that Idoc might have been responsible crossing her mind.

Near her on the ridge stood an ancient preaching cross – a cross bearing a circle – the symbol of the new religion and the old combined in one powerful stone image – a marker that had been there for centuries before the monks had come and would remain there long after they were gone. She climbed down from Hunydd and put her arms around the stone, leaning her head against it, saying a silent prayer.

What now? She did not want to go back to the cold, unfriendly peasants and beg a bed for the night in one of their cramped little huts. Nor could she return to the comforts of Castle Goreu. Her father's home was far, far away. There was still the Community of the Fish . . . but would she ever be able to find that?

Since she had left the woods, clouds had gathered. She searched the landscape that lay spread out like a quilt below her, wondering where in all that web of forest, rock and stream, crop-field and pasture, she would find what she was looking for . . .

There was a ridge of hills in the distance but the black clouds hung so oppressively low they were almost invisible. Suddenly she heard a sound above her and looked up to see that a pair of swans had risen into the air and, like white thunder, were winging their way across the landscape. Their necks outstretched, like living arrows, they pointed the way to a knoll of rock in the distance – a knoll she recognized for it overlooked the sanctuary she sought. At that very moment, as though in confirmation, the clouds parted a fraction and a ray of light caught the swans' wings, burnishing them with dazzling silver. She caught her breath. But as suddenly as it had happened it was over. The clouds closed over again. The swans landed. The moment now only existed in her memory . . . but she knew that it had been a gift and she would cherish it forever.

The landscape seemed even darker now in contrast to the brilliant white of the swans, and she noticed that the knoll overlooking the sanctuary was not the only prominence. Dark as the clouds were, she had the impression that there was a more powerful source of darkness on the earth. Its centre seemed to be a hill with a tower upon it, lying between her and the sanctuary. Towards this, like shoals of fish all swimming in the same direction, flashes and gleams of light seemed to be drawn: only to scatter in apparent confusion as they reached the black shadow surrounding the tower. Most were instantly sucked in, finding the force of darkness too strong for them. When they re-emerged they themselves had taken on the darkness and were part of the shadow that was reaching out across the land.

Shivering, she spoke to Hunydd. 'Come, we must find shelter before it rains.' She would try to skirt the dark tower, but meanwhile there was a great deal of travelling to be done.

She had not gone far when she came upon a party of warriors. They surrounded her at once, their eyes stripping her naked.

'What have we here?' one said.

'A woman ready for laying,' another replied.

'My turn first,' a third broke in.

'No, mine!' spoke a fourth.

'Let's toss for it.'

'Neol should go first.'

'After Neol we'll toss.'

Hands came out and groped her, one cupping a breast while the others whistled. She tried to pull away but they were pressing too close, and had Hunydd firmly by the bridle.

'You'll pay for this,' she said fiercely. 'I am the betrothed of Caradawc, son of Goreu!'

The effect of her words was startling.

The men drew back at once and gathered into a tight knot for consultation. Seeing them thus occupied, she encouraged Hunydd to slip away and make for the woods where she hoped she would have a better chance of hiding. But they turned and spotted her before she reached cover, and set off at once in pursuit. Once again Hunydd was urged to a gallop, but the men were upon her in moments, the leader leaning over to seize her bridle. The others encircled her – but this time silently. Only the one holding the bridle spoke, and with more respect than before.

'We apologize, my lady,' he said. 'You must be the Princess Viviane?'

'Yes.' She tried to keep her dignity, in spite of the eyes that still looked her over greedily.

'You must agree . . . dressed as you are . . . it was an easy mistake for my men to make.'

'Is any woman who comes your way subjected to the same treatment?' she asked coldly.

'We are men, my lady,' he answered, equally coldly.

'I know men who would not behave thus.'

'I know women who would not ride about the countryside pretending to be peasants when they are royal born.'

'I have been through many dangers, sir, and would be grateful if you would give me your protection and guide me to some civilized household where I may find rest and food and perhaps a change of clothes. I am sure that the Lord Caradawc will amply reward you.'

At this the men laughed loudly, and even the polite young man who had been speaking smiled grimly.

'I am sure he will, my lady,' he said quietly, but she did not miss the irony in his voice.

Her heart was beating fast as she realized that she was not among friends – but perhaps they would be held at bay by what they feared to lose or hoped to gain from Caradawc.

The young man in charge spoke briefly to his companions, sending most of them on to continue along the way they had been going, but choosing others to head back with him in the direction whence they had come. Viviane was to ride beside him, his hand still on her bridle.

'Where are you taking me, sir?' she asked calmly, though she felt far from calm.

'To my father's house,' he said.

'Your father, sir?'

'Huandaw, son of Neved.' The names meant nothing to her. She had come too recently to the area to know the enmities and rivalries of all the local houses. But she caught the pride in the young man's voice.

'And you?'

'Neol, son of Huandaw.'

'I greet you, Neol, son of Huandaw.'

'And I greet you, Viviane, daughter of Garwys,' he said coldly.

'You know my father, sir?'

'No, my lady, but I have heard of you.'

'You know Prince Caradawc?'

The answer did not come quickly this time. She could not see his face, but she saw his shoulders stiffen.

'Yes,' he said, the word devoid of any emotion.

'And his father, Goreu?'

'Particularly his father, Goreu!' To *these* words he gave bitter emphasis.

'The Lord Goreu is dead,' she said hastily, hoping that the ill feeling she could sense lay between Huandaw and Goreu, and not between Caradawc and Neol.

'I know,' he said stiffly.

They rode in silence for a while, the others keeping just behind them.

Suddenly he shouted an order and one of the men rode swiftly ahead, no doubt to prepare Huandaw for their arrival. She began to feel more and more uneasy.

'When I am guest in your father's house' – she chose the word carefully, knowing that to be a guest was to be under the host's protection – 'I would like to send a message to . . . to my father.' What had this young man heard of the murder of Goreu, the fire, her disappearance? What interpretation did he put on finding her here so far from Caradawc's lands, ragged and clad like a peasant?

'My lady, you will not be a "guest" in my father's house,' Neol replied equally carefully. 'You will be a hostage.'

Her heart sank. 'A hostage, sir?'

'Surely you must know that the House of Goreu and the House of Huandaw are sworn enemies?'

'No,' she said in a low voice. 'You will find that I am not of much value as a hostage, sir,' she continued, trying to steady her voice. 'My relationship with the House of Goreu is no longer good.'

'Yet when it suited you you claimed Caradawc's protection?' He turned and looked at her sharply.

She flushed. 'Surely you can understand, sir, a woman set upon must defend herself as best she can.'

'And when her deception is found out – what protection can

she expect then?'

What indeed?

'Sir – the protection of an honourable man: Neol, son of Huandaw.'

He reined in their two steeds, and the others came to a halt behind them. He looked at her long and closely; but in that look she could read nothing of what he was thinking.

Idoc was in his tower, staring into his scrying mirror. The images before him appeared to float in front of the mirror; they were solid-seeming, almost tangible. He bit the knuckles of his left hand. Even in rags she was beautiful: the sun catching her hair, touching the curve of her breast . . . The image was so clear he could even see the long dark lashes shadowing her green-grey eyes. The interference of Neol had not been in his plan. Who was this Neol that he looked at her so boldly? Was he contemplating taking her from Caradawc? That must not be allowed! Caradawc's body was open to Idoc in a way that Neol's would never be, for Caradawc had been under his control in that past life, and Caradawc's weakness then was his weakness now: then as now he could be manipulated – by fear . . . by jealousy . . . by loving too blindly. Neol was a colder, harder man, one who knew his own strengths and weaknesses, and those of the people around him. He would never allow himself to be taken over. Idoc strode about the chamber. If Neol lay with Viviane he, Idoc, would not be able to feel a thing. Cursing, he returned to the mirror to see what further was happening.

If Neol had made reply to Viviane, Idoc had missed it, and he was furious with himself for allowing his irritation to interfere. The group of figures was on the move again: as before, Neol leading Viviane. But the image was fading. Idoc cursed again. It was his own agitation that was causing this – his control was slipping. He was allowing his feelings for the woman he had once desired so desperately to interfere with his simple pursuit of revenge. Bitterly he put his hand over her image in the mirror, his palm against the ice-cold obsidian. He would not look at her. To look at her was to desire her. To desire her was to be diverted from his purpose.

Viviane, riding beside Neol, felt a sudden shadow cross her path and, as it touched her, it was like the touch of a hand.

It was Gerin who found Caradawc sitting on the north bank where the river narrowed and the water divided into fierce white streams rushing between huge rounded boulders. He was badly bruised and there was blood on his shoulder, but he had been very lucky to recover consciousness before hitting the worst of the rapids.

Gerin himself had crossed the river further downstream, and was making his way back towards Huandaw's house when he came upon the young king, soaked and shivering.

When Caradawc told him how he had found and rescued Viviane, Gerin thought his heart would leap out of his chest. Since the first moment he had set eyes on her he had been drawn to her, so strongly that it was almost more than he could do to hide it from his friends. It was he who had found the charred remains of Goreu with Viviane's dagger still in his back, and it was he who had removed it before anyone else could see it; confiding only in Caradawc. Had she been driven crazy by remorse for what she had done? Why else would she have plunged into the river and tried to drown herself? Why else, after Caradawc had risked his life to rescue her, would she still run from him, and bribe the ferryman to push him off the ferry?

'I'm sure she didn't mean him to kill me. She even tried to help me – but it was too late. The man was over-zealous.'

'At any rate,' Gerin said, 'we know she is alive and heading north. She's probably trying to return to her father.'

Caradawc frowned. 'That is too far! She'll never reach him on her own.'

The two young men fell silent, thinking. They had set off to solve the mystery of the black knight, but that seemed unimportant now.

Gerin stood up decisively. 'I'll be back as soon as I find Osla,' he said, 'and then we'll look for her together.'

Caradawc nodded. 'Take care,' he said quietly.

'You too, my friend. Keep out of sight if you hear anyone coming. We are very close to Huandaw's lands, if not already on them.'

Caradawc nodded, and Gerin remounted and rode off the way he had come.

Rheged was the first to find a place where he could watch the house of Huandaw without being seen. He found a tor capped with rocks and trees, and took up his position inside a huge boulder that had been cracked open by an oak tree. The tree itself was stunted and deformed, all its energy having gone into the prodigious work of splitting the solid rock.

From here, hidden by leaves and branches, Rheged could see down into the walled area of the great house: he could watch all the comings and goings in the courtyard and through the main gate. He could see a herdboy driving cattle back from the pasture, and hear the thin, high call as he summoned his dog. He could see a woman scattering grain for the chickens, and children playing around the well. The tor was out of arrow range, but there was a higher hill nearer to the buildings where he was sure a lookout would be posted. It was not the intention of Caradawc's friends to beard Huandaw in his den, or even to plan a revenge raid. They had not thought further than discovering more about the mysterious black knight: whether he was part of Huandaw's household, or whether he had arrived during the battle for some other purpose – unknown both to Huandaw and to Caradawc alike.

There was certainly no sign of his presence here in the valley.

Rheged's limbs were growing stiff in the cramped position he had chosen and he glanced anxiously more than once at the sky, where the clouds were pressing ominously low. He had just decided he would stay no longer fruitlessly watching, when suddenly he spotted a party of riders emerging from a nearby copse.

In front rode a figure that looked like Huandaw's son, Neol, leading a white horse beside his own. As Rheged suddenly leant forward he nearly pitched headlong down the tor, saving himself just in time by seizing hold of a branch. A few pebbles went skittering down the steep slope to the valley, and he feared someone watching from the other hill might notice, but any guard there was also watching the horsemen, for no one appeared to challenge him.

Rheged had recognized Viviane on the white horse.

The men accompanying her were joined by others from the house, and she was led through the gate in triumph, everyone running to stare at her, with Huandaw himself appearing at the door of the main hall.

Rheged saw her helped down from her mare by Neol, and presented to his father. They then went inside and out of sight. He continued to watch while the other horsemen dismounted and handed over their mounts to grooms and stable boys. The others who had ridden out to meet them dispersed to take up guard positions: it was clear that they were expecting trouble.

When one began to ride towards the tor on which Rheged was hidden, he knew that if he did not leave at once he would be discovered. Luckily, what sounds he made as he descended the tor were lost as the storm that had been brewing finally broke. His last glimpse of Huandaw's yard was of the children running for the house, squealing, as the huge drops of rain started to pelt down and the air rumbled with thunder.

Rheged mounted up and rode off as fast as he could, a wind driving the rain into his face and almost blinding him. Within seconds he was soaked through and exhausted, but he was confident he would not be pursued.

5

Kicva and Elined

At the feasting that night, beside Huandaw's great chair, on the right hand, where his eldest son should have been, sat Kicva, clearly as honoured by Huandaw as she had been by Goreu. Viviane's heart sank when she recognized her, particularly when she saw how the old woman looked at her.

As she was led in on the arm of Neol, arrayed in his sister's finery, green gown with gold at waist and throat, gold on her bare arms and swinging from her ears, her hair plaited and twisted high upon her head, she felt confident that she could charm these people into treating her with kindness and respect . . . And then she saw Kicva and knew that she was lost.

Neol guided her round the tables where companions, relatives and retainers sat, proudly parading her as though she was some trophy won in battle. She held her head high, allowing him the pleasure of his game; biding her time.

He ushered her to the chair on Huandaw's left side, and she looked hard at the old man, remembering Goreu. But Huandaw was not like Goreu. He was thin and spare, grey-haired and grey-eyed. His face was lined as though he smiled a lot; his manner was gracious. She wondered what he could be doing with that evil hag on his right, and a son with such cold eyes. She bowed formally to Kicva in greeting, and Kicva bowed mockingly back.

'You see, my lady, we already have here someone known to you,' Huandaw said mildly, and she could not tell from his expression if he were being sarcastic or whether he genuinely thought she would he pleased to meet an old acquaintance.

'Kicva is known to me, my lord,' she said carefully, 'but I am surprised that an enemy of Goreu should entertain his most devoted servant with such honour.'

Kicva's eyes sparked dangerously.

'It is because she was so devoted to the Lord Goreu that she is now here,' Huandaw said.

'Explain, my lord,' Viviane said coolly, trying not to let the old woman's malevolent stare unnerve her.

He gazed at her appraisingly before he answered. 'She tells me Goreu was murdered, and has come to offer her services in avenging his death.' His eyes did not leave Viviane's.

'Why would you want to avenge the Lord Goreu's death, my lord?' she asked softly. 'Surely, as he was your enemy, you would reward the man who did the deed.'

'Or the woman,' he said, watching her closely.

She kept control of her face and looked at Kicva. 'Does this Druid know who killed her lord, sir? Was she there?'

'She has the Sight.'

'Ah, the Sight!' Viviane was relieved. If Kicva's Druid 'Sight' had told her that she, Viviane, was the murderer, then Kicva's Druid 'Sight' was not worth fearing.

'Her vengeance might well serve our purposes,' Huandaw continued, 'though it is not vengeance for his *death* we seek.'

'Your son tells me, sir, that my lord Goreu robbed you of many things during his life.'

'That is true.'

'I am sure you'll find, sir, that my lord Caradawc will gladly make recompense.'

'He has already shown his "goodwill" towards us by attacking us.'

'I know nothing of that, my lord,' she said, 'but I am surprised. Goreu's son is very different from his father and does not relish conquest.'

Neol, sitting to her left, leant forward and spoke across her.

'The son is always loyal to the father, sir, though there be differences between them.'

Viviane caught a look that passed between them which intrigued her.

'I must have my lands back,' Huandaw declared. 'If you, my lady, think I'll get them back by asking – well, I will ask.'

'And when you do, you'll take a sword in the belly,' said Neol bitterly.

'Not from Caradawc!' she said quickly.

'No? Why do you run from him then, my lady, if he is so fair and just?'

She bit her lip. How could she possibly explain?

'She runs because she was given hospitality and yet she murdered her host,' Kicva said suddenly, clearly and loudly.

Viviane could hear the gasp, and see the hostility in every eye in the hall. Her composure broke.

'No!' she cried. 'It is not true!'

Kicva stood up and pointed her bony finger straight at the young woman's breast. Though it did not touch, Viviane experienced a sharp pain. She gasped and clutched her heart and sank back in her chair, her face drained of colour.

'You see!' Kicva said with satisfaction.

Viviane felt she could not breathe, as though some great weight lay on her breast. Kicva's eyes never left hers. She tried to speak, to defend herself, but the words would not come.

'It seems the Druid's accusations strike home,' Huandaw said coldly. 'Take her away,' he bade the two armed men who stood behind his chair. 'Lock her up until we decide what to do with her.'

'Locking up will do no good!' Kicva snarled. 'She is driven by demons. Kill her now . . . or let me bind her with spells.'

'Kill her!' The whisper started like a small wind rustling among dry leaves . . . and grew in volume until all were standing, shouting, shaking their fists . . . and then the wind was huge, swirling the dead leaves until the air was thick with them, and no one could see through them . . .

Viviane was dragged from the room. She saw the angry faces . . . the docile people turned suddenly violent by the dark wind that blew through the hall . . . the wind that was no wind . . .

She was thrown into a small dark room and heard the bolts slammed home. She could still hear the chanting, led by Kicva, and put her hands over her ears to shut it out. Gradually it faded and the terrible pressure on her chest began to lift . . . but not the despair. Perhaps she *was* possessed by demons? She thought back to all that had happened since she had followed that hart deeper into the forest. But in thinking back Viviane also remembered the Green Lady, and the chapel of the tree . . .

Did she imagine a light tap on the door? She listened, holding her breath. It was so intensely quiet she was aware of her
own heartbeats. Then the sound came again: as though the bolts
were being drawn back furtively, gradually.

After a few moments the door opened a crack, and a sharp
triangle of light flooded in. Viviane blinked like a night-owl
suddenly woken in daylight. It was Neol's sister Elined.

'Hush,' the girl whispered, putting her fingers to Viviane's
lips. 'I'll help you to escape if you'll take me with you.'

Viviane nodded silently, surprised, but unquestioning.

The girl slipped a dark cloak over her shoulders and took
her hand. Together they glided like shadows down the deserted
corridor. As they passed the sleeping guard, Elined smiled mis-
chievously and pointed to herself, proudly, claiming that this
was her handiwork. She knew her way through the labyrinth of
corridors, which ones to take and which to avoid, and it was
not long before the two young women were out of the house
and into the dark of the night. A young groom was waiting for
them holding ready two horses (one of them Hunydd!) and
Elined kissed his cheek lightly as he helped her to mount.
Viviane saw the adoration in his eyes and knew that Elined
would always inspire such loyal devotion, so it might be no
bad thing to have her company.

The gatekeeper must also have been dealt with by the re-
sourceful girl, for he was nowhere in sight. They walked their
horses carefully and quietly until they were well clear.

Much later, after they had put a good distance between themselves and the great house, Viviane learned why Elined had
gone to all this trouble. It was to save herself from an arranged
marriage to an old man she hated.

'I could probably talk my father out of it, but Neol would
not give way.'

'Surely it is your father's word that is heard in your house?'

'You'd think so, wouldn't you? But it is not so. I've seen
Neol get his way time and time again against father's wishes.
For instance, it was Neol's idea to attack Caradawc. My father
was reluctant.'

'You dislike your brother?'

'No, I love him, but over this matter of the marriage I am

really angry with him.'

Viviane was silent, remembering how she herself had been sent on a long journey to marry a man she had never met. But she had been lucky. The prospect of marrying Caradawc was not at all unpleasant. If only . . . She wondered if she should warn Elined of the frightening and inexplicable things likely to happen to them. She decided against it for the moment: to have a companion on her difficult journey would be a great relief.

'He's older than my father,' complained Elined. 'But Neol thinks he'll die soon, and I'll inherit his lands. Neol is ambitious to extend our family lands and doesn't care that I may have to live with that disgusting creature for *years!*'

'Has he no children to inherit?'

'No. After two wives he's still childless.'

'Then perhaps he's impotent, and won't want anything from you but your companionship.'

'Even that . . .' Elined shuddered.

For a while the two young women rode on in silence. It was Viviane who first broke it.

'We must expect Neol to send men after us,' she said.

'We'll give them the slip with the help of your demons,' Elined said cheerfully.

'My demons?'

'Yes. The ones Kicva told us about.'

'You really believe I'm possessed by demons and yet you choose to ride with me?'

'Well, I decided no ordinary means would get me out of this marriage!'

'But if Kicva speaks the truth, you are in great danger.'

Elined looked across at Viviane. 'I don't care. Nothing could be worse than marrying that revolting old man.'

'You don't know what you're saying!' Viviane was shocked that this girl could have such a casual attitude to the forces of darkness. She had obviously had no experience of them. Indeed she was very young, a virgin still, Viviane thought. What was it in a person's face that gave away this secret, no matter how closely guarded?

'*Is* what Kicva said true?' Elined asked, curious now.

'No.'

'Well, then . . . I'm in no danger.'

'Yes, you are, though not because of me . . . but because I too am being pursued.'

'By demons?' Elined sounded positively eager.

Viviane did not answer. What would be best to do now? Should she send Elined back to her father and her angry brother before too much harm was done, or should they both try to reach the sanctuary? It was almost dawn and she felt very tired; her thoughts were sluggish and confused. She hated the thought of being alone again. Two women riding together were not as remarkable as one, but with Elined to look after as well as herself . . .

She reined in. She would decide in the morning, after rest . . .

Idoc paced the octagonal chamber of his tower. On a polished brass table stood a collection of glass vessels and bottles of different shapes and sizes. Each of the table's four legs stood on a hard disc of beeswax carved with potent geometric signs. Charts of vellum hung on six of the walls, three worked all over with geometric signs and numbers, while the other three depicted hideous beings of the underworld in intricate detail. The black obsidian mirror, tall as himself, filled the seventh wall, while the eighth contained a heavy door, the lock itself an elaborate system of metal boxes, cogs and bolts, opened only by a series of keys in different metals, each preparing the way for the next. There was no window: no way of seeing out into the world by any natural means.

She had betrayed him. She must suffer – be destroyed. He would never let her be at peace again. Through life after life he would pursue her. She had sealed her own fate when she used her feminine beauty to trap him. The priests who had pronounced the spells would pay, too – but it was against her he bore the most malice. He had loved her and she had destroyed him. Well, now she would love him and he would destroy her. But to do this he must first master his own need for her. The time he had lain with her on the riverbank, using Caradawc's body, was intended only to rouse in her the desire for him that would eventually destroy her – but he had felt too much joy himself, too much ecstasy.

He would not look at her again. Striding across the room he

62

opened a heavy wooden chest and lifted out a black cloak stained with blood, the cloak he had worn recently to play the role of the black knight. He now hung it over the mirror. He would find other means of punishing her.

From the same chest he drew a sheet of lead beaten thin, and laid it on the table, pushing the glass vessels impatiently aside. He took his knife – double-edged, traced with the planetary symbols, its handle exquisitely inset with jewels in silver – and, holding it firm, began to scratch the words of a curse into the lead.

After he had done this, he looked up at the charts and thoughtfully pondered which of the many beings he should send.

At last he smiled, and began to draw on the lead sheet . . .

Viviane awoke to find her clothes drenched, and a cold, sour rain driving down the valley before a grey north wind. Startled and shivering, she staggered to her feet, wondering where she was.

She had the feeling that she was being watched, but could not bring herself to turn around and see who it was. Remembering Elined suddenly, she thought it might be Neol's men come to fetch her back. She saw the girl, asleep under a tree, out of the worst of the rain, the horses tethered beside her. Calmly, and still not looking round, she began to move towards Elined, her cloak, soaked with icy water, dragging like lead against her shoulders. The rain felt like tiny painful needles as it beat upon her face: the wind howled in her ears like a banshee.

'Elined,' she called.

How could she sleep through such a storm? The ominously creaking branches of the tree above her were being tossed so violently it seemed they would soon be ripped out of their sockets and come crashing down. Viviane nudged the girl with her foot – but she did not stir. She stooped down and shook her violently, but still she slept on. It dawned on Viviane that this was no ordinary sleep.

She spun round, clutching her knife, and crouched like a cat ready to spring.

And then she froze . . .

The crowd that pressed closer and closer was not comprised of Neol's warriors – but of foul and infernal beings . . . Bat-winged and human-faced, vulture-clawed and lizard-eyed, they flapped around her beating their webbed wings. She could feel the scalding heat of their bodies, smell their acrid and sulphurous breath.

She screamed, her tears mingling with the rain that poured over her face.

But Elined slept on, though the horses snorted and pulled at their tethers. And then, borne in on the wind, came thick black fog . . . at first in shreds and slivers, and then in waves and billows. She thought now she would surely die.

But it was not to her that death came with the fog. For it was as inimical to Idoc's fiends as they were to her. Howling as their strength failed them, they shrank . . . they withered . . .

And then it was all over. They were gone as mysteriously as they had come. She sat in silence – seeing nothing, hearing nothing. She held the sleeping Elined close, thankful for her human warmth. She could feel her peaceful breathing as though she slumbered naturally after all.

Viviane peered through the dark fog that surrounded her.

What now? She thought she saw a point of light high above her, and prayed that it was the sun trying to break through.

The point grew brighter, so bright indeed that it made her eyes water and she had to close them. When she opened them again, the point had become a rod, so bright against the darkness that it looked solid. Another appeared, and then another. As she watched, the darkness became criss-crossed with thin, brilliant rods of light. They silently moved from above to below, from side to side, diagonally . . . steadily breaking the fog into smaller and smaller patches. She stared, fascinated. She had never seen such a sight: they were like swords cutting a solid into tiny pieces. Natural sunlight would have dispersed the fog gradually. She reached out her hand curiously to touch a beam close by. Her hand disappeared. She drew her arm back hastily, staring at where her hand had been. Very slowly it began to materialize again. Then she sat very still, watching the marvellously precise way the darkness was cut away from them – until at last she stood on a clear hillside in full daylight.

* * * *

Waiting for the curse to take effect, Idoc sat hunched in his chair. His hands locked and unlocked convulsively, his mouth worked, saying over and over again the words he had carved on the lead. He gloated when he felt the creatures he had invoked rising around him like so many vulture-shadows and go streaming through the walls out into the world beyond . . .

Time passed. Time strained and pulled and tugged at him. He longed to look in the mirror, but he clutched the chair arms and refused to move. 'Now they will have found her,' he thought. 'Now they will be closing in . . . now they will be surrounding her . . .'

But something was wrong – he could sense it. He half rose, thinking of the mirror. But if he saw her he might show mercy. He forced himself down again into the chair. The curse could not fail . . .

He smelled a strange smell – at first so faint he took no notice. But soon it became so strong he could no longer ignore it. Sniffing, he turned his head and searched the chamber with dark, tormented eyes . . . From the table where he had laid the curse a thin plume of black smoke was rising. He leapt towards it. What . . .?

The smoke was gone before he reached it, and he would have thought he had imagined it but in the place of the neat leaden scroll was now a pool of molten lead still faintly sizzling. The brass table beneath was unharmed.

Furiously Idoc stared at it, then rushed to the mirror. He ripped the cloak away from its surface and glared into it. At first he was almost blinded by the flash of light that reflected off the surface. He staggered back, a shaft of pain striking him through the centre of the forehead. Screaming, he clutched his head. How could this be?

Who protected her?

Who fought her battles?

He forced himself to look in the mirror again, bracing himself for the light. But it was gone. Instead he saw a green hillside with a fringe of trees, two young women talking quietly, and two horses cropping peacefully. He spied a movement among the trees and leaned closer. Was he mistaken or did he see a translucent figure – as elusive a glimpse as the flash of crystal in clear water?

* * * *

Elined woke cheerfully, ready for any adventure, and Viviane chose not to tell her that she had already been through one. She chose also, much to Elined's joy, to keep her with her on the journey to the sanctuary.

Cai came upon them in his wanderings in search of the black knight, and he was delighted to find Viviane still alive.

Viviane told him part of the truth. She had been captured, she said, by Neol for use as hostage against Caradawc. She had escaped with the help of Elined, who was fleeing from a hateful arranged marriage, and they were now trying to reach the Community of the Fish, where they hoped to be given sanctuary.

'Women should not ride about the countryside alone,' Cai warned. 'There are all kinds of dangers. May I offer you ladies my protection on your journey?'

Viviane smiled wryly, thinking that he did not know what he was offering to protect them against, but Elined instantly accepted. Cai, with his long blond hair and light blue eyes, was for her the answer to a prayer. She was already preparing romantic snares for him. And he was by no means sorry to put off an uncomfortable confrontation with the black knight for the chance of riding through the sunlight with two beautiful women.

They set off at once, Cai having a better idea of where they were than they did. He and Elined rode ahead through green lanes and beside fields of barley and rye, startling plover and pheasants, and little, trilling larks . . . chatting together as though this was nothing but a summer pleasure ride.

Viviane followed behind, still shaken by the experiences she had been through and apprehensive as to what would happen next.

When Rheged at last found Caradawc and Gerin, he reported to them that he had seen Viviane being taken as prisoner into the stronghold of Huandaw. Caradawc insisted on going at once to negotiate for her release, in spite of Rheged's dire warnings. He assured them that he would give up all the lands his father had taken from Huandaw, if need be. Never having been in love himself, though he had lain with many women, Rheged could not understand a man prepared to sacrifice so much.

'I'd give my life for her,' vowed Caradawc passionately.

'You may have to!' said Rheged.

'Well, so be it,' replied Caradawc stubbornly, and nothing would turn him away from his purpose.

They were challenged by four armed men on their approach to the great house and escorted in to see Huandaw himself. They had expected their arrival would rouse some curiosity, but were startled by the ferocity with which Huandaw's people came running towards them, shouting abuse. They were relieved when the door of the great hall slammed shut behind them, leaving them alone with their taciturn guards.

Huandaw at last strode in with Kicva at his side. The old man's face was grey and drawn with worry, Kicva's filled with self-importance.

'What have you done with my daughter?' Huandaw snapped as soon as he saw Caradawc.

'Your daughter, sir?' he said, surprised.

'Play no games with me, sir!' Huandaw growled. 'Where have you taken her?'

'I know nothing of your daughter,' Caradawc replied. 'I have come for my future wife, Viviane daughter of Garwys, to take her home.'

'You dare to talk to me of that *witch!*' Huandaw raged.

Bewildered, and suddenly afraid, Caradawc looked at Gerin.

'Sir,' Gerin said, stepping forward. 'It's clear there is some mistake here. We know nothing of your daughter – only that you hold the princess Viviane here.'

'Held. Held her here,' Huandaw muttered bitterly.

Caradawc cleared his throat. 'Held, sir? Is she gone then?'

'Yes, she's gone!' Kicva suddenly interrupted. 'She and her vile demons have spirited away my lord Huandaw's daughter. I warned them – but they wouldn't listen!' she screeched.

Caradawc looked at her in astonishment as though registering her presence for the first time.

Huandaw was now wandering distractedly about the room, muttering to himself about his daughter.

'Why do *you* seek her?' Kicva challenged Caradawc. 'She who murdered your father, and would have murdered you if I had not been so skilled in healing . . .'

Caradawc stared at her blankly. What she said made a kind of sense to his mind – but not to his heart.

Gerin put his hand on Caradawc's arm, understanding the turmoil in his friend's heart because he shared it. But he kept better control of himself than Caradawc and demanded boldly and sternly to be told exactly what had happened.

'They brought her here as hostage, and I warned them that the only way to stop her wickedness was to use the power of spells. But they wouldn't listen. Her demons released her in the night, and out of spite she took the lady Elined with her.'

'No one knows where she is?'

'Only the dark ones whom she serves.'

'My son Neol has taken men and gone after them,' Huandaw broke in suddenly, returning to them. 'But if they are fiend-protected, I doubt they'll ever be found.'

'We'll find them,' Gerin said confidently, frowning, his eyes dark with anxiety. 'Our forces and yours, my lord, working together instead of against each other. What say you?'

Kicva laughed. 'No force of ordinary men in the world can outwit fiends.'

'We shall see . . .' Caradawc said, suddenly decisive. 'What say you, sir?'

'Together – or alone,' Gerin urged, seeing that Huandaw was hesitating. 'Nothing will be achieved if we don't go to it *soon.*'

Huandaw frowned. His son insisted that these men were his enemies, but he was not so sure.

'If you go,' Kicva insisted, 'I must ride with you. Your arms will be useless against her demons. We'll see what an old woman, Druid-trained, can do!'

'Sir?' Gerin ignored her and addressed himself still to the distraught Huandaw.

At last the old man nodded.

'We both have an interest in this. So be it,' he said.

Over the hills and forests a cold rain was driven before a gusty grey wind. The search party, pulling their cloaks tightly around themselves, set off. Trees loomed and disappeared again into obscurity. Nothing was clear-cut, nothing definite.

6

Abduction

Cai, escorting the two young women, was the first to encounter the black knight for the second time.

They were resting beside a pool in a deep ravine. A waterfall dropped like a white thread from the lip of a cliff somewhere high above them, beyond even the tops of the tallest trees. Light and shade dappled the huge moss-covered boulders around them, and ferns grew out like feathers from every surface of branch and trunk. Bird-notes pierced the shimmering green light with little stabs of sound so beautiful that they were almost painful to hear.

At noon Viviane and Elined decided that they must bathe. Cai was sent off to climb the cliff and see if he could work out the best route for them to follow, while they took off their clothes and slipped into the cool water. Like slender otters they slid through the water, turning and twisting and playing. Viviane's dark memories of the last time she was in water were dispelled by the cheerful innocence of her companion. There were no clinging weeds in this pool, only silver and crystal bubbles flowing around them, touching and teasing them.

In such a place, the trees could never be considered as wood to chop for fire or roof beam. Their slow and intricate growth, rooted in earth and reaching to Heaven, had made them the home of peaceful spirits, and as Viviane came up for air she fancied she saw the forest flowing with transparent forms, and felt their love surrounding her. She dived beneath the surface again, truly happy for the first time since she had released Idoc from the ancient spell. This was a special place. Hate could not flourish here.

Elined called her over to the waterfall, and behind it they

found a fern-covered ledge where they could sit and watch the sunlight sparking off the spray.

'We can hide here from Cai,' Elined laughed. 'He'll never be able to find us.'

'He'll be worried. I don't think . . .'

'Oh, we'll not keep him guessing long, but it will be fun to see his face when he comes back to find us gone.'

'You can hide if you like,' Viviane said, 'but I'm going back.'

'Pretend you've lost me then. See what he says.'

'You know what he'll say.'

'No, I don't,' Elined said petulantly. 'Sometimes I think he is more concerned about you than me.'

'You know that's not true.' Elined had been flirting shamelessly with Cai, and it was clear that he was now her slave.

Viviane slid down from the ledge and passed through the fine edge of the waterfall, the spray making her skin tingle. She intended to swim back to their clothes and dress before Cai returned. But it seemed she was too late – there was someone already there. Viviane turned at once and swam to the other side of the pool where she had noticed the trunk of a fallen tree, half in the water and half arched above it. The arch made a kind of cave where she could hide in shadow, only her head and shoulders out of the water. Reflected on the dark wood above her was a net of shimmering lights as the sun shone directly into the rippling water. She intended to call out to Cai from her shelter. But looking back across the pool, she saw that the figure was not Cai's. On the bank stood a tall warrior in black armour, his visor raised – and the eyes of Idoc piercingly directed into hers.

'Oh Lord,' she murmured, 'is there nowhere on this earth that is safe for me?'

'Safety is how you handle danger,' a soundless voice whispered. 'Not how you avoid it.'

If she could not run from Idoc, what would happen if she faced him?

The forest had gone deathly silent. There was no birdsong, no sigh of breeze on leaf; even the waterfall was now falling noiselessly. The shadow of Idoc had drawn the light from every living thing. Nothing sparkled. Nothing shone. Except . . . except the reflection of the ripples on the arch of tree trunk above her. Puzzled, she touched one, wondering how it had escaped – hoping this was a sign that his baleful influence could not reach her here, although he was well aware of where she was.

To her astonishment the small flicker of light seemed to come away from the bark on to her fingers. She moved her hand expecting it to be gone but it stayed with her and then she found that the whole shimmering veil of light had become separate from the arch of wood, and, almost like a filmy shawl, could be drawn about her shoulders. She glanced back at Idoc, but he had not moved. And there was no sign of Elined or Cai.

Taking a deep breath she moved out from under the fallen tree and, clothed in the shawl of rippling light, she swam back to the far bank. She was now no more than a few feet from him, and her heart was pounding so hard with fear that she did not believe she could hold her ground. His face was not Caradawc's face this time, but his own: the straight nose, the dark brow, the mouth she had kissed a hundred times . . . And she to him was Fiann in her falling robe of light, her face as it used to be when he had loved her, when she had begun to fear him . . . But no spirit-lady . . . flesh and blood, breast rising and falling with earth-breath, limbs smooth and supple as only a young woman's can be . . . He ached to touch her – ached to forgive – but something in him stubbornly clung to hate . . . the one thing he knew well . . . the one thing of which he was sure . . .

She took a step forward. She lifted her arms towards him.

'Idoc,' she said softly. 'Release me from your hate. Life is not given to be wasted thus.'

He too moved forward, and for a moment his eyes seemed less hard, less cruel. But before he could speak . . . before they could touch, Cai's shout rang out and startled the forest into noisy life again. They heard him crashing through the undergrowth as he leapt and slid and slithered down the steep hillside, bursting at last on to the bank beside them, out of breath, red in the face, struggling to get his sword out of a scabbard that had become entangled in creepers during his precipitous descent.

Viviane drew back, suddenly realizing that she was naked. She picked up the bundle of clothes and ran as hard as she could for the shelter of some rocks.

71

Idoc stood his ground, his visor now down: the black knight Cai had been seeking.

By the time Cai managed to extricate his sword, the knight had drawn his own and was waiting for him, feet planted firmly, eyes wary behind the slits of the visor. Cai flung himself forward without thinking, and was easily knocked down by a blow from the knight's metalled fist. Cai flushed with shame. The man had swept him aside like a boy too young to be a serious opponent. He raised himself quickly, resentfully struggling to gain mastery of himself.

The dark knight had moved. Somehow he was on the top of a huge boulder, overlooking the scene below: Cai clutching his sword; Viviane now in her dress but still barefoot, her hair in long, fiery strands around her.

The knight raised his sword to his forehead, then held it above his head. In the gesture there was valediction as well as a mocking promise to return.

'Stand and fight!' yelled Cai. 'You bastard! Stand and fight!' He brandished his weapon and started towards where the man had stood – but already the place was empty. Frantically Cai looked around, but there was no sign of the huge figure.

'He has gone,' Viviane said quietly.

'Why wouldn't he fight?' Cai fumed. 'I would have taught him a lesson!'

'What lesson, Cai?' Viviane asked, amused. She felt extraordinarily calm, as though for the first time she realized that what was between Idoc and herself need not necessarily be destructive.

Cai flushed again. 'I lost my footing. I would have given him something to think about!' Then he noticed that Elined was missing. 'Where is she?' he cried, gripping his sword again, though his hand was sweating so much with fear that he could scarcely hold it. Twice had the black knight refused to kill him; twice had he been humiliated by him!

'Don't worry,' Viviane said. 'We found a hiding place behind the waterfall.'

Before she could stop him, Cai rushed towards the place she indicated. Viviane picked up Elined's clothes and followed – calling out a warning – but the noise of the falling water drowned out her voice. She stubbed her bare toe on a rock and while she attended to the pain, Cai reached the waterfall and disappeared behind it.

Viviane didn't know what to do. She knew the two young people believed they were in love. Perhaps she would not be welcome if she intruded. As she hesitated – Cai found Elined. The naked girl, smiling, enticed him with her eyes.

Cai, humiliated by the Black Knight, but given confidence by the smile of the beautiful girl, stepped forward and attempted clumsily to take her in his arms. The ledge they went on was uneven and he fell against her with a greater force than he intended. Suddenly she screamed and pushed him away. This was not how she had imagined her first romantic encounter.

At this moment, Neol's warriors, accompanied by Caradawc, appeared. They heard Elined's scream and found her, naked, scrambling away from Cai.

The girl rushed straight to her brother, sobbing that Cai had raped her.

'No!' shouted Viviane; but too late. Cai was already being beaten by the very men who had seemed about to rape Viviane herself such a short time before.

'Caradawc!' shouted Viviane. 'Stop them! It is not true!' And then: 'Gerin . . . surely you . . .'

Caradawc moved forward, and with him Gerin and Rheged. At swordpoint they forced the men around Cai to stop their work.

'This is not the way,' Caradawc said coldly to Neol. 'If what your sister says is true . . .'

'If?' snapped Neol. 'You insult her, sir.'

'I do not mean to, sir – but I have known this man well for many years, and I would want to know more before I punish him.'

'And I have known my sister, sir!'

'Elined,' Viviane appealed to the girl. 'Think what you are doing. Tell the truth, now, before it is too late – before you have our blood on your hands.'

Elined merely turned away.

'Take me home, Neol,' she whispered. 'I want to go home.'

'I appeal to God Almighty and all the angels of Heaven!' cried Viviane in desperation.

'Her god will not help her,' screamed Kicva. 'She is in league with His enemies!'

As though in confirmation of her words, a sudden wind arose and swirled about their heads, roaring in the treetops, howling through the ravine – and with it came a gigantic shadow.

Horrified, everyone turned to see what caused it, and found it was cast by a huge man clad in black armour, astride a fearsome black stallion. Rider and horse stood above them on a platform of rock, almost blotting out the sun behind them.

Even Kicva shrank back.

Suddenly the black knight pressed forward, his steed leaping from the rock and thundering through them. As he passed he stooped and picked up Viviane with his left arm. Holding her in front of him, he wheeled and galloped off northwards, the whole forest shaking with the powerful thud of his horse's hooves.

Caradawc and Gerin were the first to recover their wits. Almost without thinking, they set off after him. Rheged quickly gave Cai his arm and helped him on to his horse; then they too set off in pursuit, Cai scarcely able to stay in the saddle, so bruised and battered was he.

Neol, however, held his own men back.

'There'll be time enough for vengeance,' he said darkly. 'Now it's important that we take my sister safely home.'

He set her on the saddle before him, and she curled up against his shoulder like a child.

As Caradawc rode thoughts were flashing and tumbling in confusion in his mind. He was tormented by the strangeness of Viviane's behaviour, half believing Kicva's accusations, yet with something in him refusing to accept the superficial appearance of what had happened. That the black knight had so dramatically appeared to rescue her was the most puzzling thing of all. It seemed to confirm everything that Kicva had been saying . . . and yet Viviane had not gone willingly, but had screamed and kicked and tried to resist him. He himself had seen the fear and dread in her face.

Caradawc and Gerin rode so fast they were soon far ahead of Rheged and Cai, and thus it was they who spotted the black knight first, thundering across the open hillside. Birds that had been peacefully feeding on the tall grasses now rose in clouds, screeching and twittering with alarm.

'Take the left,' Caradawc shouted to Gerin, 'and we'll cut him off the other side of the hill.' The two men separated and rode different ways around the base of the hill, but still they would have missed the knight had he chosen to give them the slip.

Gerin reached him first and shouted a challenge for him to stand and fight. The knight reined in at once, and sat, visor down, as though contemplating with amusement this mayfly that dared to bother him. Viviane took advantage of the moment to try to struggle free, but it was as though his arm was made of iron, and she was pinned close against him with no hope of release.

'Gerin,' she called out. 'You can never win. Flee while you can.'

Then Caradawc came galloping full tilt around the hill from the opposite direction, and reined up beside Gerin.

'Caradawc, go! Go, both of you! You don't understand – you *cannot* win!'

The two young men were out of breath and panting, and she could sense they were also afraid; but they did not move.

'Release her!' Caradawc ordered boldly, lifting his chin and trying to meet the other's stare.

'Release her?' the knight mocked. 'To you?'

Gerin rode angrily forward, but with one blow was knocked off his horse. Crushed against the black armour, Viviane cried out with the pain. Caradawc attacked with more forethought, and managed to land a blow against his opponent's shoulder, the armour ringing like a bell.

'Ha!' the black knight said. 'So you are serious?'

Suddenly he flung Viviane from him, and she fell almost on top of Gerin. 'Let's see what you can do, boy,' he taunted Caradawc and the two locked earnestly in combat.

Gerin picked himself up and then helped Viviane to her feet. Dazed, they stood, clinging together, watching as Caradawc took and gave blow on blow.

Suddenly the black knight, in danger of being unseated, pointed at Gerin and Viviane.

'See how your friend holds your woman,' he cried out loudly. 'Are you sure you're fighting for what is really yours?'

In the instant that Caradawc turned to look at Gerin and Viviane, the black knight could have killed him, but he hesitated as if wanting to savour Caradawc's jealousy. In that instant Viviane flung herself from Gerin's arms, thinking only of Caradawc's life. She picked up a sharp stone and flung it with all her might at the flank of the knight's charger. The huge creature snorted and reared up – and, before its rider could regain control, bolted with him.

Viviane stood astonished: as it had left her hand, the stone had hummed and spun, whistled and sung a high and faery tune, an eerie light streaming behind it like the tail of a comet. As she paused to think she realized that the black knight's steed was no ordinary horse, so no ordinary stone could possibly have pierced its side. She ran forward to look where the missile had fallen, and found there a pure double-ended quartz crystal, the colour of water and clear ice.

Wonderingly she picked it up and held the two points between her thumb and index finger. She could feel the power of it surging through her hand and almost dropped it. But the beauty of it held her riveted. Light reflected off all the crystal planes, and yet it was as clear as air. Through it she could see the trees . . . the slope of the hill . . . the clouds . . . images of the natural world reflected back and forth within the crystal, from plane to plane. She turned the crystal around and around, watching the light change . . . the reflections running into each other, becoming blurred and indistinct until, emerging from them, she saw new images . . . figures and forms of light . . . silver beings as insubstantial as gossamer yet having the strength to move mountains and fell giants . . . A thousand angels on a needle point – each one capable of overthrowing an emperor or of making a peasant into a king.

She had lost her rose-crystal sphere which had helped her to escape from the ferryman. Now she had been given a second crystal of power, a sign that she had not been deserted. Something tugged at her memory – something from the ancient days. To her people of those long-gone days pure quartz crystal was sacred and they believed it had the property of dispelling, even destroying, evil forces. She herself had helped to place protective quartz crystals on the burial mounds and places of initiation . . .

But she was not Fiann now. She was Viviane – a woman falsely accused of many crimes. She turned back to the two men – they had not moved. Silently they were searching each other's eyes. Viviane looked from one to the other sadly. How could she win back the trust of Caradawc? She knew that she had his love, for he had risked everything to fight for her. But love without trust could not last long.

'Ai . . . Aiii . . .' howled Idoc as he rode the hills . . . iron hooves on rock . . . iron heart weighing down a human soul . . . 'I touched her . . . I held her . . . but I could not feel her . . . I could not *feel* her!'

It seemed to him that the beauty of the earth mocked him. He was no longer part of it . . . yet he could not and would not leave it.

7

The pursuit

As soon as Rheged saw Viviane he called out, anxious to know what had happened with the black knight, but before she could answer, Cai slumped forward in a dead faint, falling off his horse. Caradawc and Gerin rushed forward to attend to him and amidst the confusion Viviane slipped away. She wanted more than anything to stay with Caradawc, to be taken 'home', to live as his queen and wife, to sing and play the lute and weave fine thread. And most of all, she wanted to be taken into Caradawc's arms and to tell him all that had happened, but to do that she would have to tell him that he had killed his own father – and that he was a puppet manipulated by a dark spirit from her past. She would have to tell him many things that she did not want to tell him – many things she herself did not understand.

No, it would be best for Caradawc if she left him now. She had brought him nothing but trouble.

Though she had no horse, she was determined to reach the sanctuary of the Community of the Fish. There she would ask to be allowed to complete the novitiate she had started as a girl, and then somehow take control of her emotions and her life.

Viviane knew from the position of the sun that all their journeying had been northwards, so Father Brendan's community could not be far away. Holding her new crystal tightly in her right hand, she set off resolutely. The landscape was rugged and it would not be difficult to hide in it for safety, if necessary.

Cai was now delirious.

'We must get him back home,' Rheged whispered. 'He is badly hurt.'

Cai tossed his feverish head, haunted by Elined's false accusation.

'I must find Elined,' he muttered. 'I must explain.'

His three companions pushed him back firmly on the bed of bracken they had made for him.

'He's crazy,' Rheged muttered. 'That bitch would have him castrated as soon as look at him!'

Cai fought to get up again and they fought to keep him down.

Viviane was well clear before they noticed that she was gone.

When Viviane found she could go no further she came to rest in a grove of young silver birch trees. She sank on to the thick green grass and leant back against a slender white trunk, turning her cheek to it with a sigh. The forest seemed so feminine, so ethereal in comparison to some others she had experienced recently; the very air seemed to shimmer with pearl-light between the thin stems. She could not imagine darkness touching this place. At night surely it was always full moon or starlight here . . . never darkness.

She caressed the grass beside her. If she could only afford to stop running, this is where she would like to stay.

Small strips of white bark were peeling off the tree. She pulled one off to wrap her crystal. How silky it looked, though it did not feel so. Perhaps, if she could not find the community, she would come back here and build herself a little white wood cabin with a turf roof, and live a hermit's life . . . Brendan, she was told, had lived as a hermit most of his life on a bare rock in the Irish Sea. He had spoken with angels and learnt there everything he knew. Would *she* have the courage to live alone? Could one live *alone?* Even this rustling forest of silver and pale silky green was inhabited. She could see no one, but she could feel shy presences around her.

'Could I live here?' she whispered. 'Would you have me?'

She listened with her heart and with her heart she heard the joyful answer.

Yes. She would be welcome – but . . .

There was always a but, she thought, suddenly sad . . . *But* she could not remain with Caradawc . . . *But* she could not stay in this lovely glade. She hated and feared Idoc – *but* there would

80

be no peace for her until she had finished what she had started that day in the circle of fallen stones . . . long before that . . . in that other time.

She felt desperately tired. Perhaps after sleep things would not seem so difficult. Surely there would be no harm in sleeping here in this peaceful place? She curled up in the long soft grass, her head pillowed on her arm . . . the sun warm on her shoulder . . .

It had been decided that Rheged and Gerin would carry Cai back to Castle Goreu, there to nurse him to health and to prepare defences in case Neol decided to seek the vengeance he seemed to think was his due. They promised that they would not let Cai out of their sight, and would dissuade him from the dangerous notion of going after Elined.

Caradawc set off in search of Viviane – alone.

Whether she dozed off she was not sure, but suddenly, hearing sounds, she was fully awake. Were they footsteps? Surely neither animal nor human would shake the earth in that way. She peered anxiously in the direction from which the sounds were coming. The slender trees appeared to be trembling, their silver leaves shimmering and fluttering in the moonlight, though there was no breeze.

She stood up and faced the sounds. Some instinct insisted that she should not flee though her mouth was dry with fear.

A gigantic figure emerged at last, striding slowly and inexorably towards her. She held her position, though her heart was pounding.

It came to a halt, a shadow length away, and she saw the gleam of bronze from the huge limbs and the head that carried two faces . . .

It was the being she had seen on the ferry.

He was holding her green girdle out to her as though he intended she should take it, his eyes gazing deeply and searchingly into hers.

This time she sensed no malevolence.

At last he opened both his mouths, and it was as though two people were speaking together and yet at slightly different speeds. One voice reminded her of a bronze gong that continued to reverberate long after it was struck; the other of distant thunder in mountains. Words rolled over her like water over pebbles on a beach. She heard them with her whole body rather than just with her ears. And she understood them with her heart rather than with her mind . . .

'This is a gift from the Green Lady,' the mighty being said. 'You should not part with it. It is to remind you that the strength of the green and growing earth flows through your veins. You are both of the earth and of the spirit. Keep balance between these two and you will have the courage to withstand all that befalls you.'

She stepped forward and trustingly took the green silk cord from his enormous hands. She bowed to the ground, her forehead touching the tall grass. When she stood upright again she quickly fastened the girdle around her waist. It was so light she could hardly believe it was really there.

Then she and the strange being spoke together, she asking questions fearlessly, and he answering in his deep reverberating voice.

She had been partly responsible, he said, that Idoc's progression as a soul had been halted. It was for this reason she was now caught up in these events and would not be free of him until she had undone the harm that she had done.

'But he was evil – we *couldn't* let him roam free!' she cried.

'Even I, who freely roam through many realms, cannot say what should or should not be in realms beyond my understanding. And yet you presumed to put a seal upon the door of Time and deny a living soul his right to change.'

She bent her head in shame, and there was a long silence between them.

Eventually she asked him about his appearance on the ferryboat.

'The ferryman's greed and your fear created an atmosphere – a dark whirlpool – in which you were nearly destroyed. I was sent to remind you of certain deep matters that you had forgotten, but, because you were so afraid, you misunderstood and saw me only as a malevolent figure.'

'Why do you have two faces?'

'Two eyes see three dimensions. Three eyes see four. Four eyes . . .'

He could see that she was beginning to understand. 'And two mouths speak two words simultaneously, because no one word can ever be accurate enough. Meaning springs from the strike of the one against the other – like a spark springs out as flint strikes iron.'

'You gaze on where you have been – and to where you are going.'

'I am aware of past and future.'

'Will you tell me what waits for me in my future?'

The being looked at her silently for a moment and then raised his great bronze hand, pointing over her shoulder. She spun round to see what was behind her. She could see nothing but the silver grove in the moonlight. She turned back with another question on her lips.

He was no longer there.

She was alone.

In the morning the floor of the grove was covered with white wood anemones – flowering so profusely it looked as though snow had fallen. Their tiny, delicate star-faces gave her new courage for the day.

Meanwhile, Caradawc had spent the night in a cave which must once have been inhabited by a Christian hermit, for a crude crucifix was carved on the wall and a sacred yew tree grew in front of the entrance.

He slept dreamlessly, protected by spirit forces he scarcely knew existed, and in the morning he woke refreshed, thinking again of Viviane. He was no longer confused in his emotions. He loved her, and whatever she had done would be explained when he found her once more. But where had she spent the night? He feared for her, alone in the darkness. There were many travellers' tales he had heard, of dangers natural and supernatural, that made him anxious . . . shadows that became detached from their sources and prowled about . . . trees that uprooted themselves . . . and the lord of the Celtic Otherworld who went out hunting for souls with his pack of spectre-white hounds . . .

He picked some wood anemones from a ledge that was near the cave and placed them at the foot of the crucifix.

'Protect her,' he whispered, 'and let me find her.'

Touching the red bark of the yew tree, he murmured another prayer, this time to the spirit of the tree itself – and to the soul of the hermit who had planted it. The tree was old: its wisdom well seasoned.

He felt suddenly confident that today would be the day that would change his life: the day when something that had been hidden would be brought out into the open; the day when something started a long time before would reach a turning point and proceed towards transformation and resolution.

Idoc had spent that same night preparing his dark spells.

He drew the third pentacle of Saturn on lead to invoke the spirits he needed, carefully weaving protection around himself with the fifth pentacle – for these were powerful beings and did not take easily to being any man's slaves. Then, on lead again, he worked the fourth pentacle of Saturn – and the sixth. Dread designs both. Jupiter and Mars were also invoked. Slowly, meticulously, on iron and on tin and on lead . . . the night smouldering away as the forces of these mighty planets gathered in the dark tower to await the command of Idoc.

At dawn he was ready and he set off, a shadowless shadow drifting over the lovely countryside amid his menacing horde of silent and invisible familiars.

'Ah, Caradawc,' he thought, 'this day will be the day you give back what you owe me. This day will be the day you give me life! Your blood will be my blood, your breath my breath.'

Riding into the mouth of a long valley Caradawc felt a sudden chill and looked up with surprise. There was no cloud over the sun, no breeze had sprung up, and yet the temperature had definitely dropped.

He reined in Osla, wondering if he should turn back. Some places were best avoided. Maybe there had been a particularly dreadful battle fought here at one time, and the ghost-memory of it still clung to the place. He could feel the hair on his neck rising, and Osla was trampling nervously, only restrained from galloping away by the firmness of his master's hand on the bridle.

He would turn.

He turned.

Everywhere he looked was an army of dread beings . . . dark forms that stretched and changed with every current of air, forming new shapes every moment, like black smoke billowing from a mass funeral pyre after battle . . .

He turned back again – thinking to escape into the valley – but before him one solitary figure stood across his path. One being – yet of such commanding presence that Caradawc knew he would be more fearful to oppose than all the hordes behind him.

He held close to Osla, stroking his neck, trying to calm himself by calming his horse.

'What do you want of me, sir?' he demanded as boldly as he could.

Idoc did not reply, but stood still, watching.

'Either speak or move aside, sir!' Caradawc said desperately.

Idoc smiled as coldly as a snake on its prey.

'You have something I want,' he uttered at last, his voice hollow and strange as though emerging from a tunnel.

'I have nothing here but my clothes and my weapons. If it is coin you are after . . . or jewels . . .'

'No. No coin. No jewels. Yet you've something I must have.'

'If it's my weapon you want, you may have it directly – but in your throat!' Caradawc drew his sword with a flourish.

Idoc merely smiled again. Then looking over Caradawc's shoulder he gave an almost imperceptible nod to those who were pressing in close behind the prince.

Caradawc turned at once, sword arm raised, ready to strike at as many as he could before he went down. Where now was that feeling of confidence that he had felt at dawn? Where the good spirits and the angels . . . the hermit and the yew tree?

He slashed and thrust and slashed again, but to no avail . . . the creatures he was fighting had no flesh to wound. Idoc watched impassively while they removed the prince's sword from him, his knife, his horse . . . while they carried him to a flat rock and bound him tightly with a strong web exuded like slime from their long fingers. They left him spread-eagled and then they retreated, leaving Idoc gazing down into his eyes.

'You have lent me your body before,' he spoke quietly. 'But this time . . .'

'No!' screamed Caradawc, suddenly understanding the terrible meaning of his words. Shadowy memories returned . . . the tower . . . Viviane . . . the yearning that was not *his* yearning! He twisted and turned, using all his strength against the web that bound him.

Idoc watched him as if amused.

'You are strong. That is good. But you are not strong enough.'

'Why? Why me?'

'You owe me life.'

'I owe you life? How can that be?'

'There will be a moment when you will remember . . . and in that moment you'll wish that you had died before you had remembered.'

'You are insane! I have scarcely seen you before.'

'Ah yes, my friend. You will indeed remember.'

'On the river bank perhaps. But never before that . . .'

'Long before that.'

'The black knight?'

'Before that!'

The demons were crowding around again, as though gathering for some sinister ritual. Idoc glanced at them as though checking whether they were in their proper places – whether they were ready to begin.

'Listen,' he said, his eyes gleaming with an eagerness that made Caradawc's blood run cold. 'Listen to the words they speak.' For Idoc knew that bodies can be subdued by physical force, but it is words that overcome the mind. 'Listen,' he purred.

The chanting then began – and the words wove a cunning web around Caradawc's mind that was as impossible to break as the one around his body.

He listened to the chanting. He listened . . . and he believed that he was bound . . . he believed what they were telling him. His body grew numb . . . his mind grew numb . . .

Idoc watched and waited . . . holding back until he knew that there would be no resistance . . . and then he moved.

8

The wedding and the amethyst crystal

During that same day Viviane, still travelling north, came upon a path in a valley which was hauntingly familiar. She noticed it first while resting on a grassy bank. The path snaked beside the stream and then divided; one fork continued along the stream side, while the other led off into the woods blanketing the steep slope of the hill. At the fork there stood a huge boulder totally unlike any other rock in the valley. It lay there as though it had been dropped by a giant, and it seemed to consist of hundreds of rounded river pebbles cemented together with reddish sand.

Puzzled, Viviane went up to it, and ran her hand over its surface, wondering how she could have seen it before when she knew she had not passed this way on her journey south to Castle Goreu. She stood beside it for a while and looked around her, her eyes drawn mostly to the path that climbed the wooded hill. She felt a very strong urge to climb it, but out of caution she resisted this. She tried to continue along the path beside the stream, and walked that way for a while. But she still felt so worried by the familiarity of the boulder and the steep path that finally she turned back to it. There she stood with her back to the boulder, gazing up the path. It climbed steeply, some parts of it more like a rocky stairway.

Gradually the memory, which at first had been like a gentle touch on the elbow, became more like a vigorous pressure on the shoulders. Fiann had walked this way long, long ago. At the top of this path, on this very hill, stood the tower where she used to meet Idoc!

As soon as she realized this, Viviane ran back along the lower path, her heart pounding with terror. She must leave this valley as quickly as she could: she was in greater danger than ever before. It seemed to her that behind every bush some malevolent shape now lurked; the trees, formerly so tall and shapely, seemed to have withdrawn into darkness, twisted and knotted around some secret disease. Even the path seemed rugged and hostile, and she tripped and fell more than once.

Finally, at the mouth of the valley where the path was walled steeply on both sides, she came face to face with Caradawc on his chestnut horse. For a moment she stood paralysed with fright, and then broke into relieved sobbing. The sun shone down on him and he seemed to her the most handsome sight she had ever seen. She was so tired . . . so very tired of running . . . of being alone . . . of being afraid . . .

She lifted her arms to him, tears streaming down her face.

He dismounted at once and gathered her to him, holding her close, kissing her face, her hair, her neck . . .

'Why did you run?' he asked. 'Why do you keep running from me?'

'I thought . . . I thought you would be angry with me for all that has happened . . .'

'*Should* I be angry?'

'No,' she sobbed. 'There is no cause for it. But there have been so many strange things. Oh Caradawc . . . I'm so *tired* of strange things happening to me . . .'

'Now I'm taking you home – and we'll be married. There will be no more strangeness, I promise you.'

He sounded so confident.

Perhaps he was right.

Perhaps he had grown strong with all the trials that he had been through. Perhaps he would be able to protect her from Idoc. Because she wanted to believe this she believed it, and she allowed herself to be lifted on to Caradawc's horse, and they turned towards home.

Whether it was because she was so happy, or whether it was because she had travelled in a great circle in her attempt to escape, the route back seemed much shorter than the way out. She clung to Caradawc the whole time, her heart singing that he seemed to bear no resentment at her peculiar behaviour, but was only glad – as she was glad – that they were back together.

He did not question her about anything that had happened. It was as though he had decided that what was past was truly past, and they were going to start again as though nothing had happened.

Believing herself safe in his arms, she half wished she had ventured up that path in the wood to check if the tower was really there. But then she realized what it would mean if it did exist – and she shivered.

'Are you cold?' Caradawc said, drawing her closer.

She gripped his arms so tightly her fingers went white.

'Lady,' he laughed, 'that hurts me.'

She reached up to his head and pulled it down towards her, kissing him with a desperate intensity. 'This is real!' she thought.

He swung his leg over the saddle and slid to the ground while she still kissed him. The living grass was a better mattress than any stuffed with straw. Osla settled peacefully to cropping while the two humans rolled on the earth, struggling out of their clothes and into each other.

'Ah Caradawc,' thought Viviane. 'This is what I have been waiting for. This is how love-making should be . . .' Her body arched and curved, striving to take him in deeper and deeper . . . wanting it to last for ever . . . terrified it would be over before she reached that marvellous release . . . But she need not have worried. Caradawc seemed aware of her needs and took her through that gate and back again, time and again . . . until at last she was spent and satisfied, lying damp with sweat on the grass . . . staring up at the startling blue of the sky, her eyes wide open . . . wondering how such extraordinary blissful feelings could come from such an ordinary and temporary thing as a body.

After a while Caradawc rested on his elbow and kissed her very slowly from the top of her head to her toes . . . lingering long over certain places . . . until he could feel that she was beginning to rouse from her contented lethargy. Then he made love again, but this time for himself – fiercely.

They rode into Castle Goreu when the moon was already up, and Caradawc's cheerful reply to the challenge of the guard brought Rheged and Gerin racing out into the courtyard, followed by most of the household.

Gerin at once reached up his arms to help Viviane down – his eyes alight to see her safe. But then he hesitated and drew back quickly. Rheged stepped forward to take her hand. She jumped down lightly, just holding his arm to steady herself.

'How is Cai?' Viviane asked as they walked towards the main house.

'He's very ill,' Gerin replied soberly. 'It's possible he'll die.'

'Oh, no!'

'His wounds won't heal,' Rheged said. 'That bastard Neol and his bitch sister!'

'We must go to him at once,' Viviane said, tugging at Caradawc's arm.

'You go,' he said. 'I must see what's been done to defend the place. Gerin – come with me.' And he strode off with Gerin towards the guard posts without a backward glance for her.

Vaguely uneasy, she turned to Rheged. 'Take me to Cai,' she said.

He led her to the rooms Caradawc had occupied before he inherited his father's kingdom, and she stood beside the bed looking down into the feverish face of the young man who had seemed so light-hearted, so innocent, such a short while before. His blond hair was matted and dark with sweat, his eyes wild. Blood-soaked bandages covered much of his body. She looked up at Rheged and was surprised how tender and concerned he looked – the same rough Rheged who loved to fight and hated any physical weakness. Caradawc had once told her how Rheged seemed terrified by the sight of other people's wounds, and after a battle would not even help to carry the wounded off the field to safety. Yet here he was nursing his friend with the tenderest care. Strange that Idoc, who was so evil, could sometimes bring about good in others.

She touched Rheged's arm gently. 'He needs the bandages changed, my friend. Will you help me?'

Rheged nodded. 'I'll bring water.'

'I'll need herbs too.' And she called after him: 'Send the priest to me.'

Sitting down beside the sick man she started talking softly to soothe him, his eyes looked so wild. It was evident that he did not recognize her, but seemed to grow calmer at the sound of her voice. Very carefully she started to remove the linen bandages, throwing them into the fireplace for burning. She was not more than halfway through this task when the Christian priest arrived with his little bag of herbs. They talked softly over Cai, the priest saying how Rheged had scarcely left his friend's side since he had been brought home. He explained what they had already done for the infection, but he feared nothing they could do might help while the young man seemed to have something very heavy on his conscience.

Viviane looked up sharply. 'He did not do what they accuse him of, Father.'

'I believe you, daughter, but nevertheless there is something deep in his soul that is festering outwardly on his skin. I have treated him with every remedy I know, but still it does not heal. It is up to the Lord Christ now in His mercy to forgive him . . .'

She looked at Cai thoughtfully. 'Or he to forgive himself,' she said softly.

When Rheged returned with the water, the two of them bathed the patient carefully.

'It's a pity we can't bring Elined here to see him,' she said thoughtfully. 'It is her mercy, her forgiveness he needs too, Father.'

'I'll fetch her!' Rheged said, rising suddenly.

'No, Rheged! I didn't mean that. You'd be killed . . .'

'I'll bring her!' he repeated firmly. At last there was something he could do for his friend, other than sit and watch him suffer.

'You can't go . . .'

But he had already left them, the door swinging noisily against the wall as he flung it aside. She started to hurry after him, but then she stopped. Let it be. Something had to be done.

She turned to the priest kneeling at Cai's bedside and took her place beside him.

Caradawc insisted on holding their wedding immediately, though Cai was still very ill and Rheged had not yet returned. When Viviane protested that they should wait until his friends could be with them, he argued that his people were very disturbed and anxious after recent events, and a royal wedding would settle them down and assure them that all was well.

Gerin tried to avoid her, and when he could not he forced himself to behave in a formal and distant manner. But beneath this she could sense so strongly his desire for her that she was surprised it was not the talk of the whole court.

The day chosen for the ceremony arrived in a blaze of sunlight. Apart from the spies sent out to keep watch on Huandaw's movements, and the guards alert on the battlements, Caradawc's people were all gathered in force.

The mood of uncertainty and anxiety that had followed Goreu's mysterious death, the disappearance of Princess Viviane – and the attack of Huandaw – was joyfully dispelled. Bells rang out and the roads were crowded with people hurrying towards the castle. Flags and banners fluttered from every possible post and pole, tower and pinnacle.

Viviane stood in Cai's chamber, looking out at the crowds gathering, coloured tents being put up, trestle tables laid out. She could see great spits being set up in the courtyard, where soon the beef and venison would be roasted.

Cai was still no better, and the priest was continually at his side, often in prayer, and regularly administering herbal concoctions. But to no avail: it was as though Cai had lost the will to live. Viviane was too busy now to spend much time with him, but her sympathy for what he was suffering brought her into his chamber even on her wedding morning, hoping to find him improved enough for her truly to enjoy her special day.

There had been no word from Rheged either, and she feared the worst. She regretted that it had been a remark of hers that had sent him rushing off towards his enemy.

Suddenly there came a disturbance at the gate. Viviane leaned forward the better to see what caused it, hoping that it might signal Rheged's return. But instead the guards were having an altercation with a little old woman. She seemed intent on making her way towards the door of the royal apartments, instead of joining the other guests milling about in the courtyard.

Viviane was just about to draw back from the window and leave the guards to their task when suddenly she noticed something that made her draw in her breath sharply. For the old woman was wearing a long blue cloak, much too fine for her. It was the same cloak Viviane had reluctantly parted with to the old lady in the green chapel. Without waiting another second she spun round from the window and ran from the chamber. Her hair unbound, her morning-robes half unlaced, she flew down the dim corridors and out into the blinding light of the sunlit courtyard.

'Let her be!' she called out to the guards as they bundled the old creature back out through the gate. 'I know that woman. Bring her to me.'

'What's going on here?' She heard Caradawc's voice as he came striding out to see what was happening.

'They've forbidden entry to someone I know,' Viviane protested. 'Tell them to bring her back here.'

Caradawc spoke sharply to the captain of the guard, and within moments the old woman was led before them. Viviane had judged right. She was indeed the old crone from the green chapel.

'She demanded to see the princess privately,' the captain grumbled. 'We didn't know she was known to the princess.' He gazed with ill-concealed disgust at the peasant rags beneath the extraordinary blue cloak.

Viviane held out her hands in welcome. 'Come,' she said warmly. 'We'll go inside.'

People were crowding round to stare eagerly at the scene, shuffling and pushing for a closer view.

'No,' Caradawc interrupted sharply. 'There is no time for that now! State your business,' he snapped coldly.

Viviane looked at him in surprise.

'I would guess she's a thief,' the captain said. 'That cloak is never her own!'

'I gave it to her,' Viviane said quickly and angrily. 'You may go now, sir, I need no defending from my friends.'

The captain looked at Caradawc. But the king nodded, so he left. The crowd pressed closer, marking every word.

'Caradawc, there is time enough,' she said, and annoyance showed in her voice. She turned to the old woman. 'We'll go inside,' she said and, taking her arm, she led her towards the door.

They entered a chamber full of flowers, the bower in which the bride and her women would gather before the ceremony. The old woman stared around her with delight.

Viviane took her thin hands in her own. 'Have you come from the green chapel . . . from the Lady?' she asked eagerly.

Smiling, the old woman nodded. And then she gently withdrew her hands from Viviane's and felt in a ragged pouch at her waist. It seemed she fumbled a long time, her hands shaking with age, but at last she drew out a magnificent amethyst crystal, as large as a swan's egg, and held it up to the light for Viviane to enjoy.

Viviane gasped. In its rich purple depths light glowed and pulsed. If she mourned the loss of the old woman's first gift, she was now more than comforted. Eagerly she reached out as the woman held it towards her – but at that moment Caradawc burst into the room, his eyes going straight to the amethyst.

'But this is beautiful,' he said enthusiastically, taking it from her hand. 'Is it a wedding gift?'

'Yes,' the woman replied. 'But it is for the princess alone,' she added emphatically. Viviane reached out for it, but Caradawc made no attempt to hand it over.

'I'll put it with the others,' he said. 'And now you must leave. The princess has much to do . . .'

'I have time . . .' Viviane insisted.

'No, my love . . .' he said firmly. Then he took the old woman by the arm and propelled her towards the door. 'You have had your wish,' he said. 'You have been able to deliver your gift personally. We thank you for it.'

'Caradawc, please . . .' Viviane could see that the woman was very anxious to tell her something.

But he would not listen further, and the messenger from the Green Lady was pushed out of the room and delivered into the hands of a passing servant, with quick instructions that she should be given a good place among the guests in the courtyard.

Viviane felt puzzled and annoyed by his sudden insensitivity. Surely he could see that she particularly wanted to talk to this woman – and particularly wanted to hold her precious gift. But Caradawc gave her a kiss and was gone before she could protest further.

She stood for a moment, confused, then hurried out of the room hoping still to catch up with the servant escorting the old woman. But already they were nowhere to be found, and her own maids were looking for her, to start dressing her for the ceremony. So she allowed herself to be led to her chamber, there to submit herself to the long and elaborate robing process.

After brooding a while, she called for Olwen, a trusted childhood friend, who had come with her from her father's castle, and was now in charge of her serving maids. Quietly she bade her go to the chamber where the wedding gifts were displayed, and bring the great amethyst crystal that she would find there . . .

The underslip was of fine Roman silk, woven to her father's specifications and sent as part of her dowry. The over-dress was of silk brocade from Byzantium, threaded with silver and small sapphires and a thousand or more river pearls. Her hair was plaited with sea-pearls. One the size of a grape hung from a silver chain in the middle of her forehead, while others in graded sizes led off on either side to hang over her temples and ears in a thick fringe. As she moved her head the pearls swung softly, glimmering. Beneath this costly veil hung a pair of long earrings of giant sapphires set in silver. The plaits of her red-gold hair were twisted round each other and built high on top of her head so that the queen's coronet could be mounted on it.

Viviane's shoes were pure white doeskin, trimmed with silver and sapphire. Her fingers were laden with rings, each stone brought from lands so distant that merchants and travellers could tell what tales they liked . . . and frequently did. The largest diamond, they said, had been torn from the scaly breastplate of a seven-headed dragon.

Olwen returned at last in distress to say that there was no sign of an amethyst crystal among the wedding gifts.

'Are you sure? Did you look carefully?' Viviane looked worried.

'Very carefully, my lady.'

'I think you did not.'

'Forgive me, my lady, but I did. And I asked all in charge of the gifts if they had seen such a thing, and they all denied that it was there.'

'The king himself was to set it among the gifts.'

'The king is busy dressing, my lady. Perhaps it has slipped his mind.'

Viviane looked very thoughtful for a moment. 'Olwen, when we are gone to the chapel for the ceremony, go to the king's chambers and see if you can find it there.'

Olwen looked shocked. 'I cannot, lady! The king's chambers?'

'I will take the responsibility. And when you find it, bring it to me wherever I am – even at the altar – and slip it without a word into my hand. Do you understand?'

'Yes, my lady, but . . .'

'Olwen, this is very important to me. And the king will understand. I'll explain it all to him. Don't be afraid.'

Olwen looked extremely unhappy as she slipped out of the room to wait where she could watch the king's chambers and judge when it would be relatively safe to approach.

At last Viviane was dressed, and when the trumpeters started their fanfare she was ready to head her own procession to the chapel.

The route was lined with smiling, waving people, the women and children pelting her with flowers. She thought the woods and meadows must be bare for all the flowers that were in the castle that day. Every musical instrument she could think of was playing: at least twenty flutes trilled and warbled; drummers in royal red and gold carried their drums at their hips and jauntily twirled their sticks between beating the skins; pipes and cymbals and rattles sounded everywhere. In the chapel there would be the gentler music of the harps, and high, fine singing – but outside there was a jamboree of sound, even the yard dogs joining in . . .

What did they expect of her, these people, Viviane wondered. It was not just to provide an heir to succeed Caradawc; it was that they should share her life in imagination – live through her in silks and pearls; bed with the handsome king; eat finely prepared food and sleep warm and soft. She looked at their eager, loving, happy faces, and suddenly felt a chill. If she were to disappoint them . . . if she were to live her life differently from what they expected . . . if they knew some of the thoughts and desires that troubled her – then these same faces would turn cold and hard, these same waving hands would pick up stones to throw. She felt she was a prisoner of their love. No, she was a prisoner of their *image* of love – and that bore as much relation to real love as an artist's painting of a flower bore to a living bloom.

She scanned around for the old woman in her mother's blue cloak, but she was nowhere to be seen. Caradawc had ordered her to be given a good place, so perhaps she would be among the honoured few inside the chapel.

But she was not.

At the far end of the chapel the king waited for Viviane, splendid in white and gold. The altar shone with candlelight on gold ornaments and crosses. The noise, the hot bright light, the pushing jovial crowd were shut out and she walked into a cool quiet place, rippling with harp music and drawn by a golden thread of light towards the man she loved. She was embarrassed that she had reacted so strongly over the wedding gift, and now wished that she had not sent Olwen spying into his chambers, though she could not get out of her mind the thought that the woman had come to her with this particular gift at this particular time for some purpose. But what could happen here? Caradawc was waiting for her. The priest was praying. Above them at the ends of the roof beams little wooden angels painted gold smiled down on them.

Everyone turned to look at her except Gerin. He stared fixedly at the candle flame straight ahead of him. His shoulders were straight: his bearing severe. She knew that he loved her: but he could not and would not show it.

Shafts of sunlight from the high windows crossed the chapel, reminding her of the rods of light that had cut away the black fog when she had been so sure she wanted to die. She smiled now, confident that benign spiritual beings watched over her, and now she was to have Caradawc as well, strong and human, warm and loving, to help her to face what she had so foolishly unleashed from the ancient stone circle. She began to relax inwardly and could not resist raising her lips to his when she joined him at the altar – though this was against tradition.

The priest smiled indulgently as they kissed, and then he

joined their hands, speaking the potent words of the Christian marriage spell over them.

When they walked out hand in hand through the main door the cheers were deafening. Children were held up high above the heads of the crowd, the smaller ones crying, not knowing what all the noise and excitement were about; the older ones waving flowers. Viviane could feel men's eyes on her, the women's on Caradawc. There was no doubt they would share their bed tonight with the thoughts of many of their subjects.

The smell of roasting was pungent as smoke from the spits rose high; and ale flowed freely. The mass of people ate at the trestle tables in the great courtyard; only the nobles, companions and relatives were invited into the Great Hall for a feast that would be talked about for many years. All the family's best tapestries had been taken out of store and hung around the hall, glowing with red and green and blue. Fields of blossoms in spring could not compete with the intricate working of flowers at the feet of the elegant ladies and gentlemen in the tapestries, nor Caradawc's warriors in all their armour compete with the splendour of the knights in the tableaux on the walls. All the images were caught at a moment of perfection and preserved smiling or scowling for as long as the cloth would last – making the living people below feel it incumbent upon them to strut and pose and imitate as best they could.

On three sides of the hall the warriors had hung up their polished shields, and above the great carved wooden chairs of the king and queen hung the family's emblem, an eagle, emblazoned in gold, with wings spread wide and fierce eye staring.

Course after course was brought on in procession: river trout and salmon; wild fowl; roast venison and wild boar; rye and barley bread to mop up the juices; fine wheat bread to accompany the cheeses . . . And with every course wines from France and mead from the king's own honeybees.

Viviane's cheeks were soon flushed with wine and excitement. She and Caradawc felt almost painfully aware of each other's physical proximity though apparently absorbed in speaking to others. Each found excuses to touch as they reached for wine or food; each pretending that no thrill of desire had shot through them at the touch; each savouring the apparent separation while thinking of nothing but the final coming together. Bards recounted interminable love stories; minstrels sang of love; and the dancers expressed in their movements the pleasures of the wedding night.

As the wine and mead were constantly poured by efficient and attentive servants, the feasting revellers grew ever more noisy and ribald ... Remarks were called out that made Viviane's cheeks more flushed, her body even more aware of Caradawc's. Then men and women were openly fondling each other, and some were even falling together under the table. The elegant model of the tapestries was abandoned as life's strong and untidy passions took over.

At the height of all this revelling Olwen came up to Viviane and surreptitiously slipped the amethyst crystal into her hand. For a moment she stared at the girl in surprise, having totally forgotten the old woman and her gift. The coolness of the crystal on her hot hand momentarily sobered her, and she struggled to remember why it had seemed so important to her. But Caradawc leaned across at that moment, his mouth against her ear, his breath and tongue probing it. She nearly let the crystal fall, and it would have except that Olwen, who had been to great trouble to find it and was not about to let her work come to nothing, caught it and pushed it into the tiny silk pouch that Viviane's wedding dress carried at its waist.

From her ear Caradawc's tongue found her mouth and they gave up all pretence of dignity. Tables were pushed over as the crowds rushed to get a better view. Viviane did not care that hundreds of lascivious eyes were watching them, she could think of nothing but Caradawc's touch, Caradawc's mouth on her breast, Caradawc's rising passion pushing against her.

'Lady!' cried Olwen in dismay. She tugged at her arm. 'Lady! Go to your chamber for this! Come ... your chamber!' She pulled at her frantically, but Viviane pushed her aside impatiently and gave herself totally to Caradawc there on the table among the gnawed bones and the spilled wine of the wedding feast, with the crowds all around cheering and leering ...

At the back of the hall, Gerin, like Olwen still sober, turned away and strode into the night.

Once release had come, realization of where she was and what she had done came too. Caradawc rose, pulling on his breeches, flushed and laughing, his companions slapping him on the back, praising his performance.

Viviane drew away, white and shaking.

She saw Olwen's anguished face and flung herself into her arms. Together the two women rushed unnoticed from the hall, as the men thronged around Caradawc. Some women were still locked in the embraces of their own lovers . . . others, like Viviane, drew back into the shadow, shocked and upset.

Once outside, the cool night air sobered Viviane rapidly, and she sobbed uncontrollably as Olwen hurried her towards the new bedchamber she would share with Caradawc. How she had longed for this night – to be alone and in a bed at last with him . . . not on some river bank, not beside a forest path, but in a bed with four walls keeping out the world . . . alone and to-gether and private!

Olwen gave her fresh water to drink, wiped her face and helped her out of the heavy brocade dress. Carefully she laid aside the coronet and undid the strings of pearls that held the fire-red hair in place.

'Stay with me, Olwen,' Viviane whispered. 'Stay till he comes.'

Olwen quietly took up her mistress's silver comb, and while Viviane sat naked on the edge of the bed Olwen combed her hair, crooning a lullaby as though she were a child, soothing her, calming her.

When she heard the heavy, lurching steps of the men escort-ing the king towards his bridal chamber, she helped Viviane into bed, blew out one of the lamps and prepared to leave. The queen's face was calm now, but very pale. Not knowing why she did it, Olwen paused before she left to take out the am-ethyst. She placed it on Viviane's breast and folded her hands over it.

'You wanted this, my lady,' she said – and departed.

Caradawc and his friends stayed outside the door for what seemed an age, talking and lurching drunkenly about.

Viviane lay in silence inside the chamber, clutching the crys-tal and beginning to feel very strange, as though she was floating away from her body. She was thinking about Caradawc and how much she loved him . . . not blaming him for the shameful incident in the hall because she knew that she had been as responsible as he.

Dreamlike images began to come to her, as though she were falling asleep – though she was awake enough to he aware of the noise the men were making in the corridor. She seemed to see Caradawc floating in an extraordinary starless darkness . . . reaching out his arms to her . . . calling to her for help . . . trying to reach her, yet with every movement he made towards her somehow drifting further and further away . . .

She clasped the huge amethyst on her breast, and she could feel her heart beating against it.

At last the door was flung open – and a figure stood in the doorway.

Shocked, she sat bolt upright, clutching the wraps against her breasts; her eyes wide and startled. Gone was the feeling of floating; gone the tenuous vision of Caradawc.

Idoc!

So with this new gift she could see through illusion!

Idoc!

Her heart was pounding.

He moved a step into the room and closed the door behind him. He wore the white and gold of Caradawc's wedding clothes. *She had married Idoc!* On the table in the great hall that sensual ecstasy had been induced by Idoc . . . On the path near the dark tower, again it must have been Idoc . . .

Hastily, while his back was turned, she slipped the amethyst crystal under the bed. Now she knew why he had tried to keep it from her. Now she knew why the old woman had tried so hard to press it into her own hand . . .

And when he turned back to her he was once more in the guise of Caradawc.

Viviane spent the rest of that night lying wide awake, her head pounding with the wine she had consumed and the shock she had received, her husband's heavy, inert body pinning her to the bed. Desperately she considered what to do. That she should flee once more to Father Brendan seemed the only course, but to flee again and be pursued again was almost more than she could bear. This time she must be more cunning, and she cursed herself for having drunk so much the night before – her mind was sluggish and thoughts reached for slipped away before she could fully grasp them.

When the dawn came she was exhausted, and she still had no firm plan.

The sun was already streaming through the window when her companion's body rolled off her. She lay very still as Idoc half opened his eyes, groaned, and then fell back to sleep again.

She would do it now! As soon as she was sure he would not wake again, she slid from his side and silently dressed herself in the hunting tunic and leather trousers she had worn as a young girl, lacing on the soft buckskin boots, tying a hunting bag to her hip and filling it with everything she might need. For a weapon she took up Caradawc's knife.

Just before leaving she stood beside the bed and looked down at the man lying there. He sprawled on his back, his right arm flung wide and hanging over the edge of the bed, his chest bare, his face in profile on the pillow – Caradawc's face. She stooped over him for a moment, yearning to stay with him, to creep back into the bed beside him. But the vision she had seen of the real Caradawc drifting away into the void returned, and she knew that it was urgent that she seek help from a master of mysteries at least as skilled as Idoc himself. Father Brendan was such a man and this time she was determined she would reach him. Without another backward glance she hurried from the room and down the now deserted passages.

Then, hearing loud voices in the courtyard, she drew back into the shadow of the doorway lest she was spotted. A considerable force of warriors was assembled outside. Were Neol's men attacking? She leant forward as far as she dared to catch what was being said. It soon became clear that the king himself had summoned this force to gather in readiness to attack Huandaw's castle as soon as the wedding night was over because Neol had refused to take the oath of allegiance.

'No prisoners are to be taken. No one is to be left alive; neither man, woman nor child,' the captain said. 'These are the king's precise orders. When Huandaw's estates are cleared they will be awarded to a loyal subject. Who knows, one of you might take his place – the one who proves most zealous in carrying out these orders,' he added darkly.

Viviane put her hand to her mouth with a horrified gasp. These were certainly not Caradawc's orders, but Idoc's. She thanked God that she had overheard this speech. She now had no further doubt that Idoc must be overthrown and Caradawc returned to his rightful place as soon as possible.

One of the knights broke away from the rest and started towards the doorway in which she hid. It was Gerin, sent to wake the king. Gerin, Caradawc's closest friend, his face deeply troubled. *He* would know that these orders could not be typical of Caradawc – and yet he knew nothing of Idoc's power.

She waited until he was inside the shadow of the doorway before she touched his arm, instantly putting her fingers to her lips to keep him silent. He was startled but he said nothing. Beckoning, she led him back into the house towards Cai's room. It seemed to her the safest place to talk, for if they were found it would seem unremarkable that they were visiting their sick friend.

The priest, Father David, was beside Cai's bed as usual and looked up in surprise as they furtively entered and shut the door behind them.

Viviane went at once to Cai's bedside, hoping there would have been some improvement so that he too could hear what she was about to say. His wounds at last had healed, but he lay as though in a coma, staring unseeingly at the beams across the ceiling.

Viviane knew that the family priest was by no means a man of Father Brendan's calibre and knowledge, but an ally against Idoc he would certainly prove as soon as he suspected that devilish spirits were involved. Yet still she hesitated, though Gerin was speaking questions with his eyes, and Father David was waiting expectantly for an explanation. This elderly, good-natured monk was no match for Idoc and, if the plan she was now hatching were to work, he might have to put himself in great danger.

But there was no alternative. They had very little time left. As quickly and simply as she could she explained that

Caradawc had been taken over by an evil spirit; that she knew this spirit well but could not tell them more at present; that they were all in danger and that a great many people would suffer and die if they did not find ways to exorcise him soon.

Gerin was instantly alert. It made sense of the many things that had troubled him ever since Caradawc had returned – and now it certainly made sense of Caradawc's recent cruel and ruthless orders to his warriors to massacre Huandaw's people.

The priest was flustered and frightened. He had heard of these things, and indeed had often preached about them – but now that he was faced with the reality he was terrified, and everything he had been taught to do flew out of his mind. Viviane rapidly began to regret that she had involved him.

Whether Cai heard or understood was hard to tell. His expression did not change. He lay as though already dead – yet still breathing.

'I am intending to journey immediately to Father Brendan at the Community of the Fish,' Viviane said. 'I know he will be able to help us.'

'Yes . . . yes . . .' babbled Father David in relief. 'He'll know what to do.'

'Well, can you then tell me a short way to get there?' Viviane asked. 'I've tried before but kept going in circles . . .'

'Yes, I know the way . . .' Father David muttered. 'I could show you . . . I could take you there,' he added eagerly.

Viviane realized it would be better to take him with her than to leave him behind in the state he was now in. He was a good man, and had always tried to be a good priest, but was perhaps out of his depth in the religion he tried so hard to serve.

Gerin interrupted to say he should go and wake the king as he had been instructed, otherwise suspicions would be aroused.

'When he sees that I am not there, tell him I am visiting Cai and Father David,' Viviane suggested. 'We'll prepare to leave as soon as the warriors have set out. And Gerin . . .' she stopped him just as he was about to leave. 'Try to prevent the worst happening . . . but take care of yourself. This being has no warmth in his heart, no mercy in his soul . . .'

'The Lord preserve us,' whispered the priest.

'The Lord preserve us indeed,' she said with feeling.

Gerin gave her one last long look and was gone. She was glad he knew, and she wondered fleetingly what role he had played in that ancient drama, for he too seemed deeply involved.

The warriors at last clattered off with Caradawc at their head, Gerin riding a few paces behind on his right side.

Then Father David fetched Olwen, who was rigorously instructed on how to look after Cai. It was explained to her that her mistress was riding with the family priest to visit a sick cottager, and she took her place beside Cai's bed at once.

This explanation for their leaving seemed to satisfy the few people they encountered. The groom gladly saddled Hunydd and another horse for Father David, and as they passed through the castle gate they were hardly noticed. Viviane wore a doe-skin cap over her red hair and, clad like a boy, might as well have been invisible.

Father David did indeed know a better way to cross the river, somewhere much nearer home and avoiding Huandaw's lands. Huge slabs of stone lay across the river, resting on fortuitous outcrops of rock. This had served as a bridge, he explained, since the very ancient times. 'It was mentioned in Roman writings, and was already old when they came to Britain.'

However old, it was still very strong, and they led the two horses across with no trouble. Viviane wondered what Father David would say if she told him she herself knew of her life in those very ancient times, and she had probably crossed that bridge before.

They had gone a considerable distance when Father David suddenly stopped speaking and looked around himself uneasily. Viviane reined in Hunydd at once, for she too had felt a chill against her cheek, though there was no breeze to stir the leaves.

'I would rather not go this way,' she said quickly, realizing that they were near the hill of the dark tower. Father David muttered a prayer and crossed himself, but the words of the prayer had been learnt by rote and had no resonance in the spirit-realms.

Both felt as though they were surrounded, yet they could see nothing. Viviane thought of the amethyst she had with her.

She felt sure it would give her clear-sight – the capacity to see what was normally invisible. But she was afraid to use it: afraid of what she might see. 'But that is stupid,' she told herself severely. 'To know one's enemy is half the battle.'

So she slipped her hand into the bag at her hip and felt around for the purple crystal, at the same time urging Father David to wheel his horse around, so that they could leave this place as quickly as possible.

But Father David's horse began turning round and round in circles, whinnying in terror. Hunydd too was trembling and, try as she might, Viviane could not find the crystal among all the things she had pressed into the bag.

'Come!' she called to the frightened monk. 'We must leave here.'

Whether it was because Father David was not much accustomed to riding or whether his horse was too terrified to obey his commands it was difficult to tell, but it was clear he had completely lost control of his steed. Viviane tried to bring Hunydd alongside to grasp his bridle, but her approach seemed to spook the horse even more and he suddenly bolted, the hapless monk banging about on his back like a sack of sand, plunging deeper and deeper into the thick woods at the base of the dread hill. For a moment Viviane hesitated, and then she turned Hunydd about and rode after him.

Even in the ancient days she had not approached the tower from this side and so nothing looked familiar to her. The priest was already out of sight, though she could hear him crashing noisily through the undergrowth ahead of her. Hunydd was moving fast, yet somehow making very little progress. Viviane began to feel increasingly uneasy.

Suddenly the sounds ahead of her stopped. She called out as loudly as she could, but there was no reply. She reined in Hunydd, deciding that panic was making her waste energy to no avail. She began to feel as though she were being physically pulled upwards towards the summit of the hill where the dark tower stood. She remembered what she had seen of the tower from the preaching cross on that distant hill. Everything bright and light and beautiful seemed to be drawn towards it and leave only when it had been transformed into something ugly and dark. She tried to resist, but Hunydd seemed to be feeling its influence too and was straining away from her.

When she and Father David had left Castle Goreu she had tied the Green Lady's cord around her waist. She remembered it now and with a trembling hand took hold of it. Almost immediately she found the strength and courage to resist the sinister attraction of the tower. She would like to have put a great deal of distance between herself and the tower but she could not abandon Father David. She called out again, but not even a birdsong broke the ominous silence.

Viviane ventured forward cautiously, penetrating deeper into the wood where she had last heard the crashing sound of the monk and his horse. She called his name continually, but her voice had a strange flatness as though it were not really carrying. She could just see where Hunydd was treading, but there was no sunlight shining between the trees; rather there was a dim visibility that seemed to have no connection with normal daylight at all.

Suddenly Hunydd reared up and refused to go further.

Directly in front of her she saw the body of Father David – decapitated.

She turned away, shuddering and gagging.

What had she done? Oh God, what had she done in releasing Idoc!

But she must not run away again. Indeed – there *was* nowhere to hide. She and her fellow priests – if Caradawc and his friends were in fact those same ancient priests who had worked the binding spell with her – had now been given a second chance to solve the problem of Idoc's evil in another way. Pray God this time they would not fail!

Somehow she knew she had to destroy the tower before she could rescue Caradawc – and before Idoc could begin to change.

She led Hunydd back some paces and tethered her. Then Viviane took a deep breath, clutched her green girdle for reassurance, and strode forward . . .

Darkness roared in her ears . . . She felt that she was being pulled apart . . . yet still she clung to the earth-girdle, remembering the green renewing things of spring . . . In her bag she carried two crystals – two gifts of power: the amethyst that gave clear-sight – and the quartz crystal she had thrown at the black knight's horse. With these talismans surely she could not fail!

'Oh God of all the realms . . . who was before all things existed, and will be after all have ceased . . . send me strength . . . guide me . . . protect me . . .' She screamed the words so loud that the trees in the forest seemed to bend as though before a huge wind . . . The black shapes flying outwards from the gate were buffeted hither and thither, like so many dead leaves . . .

Ahead of her was the tower.

She found the door that she remembered from that former life. She found the narrow spiral staircase winding up into the darkness. It took more courage than she knew she had to set foot upon the first step – but once having done so, she knew that there was no way back now until she had completed what she had come to do, or was killed attempting it.

She paused outside the first door, remembering – sorely tempted to peep in to see if the bed was still there, the tree still visible at the window. But she forced herself to pass it by, knowing that it was in the top room she would find what she had to do. As she passed the second and the third doors she flattened herself against the opposite wall, dreading that she would be intercepted.

Sick with fear, at last she stood at the top of the stairs in complete darkness, only touch telling her that she was now before the final door.

She pushed. The locks clicked one by one as though the very touch of her hand had set them in motion – as though her hand was somehow the key for which they had been waiting. And the door swung inwards. The dreadful inevitability of her presence on that threshold frightened her more than anything so far.

She forced herself to step inside. She was in Idoc's octagonal room. She saw his scrolls, his lamps, his table. She saw his black mirror on the wall. She felt strange, as though she were stepping out of Time, in a place not marked on any map.

She walked across the room towards the mirror.

At first she could see nothing, not even her own reflection, and then gradually, as though emerging through mist, she began to discern figures. She peered more closely. There were four figures . . . becoming more and more distinct . . . and they were indoors . . . close together . . . Rheged was standing beside Cai's bed, firmly clasping the arm of Elined . . . Olwen stood behind them. It was as though she were in the room with them. Wonderingly she put out her hand to touch them, but all she could feel was the hard, ice-cold surface of the mirror.

'Look at him,' Rheged seemed to be saying angrily. 'Are you pleased with your work?'

Elined was struggling to break from his grip, turning her head from side to side, trying to avoid looking at Cai. Cai himself was sitting up in bed, his face still deathly pale, but no longer comatose. He gazed at Elined with such despair in his eyes that Viviane longed to lean forward and comfort him.

'If only she would touch him,' Viviane thought, 'her heart might come out from behind its fear and start to feel again.'

As though Olwen had picked up her thought, she moved forward and, taking Cai's hand, she placed it on Elined's.

Viviane was startled. Was it possible that she could manipulate events as well as see them through this mirror?

Elined drew back as though she had just touched a snake, and Cai fell back on the pillows with a groan, turning his face to the wall as though this time he would succeed in giving up his life.

Furiously Rheged slapped Elined across the face, and she staggered and almost fell. But Olwen caught her in her arms and held her, as she started to weep uncontrollably. Rheged strode out of the room and slammed the door behind him, as if knowing that if he stayed longer he would kill the wretched girl.

The scene began to fade and Viviane pressed forward to see more . . . but another scene was forming across the first one and for a moment it was difficult to tell the two apart. But then there was no doubt. Viviane watched at first with horror a scene in which men were killing each other without mercy: Caradawc's warriors and Neol's locked in deadly combat. She tried to look away but could not . . . And then she found that she was fascinated: watching the death and torment of others without a tear.

How could this be, she asked herself . . . and then she knew the answer. The tower was affecting her as it affected everything that came under its baleful influence.

Another face emerged on the mirror before her eyes.

Idoc's face – coldly smiling – watching *her*.

She screamed and the shock jolted her out of the hypnotic state she had been slipping into. She found herself gripping the double-ended quartz crystal that had sent the black knight's horse stampeding, and, without thinking, she flung it with all her strength at the mirror. It hit the surface with a tremendous crack that shook the tower from foundations to battlements. Her hands over her ears, Viviane reeled back. The air was full of flying splinters as the mirror and the crystal shattered together. She flung herself from the room and down the stairs. Her hands and cheeks were cut, but she could feel no pain there yet – only in her ears as the building boomed and roared and thundered all around her.

The tower rocked, but did not fall.

Idoc, still in the form of Caradawc, might have succeeded in his murderous scheme of destroying Huandaw's people, had Neol not already been on his way with all his warriors, enraged at the abduction of his sister Elined. When the two forces met, the battle was long, savage and bloody. Caradawc's men soon discovered that far from having the advantage they were fighting frantically to defend themselves against Neol's furious onslaught.

Idoc was almost insane with frustration. The human body he had taken over was cumbersome and inefficient compared to the powerful etheric forms he had been recently assuming. He felt mortal pain as Neol's sword pierced his flesh. He even felt fear. For a moment he reeled back and in that moment Neol pressed forward. He would have killed him then if Idoc had not somehow found the strength to summon from the dark depths of his own soul a fearsome curse that made Neol pause in terror, his sword arm frozen. Then would the advantage have swung to Idoc had the curse not spread outwards like the greasy rings on a stagnant pool when a stone is dropped at the centre. Farm lads and kindly fathers on both sides were inspired to deeds of monstrous cruelty against other farm lads and other kindly fathers, while bloodless shapes, gross and grotesque, formed by aberration of soul more horrible than any physical deformity could be, fought side by side with them, urging them on against former neighbours who had now become their enemies.

The river lay wide between Caradawc's men and their home territory. There was no time to seek a safe crossing. Back and back they were driven to the water's edge. Behind them the long grey river stretched, with flexed and liquid muscles, waiting to seize and pull and twist and drown them. Deep beneath the surface among the slime and water weeds the fiendish river horses stirred, sensing prey . . .

The water was cold as Caradawc's men and horses plunged in to escape their enemies. As though unable to stop the slaughter now that he had started it, Neol drove his men after them. The bank collapsed under the trampling hooves, and earth and grass and blood mingled with the slate-grey water . . .

For some the river was salvation: those managed to cross safely and scramble out the other side. Others met a quick death with spear in chest or throat. The worst fate was slow suffocation among the river fiends, the winding weed that throttled, the terror of the unknown.

Idoc and Gerin had both gained the far bank when Neol, halfway across, suddenly drew back. Both forces had had enough.

9

The Community of the Fish

Hunydd stood pawing the ground where Viviane had left her and she flung herself upon the mare's back, desperate to get as far away as she could from the fell tower. The mare needed no urging and moved like the wind, blood from the cuts on Viviane's hands staining her white mane: the trees streaming past, their branches whipping ineffectually at rider and mount. As they rode, Viviane's fear gave way to exultation. Idoc's scrying mirror, which spied upon the lives of others, was destroyed.

At last they were clear of the woods and out upon open hillside among the tall flowering grasses. The clouds that drifted high across the sky were like gold dust in the early evening sunlight, and two playful cloud dragons engaged in a slow and rhythmic dance, twisting and coiling sinuously around the fine white pearl of the moon. From what the priest had told her before they entered the fatal woods, she knew they were not far from Father Brendan's community, and Viviane was determined not to stop again until they reached it. All the same it was nightfall before Hunydd limped exhausted through the gate of the sanctuary of the Fish.

The monastery was housed in what had once been a ruined Roman villa. It had been patched and repaired and was now a strange mixture of wood and stone and different styles of architecture. It had taken its name from the magnificent mosaic floor of the inner courtyard, which, in the old days, had contained a pool with a fountain playing over it – the fish motif provided by the artist strangely given life by the movement of the water and the smaller living fish that had swum above it. Bordering it there was still a garden: decorative flowers mingling pleasantly with the useful medicinal herbs; roses brought by the Romans from their distant country still climbed around the bordering columns . . . The old peristyle was now the cloister. Most of the red Roman roofing tiles had long since disappeared and been replaced with local thatch, but the walls were still sturdy. The main hall of the villa had been converted into a church. It too was floored with mosaic: the motif here again a fish – but combined with the Chi-Rho symbol, since the original owner had evidently been Christian.

As Viviane slid off her mare in sheer exhaustion, Father Brendan himself stepped forward and took her arm to steady her as she swayed. He was a big, loose-limbed man with kindly but penetrating eyes half shaded by enormous, shaggy eyebrows. His weather-tanned face was lined with age, yet strong with a kind of inward youth. She tried to greet him but the words caught in her throat. He took her other arm to prevent her sinking to the ground.

'Child,' he said in a deep, gentle voice, stooping to look into her tormented eyes. 'You are safe here. Put away your fear.'

'Father . . .' she murmured. She could feel the tears building up – the flood of all that she had endured now ready to break through the barriers of self-control she had so carefully and fiercely upheld for so long.

He glanced over her head to a tall nun standing near by. 'Sister Bridget,' he said quietly, 'take her. Put her to bed. Let her weep.'

Viviane next felt the strong arms of the woman around her, and for a moment almost thought she was at home with the sound of the sea in her ears and her mother rocking her to sleep.

As she closed her eyes the last thing she saw was candlelight flickering on the design of two overlapping circles decorating the wall of the chamber in which she had been placed. Where the circles overlapped they made the unmistakable outline of a fish.

Viviane's sojourn with the community was a very strange and very beautiful experience. Walls of rock rose sheer on either side of the small valley, keeping it secluded and private. That this retreat from the world had been built by a Roman surprised her, but Father Brendan smiled when she told him this.

'The Romans were individuals, too, you know,' he said. 'Not all of them were seeking conquest and power. The man who built this house was a Christian at a time when Christians were being persecuted. He chose what he believed for himself, though all the world was against him. That is why you see the fish symbol everywhere in this building.'

'I was going to ask you about that.'

'The fish was the secret sign of the early Christians, when their lives depended on keeping their allegiance to the Mystery hidden. They took the initials of His Greek designation and found that they spelled the word ichthus, meaning fish. It stands for *Iesous Christos Theou Uios Soter:* Jesus Christ, Son of God, Saviour.'

She looked delighted. 'The two circles in my chamber . . .'

'We call that the Vesica Piscis. At the crossing of the circle of God and the circle of man, the fish manifests. It was another secret sign of the early Christians. But if I were to start telling you about all the significances of the Christ/Fish symbol I would not stop talking for a week. I think it would be better if you meditated on it yourself. That way you will learn what you really need to learn from it, and not only what I think you should learn.'

As she had told him all that had been happening to her, he had listened quietly and seriously. But when she had pleaded with him that he help to defeat Idoc and rescue Caradawc, Father Brendan was silent a long time. Then he had said firmly that he could not do this – only she could. Her expression must have shown him her utter dismay at this, for he put his hands on her shoulders and continued gently but with deep conviction: 'Up to now you have been floundering in the dark, only half understanding what is happening to you. When you leave here, you will see more clearly. You will act with the power of "inner seeing" and you will find that very different from acting "blind".'

She believed him instinctively – for everywhere she looked plants were growing, people were happy. She had visited monasteries before where the atmosphere was oppressively gloomy, as though it were necessary to hate this life to be given entrance to the next. But here the inhabitants seemed to take this life gratefully as a precious gift, as if they presumed that they could only pass easily from this life to the next if the two were in harmony with each other.

Father Brendan held out a little fish made of silver.

'Go to a quiet place. Hold it in your hand. Contemplate it. Then close your hand so that you can no longer see it with your earth-eyes. See it only with your inner-eye. Let it have motion. Let it have life. See where it swims. Learn from it.'

Curiously she took the little image from his large, work-calloused hand. She made her way to the small bare chamber she had been given, its stone walls unadorned except with the Vesica Piscis; the only furniture a wooden bed and straw mattress. She sat on the edge of the bed, a shaft of light from the high, small window shining down warmly on her hand as she held it out, the silver fish catching the light and for the moment dazzling her. Then the sunbeam moved on, and the fish lay on the palm of her hand glowing faintly, as though transformed in some way by the passing light.

She started by contemplating its beauty simply as an object. Then, as Father Brendan had instructed her, she tried to see it as a living creature in its natural habitat. At first, because she was not used to meditating, her mind drifted off, picking up stray and disconnected memories . . . At one point she wondered with some impatience how this understanding of the fish symbol was going to help her to solve the insurmountable problem of Idoc. But then she pulled her mind back, for she trusted Father Brendan. Symbols were like seeds, small and insignificant, yet containing within themselves the potential to grow into mighty trees. Now he wanted her to learn how to release that potential so that the seed might grow into a tree, and so that she might see across the landscape of her life with the eyes of the bird that perches in its highest branches and not of the worm that burrows in the ground beneath it.

She shut her eyes and tried to 'see' the metal cipher in her hand as if floating in clear and translucent water at the edge of a great ocean. She saw flecks of golden sunlight touching the ripples and reflecting down on to the pure white sand. And the silver fish floated inertly in the aquamarine, catching the light, moving only as the water moved.

She thought about the world without life, and she thought about the world with life.

The fish started to move of its own volition; it made choices; it explored its environment; it reached out to the great ocean and began to swim away from the dry beach that was so inimical to it.

She began to think of the ocean as the symbol for consciousness . . . the surface with its waves sometimes tossed by wind and storm, sometimes calm, representing our normal awareness . . . the depths representing all those other, deeper forms of consciousness, we don't usually take into account. The fish swam deeply . . . to all levels . . .

She followed. She called out to him . . . she asked questions . . .

It seemed to her that the fish understood her questions but that she could not always understand his answers. She was not worried. She knew that as she grew accustomed to these new levels she would begin to understand more and more . . .

Her silver fish swam on . . . exploring deeper and deeper . . . leading her to see connections of which she had never dreamed. She followed him into caves so dark she did not at first recognize that they were in fact the secret places of her own heart – where shadows lurked that she would not previously acknowledge. There she confronted her deep desire for Idoc, realizing that it had been so strong in that ancient life that she had chosen at first to ignore his vicious cruelty to others, rather than give him up. Her so-called 'love' had made a mockery of real love. When she had finally admitted that she could no longer condone what he was doing and had then helped those who planned his destruction, she told herself that she was acting purely for the good of others, when in fact her real motive had been to remove him as far as she could from herself so that she would no longer be tempted by him. How ironic that it was still her desire for him that tormented her.

What of the others?

Her thoughts and memories were becoming strangely clear in the company of the Fish.

Caradawc, Gerin, Rheged and Cai in their earlier existences had each had a part to play in Idoc's imprisonment.

Caradawc had at first been Idoc's greatest friend and had been heavily under his influence, even, through fascination, going along with him against his better judgement. Later he had become sickened and tried to draw away, but the weakness of his own character had, like Fiann's, made it impossible for him to do so. Thankfully he had joined the others, while still professing friendship with Idoc and still apparently condoning his evil practices. Because he had not had the courage to break free independently he was still bound and would remain so until, by his own strength, he freed himself.

And what of Gerin? She saw now where he fitted in. He had been High Priest in that other life, and it had been his decision to do what they had done. But was he – even he – pure of motive? She had always looked on him as a wise and dedicated man and had turned to him with the turmoil in her heart. But one day she had seen the look in his eyes and knew that his desire for her was as strong as any she might feel for Idoc. It was the jealous man and not the High Priest who decided to pin Idoc's soul to that patch of earth.

'Ah Gerin,' she thought sadly. 'Our little schemes come to nothing in the face of all that we don't know . . .'

Cai and Rheged? She remembered them now, too.

Rheged had undertaken the breaking of Idoc's legs during the spellbinding ceremony. He had been carrying out the basic requirements of the ritual – but he had enjoyed it. He had enjoyed the suffering on Idoc's face, just as much as Idoc had enjoyed the suffering of his own victims. What difference was there then in these two men? Rheged's enjoyment of battle and his refusal to look at the suffering it caused were still a problem for his soul to work out. She thought of his present evident concern for his friend Cai and hoped that at last, through this, he would be able to free himself.

And Cai?

In this life Cai had so far mishandled all his relationships with women. Viviane frowned, trying to remember something that would give her a clue to Cai's past – something that would help her to understand his present. He had been no more than a boy when she had first met him in that former life, and his devotion to her had been obsessional. Idoc had noticed this, and used it. He had promised the lad a night of pleasure with her in exchange for certain favours to himself, and when the boy had come to claim his reward, she, unaware of Idoc's promise, had cried out in outrage. Idoc had had the boy publicly shamed and castrated, and he lived on amongst them, a eunuch, bitterly brooding on vengeance.

The Fish was swimming back to the shore . . . sunlight penetrating the water . . . light dazzling her eyes . . .

She found herself sitting upright on the edge of her bed.

'Viviane,' a voice was saying.

Dazed, she looked about her. Sister Bridget stood at the door, smiling warmly. 'It is time to return. We have a meal ready . . . then we are going to sing. Do you feel like joining us?'

Viviane felt very much like joining them. She stretched and yawned and shook herself. She was very hungry.

'Are things clearer now?' Father Brendan inquired later that evening.

'Much clearer,' she said, 'for I've seen how we're all involved in Idoc's death and punishment. And I know that we were each guilty of wrong motives in our actions then, and have to work this out now – yet what Idoc was doing was so evil he *had* to be stopped!'

'Of course. But stopping Idoc was one thing; the conflict between good and evil within each of you was another. We are accountable for what we ourselves do – not for what others do. Do you understand that?'

He could see that she did.

He smiled and touched her arm. 'Come,' he said. 'At this time I always walk – so that I don't forget the stars.'

She trod silently beside him through the garden, her eyes on the narrow little path between the rows of vegetables, brooding on everything that had occurred and everything she was just beginning to understand, and then she noticed Father Brendan had stopped walking and was staring up at the sky. Her eyes followed his and she couldn't suppress a gasp. She *had* forgotten the stars! And now they blazed down on her in their myriad; brilliant against the darkness. It seemed to her that she, and Father Brendan who had loomed so large a moment before, became pinpoints against the vastness she was now contemplating. She reached up her arms and above her the mighty wheel of gold rolled and turned, the earth beneath her feet with it, the invisible regions and realms and the worlds beyond count . . . all moving together . . .

When Idoc, in the body of Caradawc, discovered how Rheged had kidnapped Elined and brought her to Castle Goreu, he was furious, blaming him entirely for their defeat, since, due to the abduction, Neol had been armed and ready for their attack.

'If my own men work against me, how am I to withstand my enemies,' he raged. 'Take him!' he growled to the two guards who had escorted him to Cai's chamber. 'Throw him in the dungeon before he causes me more harm.'

Rheged was dumbfounded. The face of his old friend Caradawc now was hard and cold, as he had never seen it before. He struggled to explain that he had acted only to save Cai's life – but the man he thought was Caradawc was not moved. Standing beside Cai's bed as the two guards roughly pinioned Rheged's arms, he looked down coldly on the wan figure whose cheeks were hollow from fasting and whose eyes were dull and lifeless.

'What life was there to save?' Idoc growled harshly. 'The man is a vegetable. He's no use to me. Leave him. If he wants to die, let him die!' And he turned and strode out of the room.

On Idoc's orders Rheged was beaten until the blood flowed, then manacled to a greasy wall among the rats. Goreu's dungeon had housed a few unfortunates in the old man's lifetime, but since Caradawc became king it had not been used. It was dark and damp, the filth of the previous occupants still mouldering in the straw. Rheged gagged as he hung from the wall. How could this be happening to him? How could Caradawc of all people! Caradawc who had been his friend since childhood . . .

'When he thinks about it calmly he'll release me,' Rheged thought desperately. 'He must. He was so angry at his defeat he wasn't thinking straight. I'd have been angry too . . .' Yet he felt uneasy at this rage in Caradawc. He had never seen him like that before. Perhaps Caradawc had more of his father in him than they had realized . . .

* * * *

Idoc sat alone on the throne in Caradawc's great hall, his eyes smouldering with the frustrations that burned in him. He would like to cause mighty catastrophes. He would like to move whole peoples about to his whim. He would like to challenge God! But here he sat in a small castle in a small kingdom with stupid, incompetent and cowardly warriors at his command.

As far as revenge on his five enemies was concerned, things were moving well. Caradawc had been dealt with. Cai was ailing and would die soon. Rheged was suffering, and soon would suffer more. He personally would supervise the breaking of his legs which would turn gangrenous in that dungeon. Even Gerin was tormented by his passion for a woman he could not have, and it was only Viviane who had escaped him for the moment.

But despite these triumphs he still felt immensely restless . . . This place was too small for him. It was not worthy of him. Viviane's father was High King over six smaller kingdoms, of which Caradawc's was the southernmost. No doubt Goreu had had private ambitions when he negotiated a daughter of the High King for his son. Now he, Idoc, was married to that same daughter, and could easily take advantage of such family connections to manoeuvre himself into a place at the High King's right hand. And from there . . .

But for this he would first need Viviane alive and well and at his side.

And where was she? He had recently been so preoccupied with defeating Huandaw and Neol so as to put their lands under his control, that he had lost track of her. When he called for her now he was furious to discover that she was nowhere to be found.

He ordered Olwen to be brought before him for questioning.

Without hesitation Olwen revealed that her mistress had ridden off with Father David before the battle, to visit a sick cottager.

'What sick cottager?' demanded Idoc grimly.

But Olwen did not know.

'If you lie to me girl, you'll be sorry!'

'Why should I lie, my lord? My lady did not say, and it was

not for me to ask. I am sure you will learn where she went if you inquire among the other tenants.'

Idoc glared at her long and hard from beneath scowling brows, tapping his fingers irritably on the table before him.

'Send me Gerin,' he snapped at last to one of the guards.

'If you would excuse me, my lord,' said Olwen carefully, 'my lady gave me a charge before she left and I must attend to that.'

'I presume you mean the kidnapped girl,' snarled Idoc. 'The one who cost me half my warriors.'

Olwen was silent, her head bowed, waiting patiently to be dismissed. She knew that something was terribly wrong, but had faith that if she kept as quiet as possible, and went about her chores as though nothing was happening, any trouble would eventually pass her by. She was deeply worried that Viviane had not returned, but the princess had set her the task of bringing Cai back to health, and this she meant to do.

'Did the queen have any part in bringing that girl here?'

'No, my lord. She left with Father David before . . .'

At that moment the guard who had been sent to fetch Gerin rushed in and began speaking to the king in a low voice. Olwen saw the rage that flashed across his face and, without awaiting his permission, she slipped unnoticed from the room.

She arrived at Cai's chamber flushed and frightened. The door was slightly ajar but, hearing a sound, she held back and peeped through the crack. Elined was kneeling beside Cai's bed, her head resting on his left hand, bitterly sobbing. He was propped up on one elbow staring wonderingly down at her.

Olwen drew back and shut the door.

The guard's message which had roused Idoc's anger was that Gerin was nowhere to be found – and neither was Rheged. The guards in the dungeon had been knocked out cold by an unseen assailant, and had only just come round. Meanwhile two horses were missing from the stables and, on being questioned, the guards at the gate reported having seen Sir Gerin ride out in the company of an old woman in a cloak. They had not thought to question him.

'Old woman!' screamed Idoc. 'Are you mad! What would one of my knights be doing with an old woman?' He ordered the gate-watch to be severely punished and sent a party of warriors after the fugitives, warning that they would pay with their lives if they did not return with the two men. He paced about the hall, muttering to himself, his anger so great that no one dared come near him. It was as though a huge black cloud had settled over the castle. Everyone was confused and frightened. No one could understand how their king could change so utterly in a few days, and no one felt safe from his violent rages and the inexplicable changes of loyalty and fortune that seemed to be happening. Many would have liked to flee after Gerin and Rheged, but none had the courage. Instead most felt it safest to do nothing, either keeping out of the king's way, or trying to ingratiate themselves with him by carrying tales against others.

Finally Idoc decided to return to the dark tower. For there he would be able to see in his mirror where Viviane, Gerin and Rheged now were. There he would have the means to hunt them down. He put the castle under the temporary command of the Captain of the Guard, whom he knew to be an ambitious man, hinting at great rewards if the place was kept tight and safe against his return. Then he set off into the night, refusing any suggestion that he should be accompanied.

Father Brendan and Viviane were walking the path that led up the narrow valley behind the house. At first every grain of soil was cultivated, even to the ledges stepping upwards from the little stream, but gradually wild nature took over. High cliffs of limestone replaced the terraces of vegetables and every nook and cranny and ledge was rich with natural growth. The tiny pink stars of stonecrop softened the edges of fissures in the silvery-grey rock, stone bramble and holly fern flourished, while wine-red moss-campion and yellow saxifrage lent a splash of bright colour. Even where there seemed no soil to support them, spindly trees – witch's rowan and hawthorn – grew sideways from the rock, turning upwards to the sunlight, reaching towards the narrow slit of blue sky between the cliffs. The stream that ran over the boulders at her feet seemed too small to have carved this great chasm, yet it had – with minute and delicate persistence over a time so vast that the whole of man's sojourn on earth seemed no more than a moment compared to it.

At one point the valley opened up where the stream took a sharp bend. One bank was steep, the other sloping gently to the water's edge with a small grassy plain behind it. Here again trees could grow upright, and several did.

Father Brendan held up his hand for her to pause. 'We'll stay here for a while,' he said.

Viviane was glad. She could not imagine a more beautiful, more peaceful place. Here the horrors of her recent life seemed remote and unreal.

Brendan smiled as though he read her thoughts. 'Here,' he said, 'we might find that the invisible becomes visible.'

She wished she had her amethyst with her, but Brendan had refused to let her bring it. 'Today,' he had said, 'you have to learn to see through illusion to the truth beyond, without any aids.'

The air was cool and crystalline. Deep in the gorge where the sunlight touched only the highest edge of the cliffs and the very tops of the trees, the contrast between shade and light was clear-cut and sharp; but on the little plain the sun shone down directly and the trees stood in a blaze of light.

'The first thing you need to know, the river must tell you,' Brendan said. 'Sit a while on that boulder in the middle of the stream, and listen.'

Viviane was glad of a rest, and clambered eagerly over the rocks until she reached the huge rounded boulder that Brendan had indicated. She looked back at him inquiringly: what would he do while she was resting and listening? But he must have slipped away among the trees for he was nowhere in sight.

She settled down on the cool stone, glad that at least in this part of the valley the sun could enter.

She listened to the birds . . . noted the sparkle of the water as it hurried over and between the rocks . . . the green of the bushes that hung over the far bank, some of them trailing branches in the water, continually buffeted . . .

Then she began to listen to the water . . .

She began to forget herself and hear only water sounds . . . complex . . . beautiful . . . a hundred different harmonies within the same song. The water spoke, liquid-tongued, lightly lilting each tale a hundred different ways . . .

She could have listened for ever . . . but Brendan's voice was calling her . . . cutting through . . .

'What have you learned?' he asked as she joined him.

'I have learned that there are many ways to tell everything that is to be told, and that man's language is clumsy and inadequate. It can tell only one tale at a time, and that tale only one way at a time.'

He smiled. 'You listened well. Now come with me.'

He led her towards the trees.

'The next lesson, a tree must teach you,' he said. 'Choose one carefully.'

She chose an oak, the tallest she had ever seen, standing like a giant, its girth such that two tall men with long arms stretched to the limits would find difficult to encompass. It rose straight and true, branches balanced and harmonious, its crown almost out of sight. She circled it several times, and then touched it . . . She began to feel something of the tremendous forces which coursed through it, which drove it up towards the sky. She put her hands on the bark and felt through her own flesh that upsurge of energy. Totally silent and with no sign of movement, the tree yet was vibrant with action. Beneath her hand prodigious events were taking place, so minute that they could not be seen with the eye, yet so powerful that the mighty Being of the tree was continually being created and renewed . . . its roots driving deep in the earth with the strength to crack rock and tumble mountains.

She returned in awe to Brendan and sat quietly beside him, aware that within her too the energy that created the universe was coursing.

'This time I will speak while you learn, but my words will be no more than stones dropped into a still pool. It will be the rippling circles that ride out from the stones that you must note, and not the stones themselves.

'I am going to make you see a scheme, a pattern, which might help you to understand many things you need to know. But you must remember the lesson of the water language. You must try to hear the other harmonies, the other patterns, which flow through the one you will now see . . .'

'I will try,' she said humbly.

Brendan began to speak, but she soon lost the sense of whether she was hearing his words or her own thoughts.

Whether it was the extraordinary concentration of sunlight that made the tree seem to vibrate and change before her very eyes, or whether there was a kind of magic in the air channelled through Brendan, she could not be sure . . . but the natural living tree before her began to take on a visionary quality. It became for her the mysterious Tree of Life, reaching up through all the Realms of Being to the very borders of that region where not even the archangels dare penetrate . . .

She realized that the Tree was growing as much downwards from above, as though rooted in the Light of Heaven, as it was growing upwards from below, where it was rooted in the World of Changes, the World of Matter.

She saw herself as Spirit from the highest realms, rooted now in the earth, but striving to return. She saw around her the world of air, earth, fire and water: the multitudinous beings of the World of Matter. And above her she saw the non-material World of the Soul, the region of angels and of demons, of elementals and of those who are awaiting rebirth. She knew that beyond this there were other realms, still out of reach of her understanding even in her most inspired moments: the Realm of pure Spirit where the mighty archangels observe and act – known to pagans as 'the gods' – even they still far from the threshold of the Unknown, the Dwelling of the Nameless One.

Viviane felt her head burning with the struggle to understand all that was coming to her.

She envisaged the Tree with energy flowing up and down from the First to the Last, the One to the Many, and back again. She saw spheres and realms contained within the Tree, each with its precise meaning and function. She saw beings going up and down and up again, animated by the tremendous 'lightning flash' of God's desire for life, yet freely motivated by their own longing to explore before their yearning to rejoin their source drove them back, transformed and enriched.

She saw those who rose and those who fell. She saw those who tried and tried again, and those embittered and failed beings who had given up trying.

Dimly she remembered that Idoc had once described all this to her.

'Why,' she asked Brendan, 'why would a man who has seen this vision let it go?'

He knew of whom she was speaking. 'Idoc moved too fast and too unevenly . . . taking in knowledge before he had the wisdom to understand it. At first he had no motive but to seek the meaning behind all Manifestation, and, finding that he needed help, he asked for it from the realm beyond our own. To ask for such help with a pure motive is as it should be; but he soon forgot his original goal and began to think about how he could use such help to improve his earthly life, materially, and how he could use it to gain power over his neighbours. With this change of motive came a change of guidance. He refused to listen to those who tried to guide him upwards, and only to those who offered him easy and immediate rewards. He was taken over by a being whom he believed was one of the high angels, but who was not. His name was Ny-ak. Idoc followed Ny-ak's every instruction, at first not realizing where it was leading him, still believing that he was on the journey of the Return. He abandoned his own judgement, his own sense of discrimination. He started cruel animal experiments and later he experimented on humans – believing that he had the right, in the name of knowledge, to use whatever and whoever came his way. He wanted to find answers to the questions that interested him about the relationship of "mind" to "reality" and of "soul" to "body", and he chose to do this by taking the physical body apart and seeking, cell by cell, for the answer. His victims had to be alive: for dead these relationships did not exist. He suffered with their suffering at first, but excused it by telling himself how he would improve man's lot on earth with the knowledge he would gain. Increasingly he felt no pain when he inflicted pain. The rational function of his mind grew at the expense of the imaginal. He became incapable of entering any reality other than the one of his own ego.'

Did Brendan stop speaking then, or had he stopped long before?

She understood now that Idoc must be freed from the incubus he had called down upon himself – as much as Caradawc must be freed from Idoc.

127

She put her head down on her knees with a deep sigh.

She could take no more.

Brendan understood. He touched her on the shoulder, and when she lifted her head she saw that she was beside a river, with trees and bushes and little birds singing cheerfully.

'We had better return to the house,' he said gently.

She nodded gratefully and stood up, stretching, enjoying the feeling of movement in her cramped muscles, the sun on her skin. The oak tree had returned to its natural form, as splendid as any vision, with its rich depths of rustling green, its huge and powerful trunk sustaining with its strength innumerable lives . . . insects and birds . . . fern and moss and lichen . . . even the Druid's sacred mistletoe.

She walked lightly on the rocky path, listening to the river sounds with new attention, noting every colour, every shape, as though she were from another world and seeing this one for the first time.

10

The door of flame

Idoc found that Caradawc's body, though young and healthy, was sluggish after his etheric form, and his thoughts were troubled from time to time with irrelevancies. He longed for the power he had possessed before and rejoiced to feel it returning as he drew nearer the familiar valley and the rock made up of many rocks which marked the way through the woods and up the hill – the path Fiann used to take in the days when they were lovers . . .

His horse picked its way carefully through the shadows, the moonlight bright, but not enough to penetrate this tangled wood. At the top of the hill, standing clear of trees, he finally saw the tower rising tall and forbidding before him.

The tower had once been covered with the muscles and tendons of a gigantic vine, the work, he suspected, of the Green Lady, who had always opposed his schemes. He remembered how it had grown: how it had crawled and gripped and squeezed; how it had sealed the windows and begun to crack the stone. He remembered how he had broken three axes before he had been able to loosen its suffocating hold, but he had won at last and now it was nothing but a leafless, grey, brittle network of stem and tendril, powerless to harm him.

He was shocked to notice that the door was open. 'Who dares?' he cried aloud, leaping down and striding forward. He had never imagined that anyone could enter the tower without his knowledge. He now regretted even more his folly in taking on the burden of human flesh. There was so much one could not see with human eyes; so much one missed.

Inside, the stairwell was pitch dark. He ripped a branch from a nearby bush and set it alight. Silently, swiftly, he moved, determined to catch the rash intruder unawares. The lower three doors were firmly shut, but the fourth and uppermost lay wide open, the door to his octagonal chamber of power.

Without any hesitation he stormed in, his improvised torch held high. The mystery intruder was no longer there but the whole chamber was strewn with the sharp black splinters of his precious obsidian mirror. The wall where it had hung was bare. He turned suddenly and saw that he was being watched.

Small brown voyeurs, their eyes large and luminous, were crowding at the door, straining forward, eager not to miss a thing. With a curse he slammed the door shut, and heard them squealing and laughing and tumbling down the stairs.

He sat in his chair with his head in his hands.

Who could have done this? No man he knew was powerful enough to destroy that mirror. Without it how was he going to trace his enemies, Gerin and Rheged? Without it how was he going to find Viviane?

He remembered the creatures he had closed out when he flung the door shut. It was possible they had witnessed the destruction of the mirror. They seemed to appear everywhere – perching, prowling, watching everything that went on; relentless sight-seekers, sniffing out trouble and rushing to where it was to pry and peep; slobbering greedily over sexual couplings and gloating over suffering. He had even been half aware of them during the battle, shrilling to each other excitedly to come and see some young man horribly dismembered, clucking their teeth in hypocritical disapproval even as their eyes swelled larger and larger with excitement. Perhaps he could use them in some way to his advantage, though he hated the thought of relying on anyone – let alone such inferior creatures. The tower had always been his private space – where he could watch but not be watched; where he could make decisions that plunged others into misery, but never have to meet their eyes. He was determined to find out by whom his privacy had been violated.

He strode to the door and flung it open again. The macabre little sight-seekers, the voyeurs, were still crowded there, their bowl-shaped ears pressed to the wood, fighting over which should get its eyeball to the keyhole. When Idoc appeared they immediately fell back in terror, but he managed to seize one by its thin, bird-bone leg. Its mates shrieked with excitement as he dragged it into the chamber, then they surged forward again, obviously feeling no sympathy for the victim, only delight that they would have yet another drama to enjoy.

The voyeur itself was not so happy about being forced to take a central part in the action for once. It squealed and bit and scratched its oppressor, the weasel teeth and small filthy talons uncomfortably sharp. Idoc held the creature at arm's length and shook it violently until it hung from his hand like a dirty rag. Its whole being seemed to shrivel with despair. Even the bulbous eyes, which had been such a feature of its face, retreated into the skull, leaving only two heavily lidded slits, through which Idoc could catch the glint of a venomous stare.

Idoc felt disgust at handling the creature, and looked around for something to use to tie it up while he interrogated it; but as he did so he noticed something that made him totally forget his prisoner. His grip loosened and the voyeur fell to the floor, as Idoc stooped to pick up a piece of broken mirror the size of a plate. For in it he could see as complete a scene as he had ever seen in the full mirror on the wall. Then he picked up another piece: in this too was a complete scene. He scrabbled on the floor picking up pieces one by one. Each, however small, gave back as much as the whole mirror had done. Now he had a hundred scrying mirrors – some small enough to fit into his pocket and carry about with him. Whoever had dared this dreadful deed had thought to cripple him, but in fact had served to make him even stronger. Smiling triumphantly, Idoc sat at his table holding up a piece of mirror the size of his palm. He was no longer limited by Caradawc's human vision, no longer tied to the tower for his source of information.

Forgotten, the dying voyeur oozed yellow blood, watched by its companions to the last fluttering movement of its tiny hands.

Gerin carefully related to Rheged everything he knew about Idoc as they rode away from Castle Goreu. Rheged was relieved to know that it had not truly been Caradawc his friend who had treated him so harshly. His back was still very painful from the thrashing, and his arms and shoulders ached from the torment of the manacles. Their priority now was to get as far away from Castle Goreu as they could, and seek a safe place for Rheged to regain his strength while they thought and planned what to do next. Rheged's first thought had been to attempt to kill Idoc, but Gerin pointed out to him that this would be useless, for all they would achieve would be the destruction of Caradawc's physical body. Idoc himself would still exist: he seemed capable of taking on any form, of appearing anywhere.

'No,' Gerin said. 'This needs careful thought.' Perhaps they should join Viviane at the Community of the Fish, and all decide together what had to be done.

'And what about Cai?' Rheged protested, 'We can't leave him behind.'

Gerin was silent.

'I'll go back for Cai as soon as I have you safely in Viviane's care,' he said finally.

'No, you go back now. I can manage.' But Rheged was swaying dangerously in the saddle, fresh blood from the lash wounds seeping through his shirt.

Suddenly they heard the sound of riders coming their way, galloping fast and calling out to each other. They could hear hounds, too. A hunt was on, but not for deer.

Gerin took Rheged's bridle. 'Hold on tight. We have to get away!'

He led the two horses into a stream, and they worked their way along it as fast as they could, hooves slipping and sliding on rounded pebbles. This ploy must have lost the hunters a little time, for the sound of them faded for a while – but not for long.

Their next ruse when they heard their pursuers closing in again was for Gerin to take Rheged on to his own horse, and send Rheged's mount galloping off in another direction.

Their final desperate trick, when they feared at last they had been cornered at the edge of a precipice, was to send off Gerin's horse too, while they themselves climbed over the lip of the cliff, clutching frantically at small outcrops and fibrous roots until they found a ledge just wide enough to hold them. There they stood, trembling and panting, backs pressed against the rock, praying to all the gods they knew that their pursuers would not dream that they had been crazy enough to climb down there. Luckily, above them a hawthorn bush in full leaf corkscrewed out of the cliff, affording some kind of screen.

When Olwen returned to Cai's room, Elined was sitting close to Cai, on the edge of his bed. They held each other's hands and Elined was speaking fast and earnestly as though she had to make up for a hundred years of silence. She had created a burden for herself with her lie, which, with every passing moment, had increased in weight until it almost crushed her. Now she was trying to free herself of it.

Olwen stood unnoticed in the doorway for some time, unwilling to interrupt them yet aware of the importance and urgency of the message she must convey. At last, when she cleared her throat and stepped forward, they turned to look at her.

She had decided, though she understood very little of it, that something was very wrong in Castle Goreu. It was clear to her from the king's behaviour, and Viviane's earlier agitation, that the princess had not really gone to visit a sick tenant, but had fled for safety. And so, too, had Gerin and Rheged. The king was behaving very unpredictably and everyone else was confused and afraid. She felt bound to warn Cai of her fears now that he seemed to have regained his senses.

Having seen her vision of the many Realms of Being, Viviane realized that her next task was to find Caradawc before his disembodied soul finally lost its normal desire to return to life in this realm, and drifted off seeking premature entry into the next. Brendan had already explained that this would be disastrous for Caradawc. 'Because,' he said, 'although we talk of "realms" and "worlds" and "regions" and see them in images drawn from our experience on earth, they are not actually places where one can go, but states of being. And I fear Caradawc is not ready for this next state yet.'

'But surely he could be born again on this earth in another body, and try again to reach that "readiness"?'

'It's not as simple as that. Death occurs always at a very precise moment in one's "greater life", no matter how random and ill-timed it may seem to one's "lesser life".'

'But surely . . .'

Brendan held up his hand.

'No more questions. I have no more answers for you now. I think it would be wiser to retrieve him as quickly as possible, before too much damage is done to his unprepared soul. Now, we'll go into the chapel and I'll light a candle for you. I suggest you look into the flame as you meditate and pray.'

'You won't leave me?' she pleaded.

'I've explained before,' he said quietly. 'I cannot act for you. It is you and Caradawc and Idoc who have the responsibility for these events on your shoulders and it is you and they who alone must lift the burden of them.'

He led the way to a small stone chapel, much rougher in construction than the main villa – where a hermit had once established his cell long after the Roman family had left and the house had fallen to ruin – but before Brendan had come from Ireland to establish his own, unusual, community there – a community that did not fit comfortably into the established church.

The walls were simply built without mortar, and Viviane could envisage the man choosing its stones in the valley, carefully and meticulously, knowing exactly which ones would suit and which ones not. She could see him toiling day by day, alone, lifting and fitting, patiently and lovingly, constructing a sacred place where it would feel right to him to pray.

Around the walls there were several small apertures, where stones had been omitted, too small to be called windows. She noticed that one of them on the west wall was now admitting a thin but brilliant beam of light from the setting sun, the very narrowness of the gap serving to concentrate and focus the ray. Around the walls were panels of rough carvings. She moved towards one and peered closely. It seemed to represent a mother holding up a babe.

Brendan, standing close behind her, traced the lines of the worn carving with his finger so that there could be no mistake.

'The rays of the setting sun at midwinter fall there,' he told her, 'so that at the nadir of darkness there is a promise that the light will return.'

He took a candle from the small stone slab that served as an altar and lit it. Holding it high, he beckoned her to follow him.

One by one, he illuminated other carvings around the walls, twelve in all, each illustrating an important moment in the life of the Christ when He was on earth as the man Jesus. Brendan explained how the apertures were so skilfully placed that each of the twelve carvings was separately lit at a certain significant time. It was as though the sun's finger were pointing to them, reading them off in sequence. The hermit could thus regularly follow the teachings they spelled out.

An ancient memory began to flicker in the candle flame. Had she herself not once been part of a culture that built great initiation chambers for the living and the dead where the sun's rays were used in just this way?

Father Brendan placed the candle back on the altar. It was now almost nightfall and the chapel was suddenly very dark. He knelt down in front of the altar for a few moments, bowing his head. And then he departed, pulling the rickety door closed behind him, so that she was left alone.

She was frightened, thinking how terrible it would be if the candle flame went out, because Brendan had not left her the means to rekindle it. But then she told herself that she was being foolish: after all the chapel was nothing more than a small stone room, with a door she could open, and beyond that lay the buildings of the community and all the light and warmth and human companionship she could need. But no matter how firmly she reassured herself of this, she still could not shake off the feeling that she was somehow utterly alone – far, far from anything or anyone she knew . . . and about to embark on a dangerous mission into an unknown which even Father Brendan seemed unclear about, though no doubt he had given her as much support and protection as he could to prepare her.

There was one small yew-wood bench in the chamber and she sat herself down on it now, directly in front of the faintly flickering candle. Straightening her back, she placed her feet together flat on the flagstones of the floor, her hands folded quietly in her lap. The discomforts of her body must not interrupt the work she was about to do.

Then she began to stare into the candle flame, taking deep breaths to steady herself. Her heart was beating uncomfortably fast at first, then gradually slowed down. The flame seemed brilliant in the darkness – and within it that deep and unfathomable blue she always associated with the Realm of Spirit.

For how long she sat and stared, she could not tell, but it seemed to her the candle flame grew and grew, very slowly but steadily, until it towered above her. She was now looking at a door of fire, and knew that she must step through it. She knew also that the only way she could pass safely through it was to aim at the centre – the deepest and most vibrant part of it, the blue of the Spirit Realm.

It seemed to her that she stood up and stepped forward . . . Now she was ready to search for Caradawc, so she called his name, forming his image in her heart. Yet as she stepped into the door of flame she glanced back and saw her own body still seated immobile on the bench, eyes still fixed on the candle. For a moment she was startled and fearful, wanting to return. In that same moment the white-gold edge of the extraordinary door flared inwards, and she felt the searing pain of burning on her arm. She cringed, and almost drew back – but then a thought came to her: 'You would not have been burned if you had not feared. So trust.'

She stood firm then, trying to master her fear, determined not to fail Caradawc. The flame still roared around her alarmingly, but the numinous blue light protected her in the centre. She moved forward again, and the flame seemed to flow away from her like water past a fast-moving boat.

On the other side of the door of flame she was confronted by what appeared at first to be a black void, totally without form or feature. She remembered she had seen a vision of Caradawc floating in such a darkness, calling for her help.

Again she could feel the fear welling up inside her, and now she feared to fear. She tried to remember instead her magnificent vision of the Tree of Life, and a thought came to her . . . Caradawc may have left the realm of Matter, but he probably had not yet passed totally beyond the reverberations of Time into Eternity. She was aware that there was quite a traffic between the realms closest to each other, and that if angels and demons and strange unearthly beings could pass freely from one to the other, surely Caradawc would still be able to share that facility.

Gradually it seemed to her that within the darkness, which

had seemed so absolute before, there were gradations and variations. She could now distinguish clouds billowing around her, made up of creatures of every conceivable form – some reaching out to her, calling to her for help. She was filled with pity, but could think of nothing but the rescue of Caradawc. How would she ever find him? And even if she did, how would they ever be able to return to earth? She could nowhere see the door through which she had come.

She was becoming increasingly jostled – long fingers were tugging at her – spindly arms and legs were twining around her own like bindweed. She tore them off and pushed them away, but as fast as she rid herself of one, another was in its place.

'Caradawc!' she called frantically. Her voice seemed to go nowhere, but returned in a thousand different mocking guises.

'Oh God,' she thought, 'what if I'm trapped here forever . . . neither alive nor dead? What if Father Brendan is an agent of evil and not of good, and has lured me here to my destruction?'

Despair is one of the most dangerous conditions of all, for in despair one is completely defenceless: all doors wide open and unguarded, an invitation to any trouble-maker to enter and take over.

For a moment Viviane hovered on the edge of despair, on the edge of 'no return'. But then she rallied, forcing herself to envisage the mighty realms above, and all the splendours of existence. In that moment it seemed her strength increased and, in the distance, she saw a beam of light. She struggled towards it, believing now that she would surely find Caradawc. The would-be parasites that had beset her fell away, seeking a host easier to overcome.

As she approached it, the shaft of light seemed like a ladder passing through the darkness from the realms far above, to the realms that lay below. It was crowded with beings passing up and down. The impression they gave was very different from the one she had received from the other inhabitants of this region. Here there was no despair, no desperation: only a sense of hope and purpose.

She found Caradawc at last, hovering at the very edge of the light-beam, but seemingly incapable of making the final effort that would carry him into it.

She took his hands at once, and they turned and turned together, free floating now in light, spiralling close together, twining round each other as though they would never be parted . . .

Suddenly Viviane found herself seated again on the yew bench in the little chapel. Dawn light was shining through the tiny window behind the altar, shafting down on to the little pool of melted wax that had been the candle. She started up and looked around. *Caradawc?* Her arm was hurting, and when she looked down she saw there was an ugly red burn on the skin.

She leapt up.

'Caradawc?' she called. 'Caradawc!'

Had she failed, then? It had all been so vivid – so how could it have been just a dream? And her arm was visibly burned. She *must* have passed through that door.

Then the door of the chapel creaked open and Father Brendan stood silhouetted against the morning light.

'I see you found him, then,' he said cheerfully.

'Where is he?' she cried. She looked all round the tiny room but could see no sign.

'I am here, my love.' She heard his voice in her head, but could not see him. Frantically she turned to Father Brendan.

'I want to *see* him! I want to *hold* him!'

'You have brought him safely back to this realm, my child, but he has not yet returned to his bodily form.'

She could bear no more. Picking up the candle-holder she flung it with all her might against the wall, then crumpled onto the bench and sobbed.

'I can't do it! I can't! *Why* won't someone help me?'

Brendan stood beside her, letting her rage and weep. At last, when she was quieter, he murmured, 'You are being helped, but not always in the way you think you ought to be. Remember, you cannot see the whole scene . . . only a very small part of it.'

Gradually she pulled herself together and wiped her face on her sleeve.

'And Caradawc? Can you see him?'

'No, but I know he's here.'

'How will we ever save him?'

'Come, you are very tired. You must sleep. Decisions made in haste and weariness are not well made.'

'I can't leave Caradawc . . .'

'You won't have to. He will be with you – even in your sleep.'

She suffered herself to be led away, exhausted.

The men in pursuit of Gerin and Rheged were obviously perplexed by the sudden disappearance of their quarry. For a while they milled about at the top of the cliff. Then they must have picked up the tracks of Gerin's horse, for they moved off suddenly in a great hurry. Several of them had peered over the cliff edge, but the hawthorn bush hid the fugitives from view.

The drop down to the valley floor was precipitous, and the two young men were anything but comfortable on their precarious perch. As soon as they were sure Caradawc's men had gone, they started to look at the possibilities of escape. It seemed impossible now that they had ever climbed down there, and equally impossible that they could ever climb up. Rheged groaned as the rock pressed into his wounds, the ledge being too narrow for him to shift his position. Gerin worried that if he did not get him off the ledge soon, he might faint and plummet to the rocks far below them. He anxiously scanned the cliff face for any handhold.

Catching a movement from some bushes further along, he peered more closely, wondering what animal could live or hunt on such vertical terrain. For a moment he stared astonished. Every bush and outcrop on the cliff face, above and on either side of them, seemed crowded with little brown creatures with spindly legs and arms, bulbous bellies and bulbous eyes. He had never before seen anything like them. Their faces were strangely human, yet he knew that they could not be. They sat on twigs and plants that surely could not bear an ounce of weight, swinging their legs, chattering, eagerly watching, as though the two men in their adversity were some kind of freak show put on specially for their entertainment. Then Gerin blinked, and when he looked again they were gone – or rather he had the feeling that they were still there but he could no longer see them. He blinked again, several times, staring and peering but there was now no sight or sound of them. Deciding he must have imagined them he tried to concentrate on the problem of getting off the cliff face safely. If they had got down, there must surely be a way up. But they had slithered down without thinking, carried by the powerful instinct of survival. Now with his conscious mind he could see no way for them to go. Beside him Rheged was trembling with the effort of keeping his position, so he must think of something soon. If they could not go up again, was it possible to go down? He turned his attention in that direction. It was a long way to the valley floor and seemed just as difficult as the way up. But then he spotted something that might be of help. A long slanting fault traversed the rock face from left to right about ten foot below them. If they could only reach that crack they would be able to work their way along it until the cliff crumbled into a scree of boulders to the west. From there it would be relatively easy to clamber down. Gerin searched until he found the foothold he needed. Carefully, painfully, inch-by-inch, they eased themselves down the rock face until their feet at last slid into the cliff's long scar. From there it was a matter of patience and persistence, until finally they were slipping and slithering down the scree to the valley floor.

They were safe, but on foot – and a long way from where they wanted to be.

Olwen's father was a younger son of a minor nobleman at the court of Garwys, the High King, and although she had no riches she had possessed a certain status at court which made her a suitable choice for companion to the princess in her new married life. Olwen was well used to making decisions and giving orders among the other women who attended Viviane, and she could see that she would have to make decisions and give orders now. Cai, though much improved, was still in no fit state to think and act coherently, and nor was Elined. So Olwen resolved, Caradawc being in the dangerous mood he was, that they should follow the king's other friends and make good their escape.

For a long while Viviane lay in the little bare room at the monastery, listening to the songbirds and the honk of wild duck as they passed overhead. Occasionally she heard a voice calling or the clank of cooking pots and at regular intervals the faint sweet sound of singing. She tried to forget all the dreadful beings she had seen and remember that there was always that ladder-like beam of mysterious light for any who sought it. Finally, too tired to worry any more about her problems, she fell asleep.

Caradawc and she were walking together in an apple orchard. It was spring and clouds of blossom surrounded them. They were intensely aware of each other and of every detail of the scene around them: the waxy-white petals with the dark pink underflush; the small birds hopping about on the mossy bark, prising out minute insects with their sharp little beaks; the sky extra-deep blue between the clusters of blossom: sunlight on grass, sunlight on Caradawc's hair, sunlight on the hand that rested on her waist. She was completely happy. They were not talking, yet communicating perfectly. Both knew when the moment was right, and they turned simultaneously to touch lips. They lay in the grass and explored each other tenderly and carefully as though making sure that everything about each other was known and loved; every hair, every nail, every cleft . . . it was not so much passion as contentment . . .

In a way she knew while it was happening that it was a dream. Yet she knew also that it *would* happen, detail by detail . . . exactly and precisely . . .

It was this idyllic scene that Idoc witnessed in his shattered fragment of scrying mirror; and it was this scene that finally made him put his head in his hands and despair. Did Caradawc mean so much to her then, that she would dare even those dark regions to rescue him? He, Idoc, had Caradawc's physical form but it seemed that it was not enough. Had he, Idoc, ever had her love? Even in those ancient days? She had desired him, yes, but had she ever loved him as she now loved Caradawc?

As Olwen rode out with Cai and Elined, her thoughts were mostly with the handsome Gerin, for, since her first arrival at Castle Goreu, she had nursed a hopeless passion for him. She had no illusions that he shared her feelings, for she had seen the way he looked at Viviane. Indeed, apart from Viviane, Olwen was probably the only one at court who suspected Gerin of his attachment for Caradawc's princess.

Were he and Rheged now safe from pursuit? Where would they hide? In all this land, where would they be safe from the king's wrath?

She looked at Cai and Elined, and sighed. They seemed so unaware of the danger they were in – riding close together, taking every opportunity to linger . . . to touch hands and to gaze into each other's eyes. She could see they were weaving a golden cocoon of dreams around themselves no less inimical to them than Elined's lie.

It was clear to Olwen that it was she who must be strong and sensible. It was not the time to be dreaming about Gerin.

At last she felt they were safe enough to take a rest. Immediately the two lovers locked themselves in each other's arms, while Olwen took the horses down to the stream to drink. On the north side of the stream rose a precipitous cliff, its rock face cracked and scarred and veined. There were rust-red drip marks where the rains had leached out the irons, and huge areas of the surface were mapped out in orange and yellow lichen. On the south side, however, the landscape opened out and rolled away in gentle hills and wooded valleys.

Olwen sat on a boulder beside the stream while the horses drank. She was tired and discouraged. She was no longer sure what to do, and wondered if they'd been wrong to leave the castle. She had thought to take Elined back to her father, but she saw no prospect of reaching Huandaw before nightfall. She wondered if Caradawc was back at Castle Goreu yet, and what measures he would take to retrieve his bride and the other fugitives. She laid her head back against the trunk of a tree wearily, and began to drift off to sleep.

In her dreams the forces pursuing her were demon-faced. She saw black cloaks billowing out like wings behind them.

She woke with a shriek.

In front of her stood two men: Gerin and Rheged.

'Whoa,' said Gerin gently. 'Steady. We'll do you no harm.'

She stared at them in astonishment. 'I . . . I thought . . .' she stammered.

'What are you doing here?' he asked, obviously puzzled.

She wondered if he would notice how her pulse was racing and how flushed her cheeks were. He leant over, reaching out a steady hand to help her to her feet, his eyes deep blue in a tanned face, his hair as black as her own and curling against his neck. Her own hand was trembling as she took his.

'I thought it best to leave the castle . . . The king is not himself . . .'

He smiled grimly. 'I had noticed,' he said. 'But surely you would have been in no danger?'

'Perhaps not – but I was afraid for Cai and Elined.'

'Cai? Is Cai here?' Gerin looked around eagerly, and she felt she had already lost his attention. He had held her hand no longer than he needed; he had not gazed into her eyes as she had gazed into his.

'I left them in that grove of trees there,' she pointed. 'They . . . we were all very tired,' she added, loath to let him go. But without another word he turned and strode away towards the trees, leaving her alone with Rheged, who sank on to the grassy bank beside her with a groan. She noticed for the first time how pale he was, and how awkwardly he was sitting, hunched with pain. She had heard of the dreadful beating he had received, and could see now how his clothes were sticking to the dried blood on his back. He flexed his shoulders very gingerly as though trying to release them.

'Wait,' she cried. 'You need water for that. Come.' She drew him nearer the stream and carefully soaked the fabric until it loosened, then she took off his shirt and bathed his back.

'These weals don't look infected,' she said. 'I think you've been lucky.'

He laughed ruefully and, realizing what she'd said, she laughed too. 'You know what I mean . . .'

He grinned at her gratefully. 'It feels better already. Could you give me a drink?'

She stooped to the water and brought up her cupped hands. Gratefully he drank from them. She did not notice Gerin and the others close behind them until he put his hand on her shoulder, and her body seemed to melt with delight under it.

'We've a lot to thank you for, Olwen,' he said, and took his hand away, not noticing how it had left her trembling. 'It's a godsend to find you here. But we should move on while we can and try to reach the Community of the Fish before nightfall.' He looked musingly at the sky. The long summer day was coming to an end and no amount of wishing would extend it.

Cai seemed well recovered now that he was with his friends. He and Elined took one of the horses, Rheged another – and Gerin and Olwen, the third. Above them the swallows darted and swooped . . . marking the air with their invisible calligraphy. When she was a child Olwen had pretended she could read what the swallows wrote in the air with their swift, sure movements; and made up songs for her little sister, claiming that they were the swallows' songs. Sometimes she had even convinced herself. She smiled wryly. Those days seemed very far away and she could no longer read what the swallows wrote. Nor could she read what was in Gerin's thoughts as he held her lightly against his chest, his chin against her temple, his eyes staring straight ahead.

11

The destruction of the tower

When Viviane awoke she knew part of what she had to do to help Caradawc.

She could not remember dreaming it, nor being told; she just seemed to know. She must return to the dread tower, and somehow contrive that both Idoc and Caradawc were present at the same time. She did not have any idea how she was going to bring this about, nor what she had to do then, but she sensed it was crucial for Caradawc's 'return' to the present world. Father Brendan had told her that she could hold Caradawc within her for a while by the power and sincerity of her love, but this hold was dangerous to both of them and must not be prolonged.

In the early afternoon she began to feel dizzy and nearly missed her footing on a step. She found she had to lie down for a while to recover, but as she lay her body began to feel as though it were dematerialising . . . as though she were drifting away from it. She was frightened, and struggled to regain control.

'No,' she prayed, 'please . . . don't . . .'

She was not sure what was happening, but it seemed that Caradawc's thoughts and not her own were now occupying her mind. Like a drowning man who holds too tightly to his rescuer, Caradawc was clinging so desperately to her that she was beginning to lose her own identity to his.

A voice suddenly recalled her: the rich, commanding voice of Father Brendan. Speaking her name repeatedly, he seized her by the shoulders and shook her awake. She could feel the calloused strength of his hands.

She opened her eyes in relief, and turned to thank him – but there was no one there.

She rose up at once and hurried outside.

Seeing Sister Bridget gardening, she asked her where Father Brendan was.

'He's in the hermit's chapel,' the nun replied, looking up, trowel in hand, surprised at the agitation in Viviane's voice.

'How long has he been in there?'

'At least an hour.'

'He did not come out a few moments ago?'

'No. But if you want him urgently . . .'

Viviane did not wait for her to finish, but hurried away towards the stables. Bridget looked after her, alarmed. She put down the heavy iron tool and hurried towards the chapel, dusting her hands on her skirt as she went. At the doorway she looked back just in time to see Viviane leading her white mare out into the yard.

This decided Bridget. She tapped gently at the door and, without waiting for permission, eased it open. Father Brendan was on his knees, deep in prayer, before one of the wall carvings which was brilliantly illuminated by a sword of light . . . It was of the Christ as Jesus walking on the water . . . the faith that could move mountains.

Bridget stood awkwardly at the door, not knowing what to do. She knew that Viviane was quite at liberty to go off riding on her mare if she wanted to, or, indeed, to leave the community at any time. It was just that her expression had been so distraught . . .

Brendan rose and came to stand beside her, looking out into the yard in time to see Viviane and Hunydd leap the low wooden gate and go off through the trees and down the valley towards the outer world.

'I'm sorry I disturbed you, Father,' Bridget apologized, 'but she looked so frantic.'

Brendan's face was thoughtful. Bridget expected him to call out to someone to follow Viviane, but he did not.

'Should not someone at least go with her?' she asked anxiously.

'No, not now,' he said. 'There's something she has to do. We can only pray that she'll be guided by our Lord – and that she'll not forget what she has learned. It is essential that the choices she makes now are her own.'

Bridget and the rest of the community had not been told the full story of Viviane's reason for being with them. For the most part they had respected her privacy and made no inquiries. But at this moment Bridget's curiosity was too much for her.

'How can I pray for her if I don't know what I'm to pray for?' she asked.

Brendan smiled. 'You know all you need to know,' he said firmly.

She bowed her head. He had chided her many times about underestimating the 'unseen' part of herself. She sighed – sometimes it all seemed too difficult. At this moment she would much rather leap on a horse and follow Viviane than stay behind and bring the different levels of her consciousness under enough control for prayer.

Viviane had one thought in mind: to reach the dark tower and bring this whole nightmare to resolution. She dreaded the thought of returning to that place, but she knew she had been 'told' to go there, and go she must.

Caradawc was with her – within her. This time she was not alone.

As she rode she began to feel excited and confident, believing that now she understood the problem it would be easier to resolve. Her reluctance to return to the tower changed to eagerness, and she urged Hunydd to hurry.

She fancied at one time that she heard Caradawc's voice warning her not to go further, but she took no notice.

It had been Gerin's intention to reach the Community of the Fish before nightfall, and he did everything in his power to do so, driven on by the thought of seeing Viviane again: but it was not to be. They took several wrong turns and found themselves with still a long way to go, and the afternoon closing in fast. Elined was very tired and pleaded for rest. Olwen could have gone on forever as long as Gerin was with her, but she agreed to the rest, thinking to prolong her time with Gerin and put off the moment when they rejoined the princess.

They had seen no sign of their pursuers, and hoped that they had given up the chase. An occasional peasant crossed their path, but none that they might fear. The only hostility they encountered was from a fisherman standing as still as a heron on the river bank, who scowled and looked at them as though they were mad when they asked the way to the Community of the Fish. Afterwards they laughed about it, realizing how the question must have sounded to him; but now it was the end of the day and they were worried when they realized they had nowhere to spend the night. The sky looked as though it had been covered with a pink veil, now roughly torn aside. Filmy shreds were still drifting and floating. The birds were winging home . . . long whip-like strings of starlings high in the air – moving together as though they were one being, clouds of smaller birds – bobbing in unison – below them. The strange, intensified light of evening picked out trees individually and cast their shadows extraordinarily long against the vivid, almost luminous green of a grassy hill. They heard the high, ululating call of the herdboy, and watched him, first as a moving speck behind his cows, gradually taking shape as he approached the valley. They were now in shadow, while the peak of the opposite hill was still in a blaze of light.

Gerin and Olwen rode ahead of the others and came to a halt at the point where the boy would join the path.

The cows flowed around them on either side like water parting around a boulder in a stream. The herdboy stopped and stared at them. He was an ungainly lad, the kind that has grown too fast for his clothes. He slouched as though ashamed of his height, and the hand gripping the hazel cow-switch seemed too big and bony for the skinny wrist that protruded from his ragged sleeve. Without the openness usual in people who spend a great deal of time in the hills, his expression was sullen, suspicious and surly.

Gerin asked him the way to the nearest farmhouse, and whether the farmer would give them shelter for the night.

The boy stared at them balefully for a while before replying gruffly. 'There'll be no shelter there. You'd be best going back aways.'

'We saw no houses back there,' Gerin complained.

'Morgan's farm,' the youth insisted.

'We saw no farm.'

'Them what's blind can't expect to see,' the herd-boy grunted and turned his back on them. Cockily he whistled to his lumbering charges, who had taken advantage of the pause to start cropping the verges.

At this point the others joined them, and Elined slid down from her horse and ran up to grasp his arm.

'Please,' she said, tears in her appealing blue eyes, 'I can go no further. I am almost ill with weariness.'

As he looked at her he unconsciously straightened his back until he was taller than she. She was a fine lady with skin as white as a rose petal and hair the colour of wheat at harvest.

'There's no comfort there for the likes of you,' he said at last, grudgingly.

'I need no great comfort,' Elined said. 'A barn would do . . . anything . . .'

'A barn would be all you'd get,' the boy said, his eyes moving up and down her figure, lingeringly.

Cai moved forward aggressively. 'We're coming with you, whatever you say. The farmer himself will decide the issue.'

The boy merely shrugged and turned back to his task. They followed slowly behind: so slowly indeed that they found it difficult to contain their impatience.

At their approach the farm dogs came racing out to meet them, barking furiously, as bad tempered as the boy himself.

Two small, unkempt girls came timidly from the house and stood staring at them solemnly. Olwen thought she detected just a glimmer of friendliness in their eyes, but they were too afraid to follow it through. Behind them suddenly loomed a large man with a shaggy grey beard, to see what the commotion was about. His resemblance to the herd boy, even down to the sullen expression, was unmistakable. He snarled at the dogs, giving the nearest one a brutal kick. They both retreated instantly, whimpering.

As Gerin asked about shelter for the night, Olwen was already pulling at his sleeve and whispering that she did not like the feeling of the place, and that they must move on.

'There's no lodging here,' the man growled. 'The wife is ill.'

The boy was moving off with his cows, but he gave a backward glance, as much as to say: 'I told you so!'

'It's a warm night,' Olwen murmured to Elined. 'We can easily sleep in the woods.'

'Not I,' said Elined, moving towards the man, and swaying slightly as though about to faint. 'Please, sir, I too am ill – with weariness and lack of food. Surely there is a place at your hearth for friends of the king? You will be well rewarded, I promise.'

The charm worked and they were shown into the house, the two nervous little girls clinging like limpets to Olwen's skirt.

The low farmhouse was built of stone and wood, the thatch roof in bad repair and green with moss and grass, the smoke from the kitchen fire seeping out where it could. Inside, several lamps were lit, but it remained dim and gloomy. There was just one long room for all purposes, and the children's pallets lay on the floor. But one area was curtained off, and they presumed that it was here the farmer's wife lay ill. At a great iron stove the eldest daughter, a slatternly thirteen-year-old, was stirring a cauldron of steaming broth. The smell of it made Olwen quite faint with hunger.

An old woman, probably grandmother of the children, was laying out wooden bowls and wooden spoons for the evening meal. She peered at them suspiciously through wrinkled eyelids that had no lashes.

She was informed brusquely that they had guests and must look after them, then the farmer strode over to the curtained area and disappeared behind the heavy homespun cloth. They could hear a steady groaning from behind it.

Olwen touched Gerin's arm. 'I really think we shouldn't stay.'

'We're staying,' Cai said firmly. 'Even if we have to sleep in the barn. Elined must have shelter.'

Neither the old woman nor the girl said anything. The girl continued stirring, her mouth set in the hard line that continual despair sometimes brings to a face. She had the look of one who had never been allowed to be a child, and was no longer expecting it.

The old woman hobbled off to fetch some more bowls and spoons from a shelf stacked precariously high with bags of flour and beans, twigs and sheaves of dried herbs, cracked earthenware jars and sagging baskets.

'Let me help you.' Olwen hurried over, reaching up to the shelf for her, while Elined and the others sank down on the wooden bench beside the table and eyed the cooking-pot ravenously.

The farmer did not return for the meal, but the herd boy came in and sat down at the table, his hands still grimy and his boots still muddy from the fields. He fixed his eyes instantly on Elined and did not look away from her all the time he was shovelling broth into his mouth. The two little girls ate fast and timidly, as though they half expected their food to be snatched away from them, and glanced nervously at their brother from time to time. Their fears seemed well grounded, for as he swallowed the last of his own broth, his arm shot out to seize the unfinished bowl of one of his sisters. She tried to hold it away, but her grandmother struck her hand with a wooden spoon and she withdrew. Her sister hastily pushed her own bowl towards him and he gulped that as well. He then took a hunk of bread and scoured out the serving bowl. The guests were not offered second helpings.

Meanwhile the groans behind the curtain were turning to intermittent shrieks. Several times Olwen offered to go and see to the poor woman, but the old crone sharply told her that her son could manage well enough.

At last Olwen could bear it no longer, and dashed towards the curtain before the old woman could stop her. Behind it she found Kicva, Goreu's witch-woman, with blood up to her elbows. She was holding a newborn infant by its feet, its head immersed in a leather bucket of water. Olwen leapt forward and grabbed the child from her, the surprise of her unexpected arrival giving her a momentary advantage.

'What are you doing?' she cried. 'You'll drown it!'

Candles sputtered around the bed and the farmer's wife lay twisted awkwardly, her face deathly pale, watching the scene with dark and desperate eyes. Beside her lay two creatures like skinned rabbits. Her husband stood at the foot of the bed, arms folded on his barrel chest, and his face stony.

The candlelight beneath it, Kicva's furious face was grotesque with shadow. Olwen reeled back and the farmer seized her roughly by the arm.

'This is none of your business,' he snapped.

Olwen could see now that the newborn infants were all female. She had heard that ignorant people often looked on triplets, particularly females, as unnatural, boding misfortune for the family. She had even heard tales that the extra ones were drowned like kittens, but she had never thought to come upon such barbarism herself.

She wrenched her arm away from the man's grasp, and flung herself forward to face Kicva, still clutching the tiny, mewling creature she had rescued.

Gerin appeared suddenly behind the angry farmer, in time to hear the stream of curses Olwen was being subjected to.

Instantly he seized Kicva's shoulders and shook her violently. 'Take back your curses, old woman,' he yelled. 'Or they'll return on your own head!'

Kicva laughed scornfully. 'It's too late,' she sneered. 'Too late! She'll never be loved by a man! She'll never bear children!' Her bony finger pointed straight at Olwen, who shivered at the old woman's words, but did not turn from her task of trying to save the lives of the three hapless infants. Two of them were howling lustily, but the third, after being so roughly treated, was scarcely breathing.

The farmer's wife had already borne him six daughters in all, and only one son. Three of the girls had died, to his great relief, but now the cursed woman had presented him with female triplets. He and the midwife Kicva had agreed that the three were too sickly to live, and neither felt any compunction in hastening what to them was an inevitable and indeed a desirable outcome. His wife did not dare protest. She lived in terror of her husband's rages. But now, angry as he was at the interference of the strangers, he was hesitant to continue with his original plan in front of them. He stood irresolute, no longer taking an active part in the affair.

'If you let them live,' Kicva warned Olwen darkly, 'there will be nothing but trouble in this house. Three curses will fall on it. Three times three will be their sorrows.'

'How can you say that?' cried Olwen indignantly. 'Three

daughters: three times blessed. Three times three will be their joys!'

Cai and Elined had now come to see what the commotion was about and, on seeing Elined, Kicva instantly cried out. 'My lady Elined! What are you doing here?' And then she noticed Cai and looked horrified.

Elined at once put her arm through his. 'It's all right, Kicva. It's all right now. These are my friends.'

'What have they done to you, lady? They've turned your mind!'

'No. No, truly. They're my friends.'

'Your father and your brother are frantic with worry. Hundreds have been killed in trying to rescue you! And here you stand and talk of *friendship*!'

Elined put her face against Cai's shoulder and began to sob.

'Leave her alone!' Cai warned fiercely. 'If Huandaw had not been so impatient to rush to war without finding out the true facts, those men would be alive today.' He drew Elined gently away from the fierce and accusing eyes of the old woman.

Kicva glared after them for a moment and then turned her attention back to Olwen, who had meanwhile started quietly and competently clearing things up. She had ordered the farmer to fetch water and he, somewhat caught off guard by the turn of events, had sullenly gone off to the well in the yard. Gerin was helping her to arrange the woman more comfortably. The candlelight fell on a scene in which Kicva now had no part to play.

She turned on her heel and picked up her shawl. At the door she paused and looked back. 'You'll be sorry,' she warned darkly. 'You'll be sorry.' And then she left.

Through the open doorway they could see the blackness of a night without moon and without stars.

Suddenly a flash of lightning rent the sky.

Idoc was waiting for Viviane in his tower. It was he who had put the thought into her mind to come there, and he watched her progress on Hunydd with amused interest. Not once did she hesitate, though he knew that Caradawc was trying desperately to turn her around. He was pleased that he had not lost his old skills though he was encased in the body of someone not a master of invocation nor a high adept in sorcery. He leant back in his carved ebony chair and put his feet up on the bronze table. He was totally relaxed, totally confident. He intended to drive that spark of consciousness that was the soul of Caradawc to such depths of despair and frustration that it would choose to give up the Great Journey and abandon itself among the flotsam and jetsam of outer darkness. Viviane he would bind to himself so utterly that she would have no hesitation in following him wherever he would lead, nor cast a backward glance to the lost soul of her handsome, immature lover. He had the spells prepared, he had his infernal helpers ready. All he need do now was to wait. He could not proceed until they arrived, for, just as the ancient stone circle with its powerful energies was the only place his enemies could have cast that particular binding spell on him, so this tower with its particular concentration of energy was the only place in which he could be sure his present scheme would work.

Viviane finally reached the foot of the hill beneath the tower and, for the first time, paused to consider what she was doing. At first very faintly, but more vividly with every passing moment, she began to remember the Green Lady who had given her the green silk cord she now wore at her waist. Nervously she fingered it, wondering at the words spoken by the being who had returned it to her in the grove of silver birch trees. She looked around and it seemed to her that on the slope leading up to the tower much of the plant life was pale, weak and struggling. The only things that grew with any vigour were poisonous plants: henbane and black nightshade, hemlock and bittersweet. If she stepped down, as she would soon have to, burs and thistles, stinging nettles and brambles were waiting for her. She looked back and saw that beyond the reach of the tower's shadow, the countryside was lush and fertile. Each plant, each tree, each blade of grass seemed to have taken on a rich distinction: a glow, a certain magic. She could feel her skin prickling as though she were in the presence of a great being. Did she see a movement there among the trees, the bare shoulder of the Green Lady as the sunlight blazed through the leaves?

Idoc suddenly leaned forward in his chair, concentrating on the shew-stone in his hand – the piece of broken obsidian mirror. Surely they were not going to slip through his fingers after all? Damn that Caradawc! He must have learned something as his apprentice in those ancient days, and was using his knowledge now to break through Idoc's calling spell. Damn that interfering Green Lady, the Earth Spirit whose powerful energy could transform bare rock into garden, desert into orchard. She who reclaimed sacked cities and battlefields with nothing more than the lily and the poppy; she who covered graveyards with daisies and distilled pure water from cesspits. Damn her!

Viviane shivered; feeling his malevolence – torn between a growing sense of unease and her conviction that the only way to rescue Caradawc was to confront Idoc in the tower. If the Green Lady did not want her to proceed, why did she not come forward to stop her? It seemed to her that the green fields and the forest were calling to her, but the tower's call was stronger. She dismounted slowly, gingerly stepping down among the thorns and nettles, her heart beating wildly. She assured herself that though she had hitherto been riding 'blind', she was now very well aware of what she was doing. She might have been lured as far as this by the power of Idoc, but she was determined to stay on her own terms. She could feel Caradawc's fear, his doubt that they could ever outwit Idoc on his own ground. It made her waver momentarily, but she knew that what had to be done had to be done soon, or it would be too late. She had come this far, and was not prepared to back out now.

Idoc relaxed again. 'They'll come,' he thought with satisfaction. 'Let her bring whom she will to help her. They can do nothing against me in this tower.'

He began to walk the chamber, tracing on the floor, with fine sulphur powder, the various figures he required for his spells. On either side of the door he placed one of his familiars ready to seal it as soon as the two invited guests had passed through.

Viviane took out her amethyst crystal and held it up for clear-sight. On every branch of every tree the little brown sight-seekers, the voyeurs, were perched, their eyes bulging with anticipation, their ears flexing constantly for every sound. How she hated them! She detested the feeling of always being watched.

'*Don't be distracted,*' Caradawc whispered urgently. '*Call for help. We can't face Idoc alone.*'

She sent out the call . . . but even as it left her she felt an irresistible pull towards the tower.

'They'll come,' she said to Caradawc. 'But we can't wait for them . . .'

Ignoring the thorns that tore at her flesh and the nettles that stung her, she set off up the hill.

'*Viviane!*' Caradawc's disembodied voice was like the call of a distant bird – a cry so distant, so sad, it would have brought tears to her eyes at any other time. But now she hardly noticed it. Another voice was calling; strong, powerful, commanding – a voice she had loved, a voice she still thrilled to in spite of everything.

'Viviane!' said Idoc quietly at the centre of the pentagram of calling, and smiled to see the eagerness with which she rushed towards him. Was there something left, after all, of her old desire for him? A desire Caradawc could not completely satisfy, just as he himself could not completely satisfy her need for a steadier, deeper kind of love. Well, if it was so, it would make his task that much easier.

She took the stairs two and three at a time, and only paused at the threshold of the final door. It lay open, the chamber beyond well lit with lamps. The blank wall where the obsidian mirror had been was hung now with a tapestry of rich and glowing colours. She could not see the design, but was instantly curious. There was no sign of Idoc, and she was shocked at the disappointment that she felt.

As she took a step forward into the room she experienced an extraordinary chill. Her skin was suddenly goose-pimpled from scalp to toe; her teeth began to chatter. From a hot summer's evening she had been plunged into mid-winter. Terrified she tried to withdraw, but the door had swung shut behind her. She could hear the wheels turning in the elaborate lock, though there was no hand there to turn them.

'*We're trapped!*' Caradawc's panic almost choked her.

'No, we're *not!*' she replied fiercely, trying to convince herself as much as him. The sudden chill had passed, yet she still shivered.

'Welcome,' said a smooth voice, and she spun round to find Idoc standing there after all. It was strange to see him, knowing that he was Idoc, yet his every feature was Caradawc's: those sea-blue eyes; that curly chestnut hair; the slender yet muscular figure. Idoc himself had been a much heavier man, even when young: a man of dark, penetrating eyes and hair the colour of a raven's wing . . .

She still clutched the amethyst that gave her clear-sight, and, with its power, she saw behind him, and partially enclosing him like a sheath, another figure, almost transparent, the colour of smoke from rotting rags, its face so hideous that she could not bear to look upon it, an angel of darkness, long enemy of the light. This was their real antagonist: and Idoc did not even know that he was there. How could a man so brilliant and so skilled be so deluded?

She looked around the chamber hoping to find some hint of how she could start the process of disentanglement; perhaps something that would let her stall for time until those she called on would arrive. Her eye fell on the tapestry that had not been there before.

Idoc smiled and held out his hand to her. 'Come. It is my latest acquisition. Look at it closely. Is it not beautiful?'

She did not take his hand, though it looked so like Caradawc's she found it difficult to resist. But she stepped nearer the tapestry, and Idoc held up a lamp so that she could see it more clearly.

It was a finely stitched representation of a forest, with a hunting party in the foreground. The lords and ladies were dressed in richly embroidered clothes, their steeds expensively caparisoned. Every detail of the forest, the leaves on the trees, oak and ash, hornbeam and hazel, the markings on the bark, and the flowers underfoot . . . delicate white asphodel, violets and celandine, wood anemone and arum, broad buckler fern unrolling its thick brown tendrils, even the tiny stag-horn mosses and the silver-grey lichens . . . Viviane had never seen such a detailed record of a forest in tapestry. Something caught her eye in the thicket off to the left, and she saw that it was a hart. She put her hand to her mouth with a gasp. The hunting party was Caradawc's; the young woman breaking away from the party to follow the hart was herself.

'I thought you would appreciate it,' said Idoc close behind her. 'It is a wedding gift.'

She felt a touch on her hand and looked down at once. Deftly and neatly he had removed the amethyst from her grasp. She reached for it at once.

'Thank you, my dear love,' he said. 'I see you have brought a gift for me.' And he moved it quickly out of her reach.

'No!' she cried. 'No!' She tried to seize it back, but he laughed and held it above his head. To take it she would have to come right up against his body and she knew that if she did, she as well as Caradawc would be lost for ever. The monstrous being that overshadowed Idoc was no longer visible to her, though she was still very well aware of his presence. The figure of Caradawc stood before her, but from his eyes Idoc's soul looked out.

She had a sudden inspiration. 'Yes,' she said, withdrawing her hand. 'It *is* a gift – but I wanted to give it to you in a special way. I wanted you to use it to see something.' She picked up the sheet of obsidian from his table and held it before him. 'Hold the crystal in front of you,' she said, 'and look in the mirror.'

'I'll see nothing there but my love for you,' he was smiling into her eyes, and, for a moment, she could have believed he spoke the truth.

She touched the green girdle at her waist. 'Hold on! Hold on,' she whispered to herself. 'Hold to this lifeline. Be not seduced by words, by ancient feelings, by dreams of what might have been . . .'

'Look in the mirror,' she urged him, trying to keep her voice steady. 'You will see something even you have never seen before. It is my gift because I loved you once . . . because I still . . .'

She broke off, for he seemed to be engaged in a terrible struggle with himself . . . his skin flushing dark red and then, as though suddenly drained of blood, becoming deathly pale . . . his eyes were changing, Caradawc's sea-blue becoming almost black. She heard the sound of a rushing wind and small objects in the closed chamber began to fly about. The flames of the lamps and candles guttered and sputtered; heavy jars fell to the floor.

She could see all the veins and muscles in Idoc's neck and

face stand out as though he were undergoing great physical strain in trying to turn his head towards the mirror. Her own arm was being mysteriously pressurized to drop it. With every ounce of strength in her body, and calling on Caradawc's soul and all the powers of Light to help, she strove to hold on and to bring it nearer to Idoc's eyes. She knew now that she was doing the right thing. The being that had taken over Idoc did not want him to see himself through the power of the amethyst.

She summoned all the love she had felt for him in those ancient times when he was young . . . She called up the image of him as he had once been, before he began to invoke dark spirits . . . She visualized Caradawc and Gerin and Rheged and Cai and herself in their ancient forms, holding hands and circling him – chanting not the fatal binding spell, but what they should have chanted in the first place: the releasing spell, the spell of exorcism . . .

For a split second Idoc saw through the amethyst to the dark obsidian mirror.

He saw himself and he saw that of which he had become the prisoner.

In that instant the room was rent by lightning.

For the most rare and powerful energy of all had been released: the energy of the living being seeing truthfully into its own nature.

The amethyst crystal turned to dust in his hand – as did the fragment of mirror in Viviane's. In that moment of tremendous revelation, Viviane knew that Caradawc's soul had returned where it belonged – and Idoc was a bodiless shade once more – no longer sustained by a being of hate but cringing in a corner like a creature that had lived all its life in a dark cave and was suddenly exposed to the full light of the sun . . .

Around them raged the lightning of a supernatural storm. Thunder whipped and roared. The tower swayed in a wind that no earthly conditions had ever engendered.

Stone by stone it cracked and crumbled, sliding slowly down the hill, the dry dust of centuries rising in a column of cloud that reached high into the sky and then mushroomed out over the whole land . . . a fearsome sound rolling and rumbling around the hills, penetrating to the furthest valleys . . .

At the heart of its vast shadow Idoc's wax discs, bronze table, chair, charts and flasks, noisome liquids and infernal instruments shattered and splintered, slid and slithered and fell – and with them Caradawc and Viviane spiralled and turned in the dust . . .

12

The rebuilding of the tower

When Viviane regained consciousness she discovered that she was miraculously unhurt. All around her the dust of the dark tower had finally settled, and there was nothing left of it but jagged piles of rock. The storm had subsided and the moon was sailing large and magical above her, filling the landscape with light. Even in her bemused state she wondered that moonlight could be quite so bright. She turned her head to look for Caradawc and saw instead a sight so beautiful her heart almost stopped beating with the sheer pleasure of it. The Green Lady stood there, and behind her hovered three shining beings. She could feel their caring and their love as though it were the warmth of sunlight on her skin. The light that shone from them was so subtle, so full of the *hint* of colour and yet not coloured, that it reminded her of mother-of-pearl. Their forms and features were each different and individual – yet later, when she tried to describe them, she could not find the words. She remembered nothing of them but the light and the feeling they gave her of being loved and protected . . . the feeling that they were pleased with her . . . that she had done well.

The Green Lady stepped forward, and as her long mantle brushed the dark stones of the fallen tower, mosses and small plants seemed to grow up around them, fern fronds uncurled out of cracks. She reached down and gently helped Viviane to her feet.

'Caradawc?' Viviane murmured, looking anxiously around her.

The Lady smiled.

'Those you love are safe – for the moment. But we cannot stay here.'

Caradawc groaned at that moment and Viviane clambered over the rocks to him and gathered him in her arms, his head falling back against her shoulder, unconscious. She looked up in distress.

'He will live,' the Lady said softly. 'He has been through a great strain . . . He is weak now and you must help him.'

'And Idoc?'

'He too must be in your care for a while. He has lost his strength, his confidence . . . and he will fall into despair and try to abandon the Great Journey. If he does so he will be lost in the outer darkness as he intended Caradawc to be. Your love and courage could sustain him until he is ready again to start the upward journey by himself. But can you do this – after what you have suffered through him?'

'I think so,' she said haltingly. 'After all, it was not Idoc himself – but that . . . that . . .'

'That being of darkness you saw was indeed the true enemy, but he would have had no power had Idoc not permitted it – had Idoc not given up his own will to his.'

'Was he destroyed with the tower?' She shuddered.

'Ah, no – if only it were that simple! He is not mortal. He has been driven off for a while by the strength Idoc found in that moment of truth, but he will be back. He will not leave Idoc alone until he has what he wants, or until Idoc is too strong for him. The forces of darkness do not easily give up their willing human vehicles. If you choose to protect and care for Idoc through this dangerous time, you yourself will be in great danger. But no one demands this of you. It must be your own choice.'

Viviane lowered her face to Caradawc's and rested her forehead on his. If only they could go home now and live together as man and wife, forgetting Idoc and his problems. Surely they had done enough to atone for their bitter mistake so many centuries before. The choosing of the dark way had been Idoc's own mistake. Let *him* atone for it! But then she remembered the cowering, whimpering shadow she had glimpsed before the tower fell, and she remembered the young Idoc she had loved before he had taken the wrong path. There would be no hope for him if he were left alone. He would either sink downwards in despair and become the least and most hopeless of beings, or he would allow the creature of darkness back and become a potent force for evil once again. With her, he might stand a chance of recovering his own will and his own dignity.

Her love had not died. She could not leave him.

Her tears fell on Caradawc's pale cheek. She loved them both. What would her staying with Idoc mean to Caradawc?

Sadly she lifted her face to the Lady.

'I will help him,' she said simply. 'But must I be alone?'

'You are never alone,' she replied quietly, 'but what you will be trying to do this time is one of the most difficult tasks on earth . . . to halt the force that drives a soul on the downward spiral, to turn that soul and start it on the upward spiral. You will have every dark being in the universe against you.'

'How can I possibly . . .?' Viviane began despairingly. The shining beings behind the Green Lady had disappeared and she felt it would not be long before she too was gone.

'There is something that would be of great help to you,' the beautiful Earth Spirit said. 'And to me,' she added in a thoughtful undertone. 'But to find it will not be easy.'

'What is that?'

'It is an emerald. It was once fixed in the crown of the great archangel Lucifer, the Star of Morning, before he chose to rebel against the Most High and set up his own kingdom. It fell from his crown and without it he can never return; and without it his archangelic power can never be complete.'

'An emerald like the ones we have here on earth?' asked Viviane in astonishment.

'No – but when you see it, you will see it as though it were an emerald of this earth.'

'How can this emerald help me to save Idoc?' Viviane asked wonderingly.

'When Lucifer lost it, he lost the ability to see with the range and the clarity of an archangel. He took on the limitations of a much lower being. Whoever finds it would be able to see the whole pattern of creation in all its splendour. Whoever finds it would know truth directly.'

There was something in the Lady's eyes . . . a sadness . . . a longing.

'Have you ever seen it?' Viviane asked softly. The Green Lady held out her hand – slender and green as a leaf – and regarded it thoughtfully. 'Once,' she replied dreamily. 'Once I wore it on my finger.' Viviane waited almost without breathing for her to continue. 'The earth was paradise in those days – all things in harmony . . .' She fell silent, and a tear like an emerald itself appeared in her sad eye.

'What happened?' breathed Viviane.

'I gave it as a gift to the one I loved,' she murmured. 'But he . . . he did not appreciate it. He exchanged it for a sword. All things became disordered then and out of harmony . . .'

Viviane hardly dared ask the next question, but a feeling that she knew the answer was growing in her.

'His name?' she breathed,

'Ny-ak,' whispered the Lady. 'Ny-ak who overshadows Idoc. Ny-ak who believes that he can rule the earth by denying everything that makes the earth live.'

Viviane shivered. She had believed that what was happening to her and Idoc was important – but now she knew it was only a small part of a much greater drama.

The Lady reached out her arms to Viviane, and her expression was full of love and tenderness, her voice like the sound of a spring in a deep green forest.

'Child, those shining beings who were here have told me that the time may be right for the emerald to be found again – and that you may be the one to find it.'

'*May* be?'

'I know no more than that. Success in finding it depends on a delicate balance of many different energies. There can be no certainty.'

'And the emerald – if I find it, how will I use it?'

'When you find it, you will know,' came the quiet answer.

'Will it be more powerful than the crystals I have already had?'

The Lady smiled as though this were a foolish question.

Viviane swallowed hard. She was afraid.

The Lady touched her gently on the head, and her fear was gone. Peace flowed through her like a silver stream.

'Come,' the Lady said softly, 'gather up the two you love,

and leave this place. It is not safe to remain here any longer.'

Viviane looked down at Caradawc, about to protest that she could not possibly bear his weight alone, and found to her delight that he was regaining consciousness.

'Can you stand? Do you feel all right?' She helped him up and he managed to stand, leaning heavily on her. He gazed around in awe at the piles of tumbled rock, the remnants of the shattered tower. The Green Lady was no longer visible, but the faithful Hunydd was cropping grass not far away, as though nothing untoward had happened.

'We must first find Idoc – then we must leave,' she said. 'Can you stand alone?'

'Idoc must surely have been destroyed . . .'

'No – and we must take him with us.'

'Why, in God's name, should we do that?'

'It's a long story, and I'll tell you when we've time. But meanwhile trust me – we *have* to find him.'

Caradawc looked around helplessly at the debris. 'He could be anywhere under there!'

She stood still and tried to remember something she had once known, long ago, which she had almost lost. Gradually . . . faintly . . . it came back to her. She remembered that the vibration of the sound of any name on the 'conscious' plane could be used in a calling-spell if you could match it with the correct vibrations from the 'super-conscious' plane. On that plane there are no barriers to the flow of thought from one being to another.

Tentatively at first, then gaining in confidence, she chanted the spell that contained Idoc's name . . .

Hunydd lifted her head and listened. Caradawc frowned, wondering if he should trust her, knowing how she had once loved Idoc.

There was a strange stillness as though every living creature had paused in what it was doing and was listening . . . The spider, the tiny ant, the brown and fibrous roots of grass and bush . . . everything . . . even the crystals in the rocks . . .

Idoc heard it too, and rose groaning from the dark and dusty cleft in which he had been lying. He was hardly recognizable to them. There was something of the form and features he had possessed when they had both known him in those ancient days, but now so shrivelled, so twisted, so hunched and cowering, that he appeared to be half their size. He covered his head as though he expected a blow.

Viviane went over to him and held out her hand.

'Come,' she said quietly.

For Olwen the night was a restless one. The storm threatened but never quite broke. She lay on the straw in the barn loft and stared into the darkness. At one time they all sat up, startled, as the silence of the oppressive night was shattered by a violent and unusual sound which set the horses to pulling at their tethers, and the cows to lowing and jostling against the barn doors. But as suddenly and mysteriously as it had come, it passed, and the animals and humans settled down again. She could hear Cai and Elined murmuring to each other, and then the rhythmic creak of the loft joists as they made love. She turned her face to the wall, very much aware that Gerin was lying not far from her.

At last, exhausted and with tears against her cheek, she fell into an uneasy sleep.

Just before dawn she woke suddenly, her heart pounding, wondering where she was. She was cold and uncomfortable, and the arm she had been lying on was numb. She felt that she was being watched and sat up to look around.

The patch of sky seen through the square window at the end of the loft was no longer as dark as before. Were the others awake too? She peered into the darkness and could just make out Gerin's shoulder, but his breathing was deep and there was no sign of his waking. The others were deeper into the loft, where it was too dark to see, and there was no sound or movement from any of them. No, she felt very strongly that there was someone *else* present.

She thought of calling out, asking whoever it was to reveal themselves. Then she noticed a kind of glow hovering by the main beam that held up the roof. She peered intently as it began to take on shape. Was she imagining it or could she dimly make out three forms? The glow intensified and at the centre of it she could now quite clearly see the figures of three young women.

There was something unearthly about them, their skin pearl-white, their features identical. On each head was a crown: one of silver, one of gold, and one of leaves and flowers.

They reached out their hands to her, the fine, almost transparent silver fabric of their robes falling from their outstretched arms like the water of a waterfall. As they opened their mouths to speak, she leant forward eagerly to catch what they were about to say. But suddenly the barn door below them crashed open, and the farmer's harsh voice shouted that it was time for them to be up and about their business. The herdboy was with him and began to whistle out the cows.

Olwen's attention was thus momentarily diverted, and when she looked back, the three figures had gone. The loft was rapidly filling with daylight and her companions were yawning and stretching near by.

By his surly behaviour the farmer made it clear that they were not invited into the house again for breakfast and, in spite of Elined's complaints, they had to be satisfied with no more than a drink of water from the well in the yard before they set off. Olwen feared for the three infants, but the others persuaded her that there was nothing more she could do about them, and that the sooner they left this inhospitable and unpleasant place the better.

Just as they were turning through the gate, the two little girls ran up to Olwen and nervously presented her with a loaf of bread. As they ran back quickly to the farmhouse, she wondered if their grandmother knew what they had done. At least this would help to stave off their hunger for a while, but even the consolation of riding with Gerin did not set her mind at ease, and she worried silently for a long time about the lives of the three little infants, and the strange visitation she had received just before dawn. The coincidence of the supernatural figures being three young women of identical appearance with the fact that the triplets were three females did not escape her; but the significance of it she could not fathom.

After a few hours they passed a strangely isolated hill at the top of which lay the jagged remains of a stone tower. At the foot of it they found the fallen blocks of stone of which the structure had once been made. The side of the hill was badly scarred, branches ripped off and trees uprooted.

They had noticed for some time a cloud of what appeared to be crows circling the area, but when they came nearer, they were shocked to find the creatures were like nothing they had ever seen before.

At first they seemed to hover over the place in distracted bewilderment, rather as wasps hover around the place where their nest was located before it was destroyed. But by the time Gerin's little group approached, they had set about trying to rebuild their 'nest'. Many had alighted on the fallen blocks and were tugging frantically at them, trying to free them from the creepers and vines that were already growing over them. Some even managed to lift the lighter blocks between them to the top of the hill.

'What *are* they?' muttered Rheged in fascinated disgust. They paused to watch, though their instincts told them that infernal work was being done and that they should get as far away as possible while they still could. But suddenly they themselves were noticed and a swarm of the revolting creatures came crowding around them. The horses reared in panic. Gerin and Olwen managed to hold on, but Rheged and the other two were thrown, their steeds dashing away riderless.

Some of the creatures pursued Gerin and Olwen as they fled, trying to get a grip on their hair or clothes to drag them off the horse. With one arm Gerin held firmly to Olwen and the reins, while with the other he took out his knife and slashed about in the air.

'Keep down!' Gerin cried, pushing her closer to the horse's neck, his own body covering hers protectively. He stabbed wildly at one of the creatures that had sunk its fangs into the horse's ear. Another fastened on his own neck, and he flapped at it angrily but could not dislodge it. He felt a sudden searing pain and was overcome by dizziness. His vision seemed to darken round the edges and gradually reduce to a pinpoint. Olwen felt his body go slack on hers and its weight increased so that however much she struggled and twisted she could not free herself to reach the creature that was sucking his blood.

As Gerin weakened other creatures managed to get a grip on him, and she knew that if she did not do something soon he would be dragged off the horse.

Desperately her thoughts darted hither and thither seeking a solution. Then she remembered the little purse of medicinal herbs at her waist, including some in powdered form. She struggled to find the bag and loosened the cord that held it closed. Then she twisted herself around as far as she could and flung the contents into the air, hoping that some would land in the eyes of their vile assailants. Her ruse must have been successful, for she heard shrieks and screams, and many of their pursuers fell back in panic. Then the creature fastened on Gerin's neck loosened its grip and went into convulsions.

For a while they were still pursued, but their tormentors were less persistent than before, and easier to fight off. Some began to flail about helplessly, as though losing strength and momentum when further away from their fellows. She dreaded to think what might have happened to her other companions – but at least she and Gerin had broken free. Soon the last creature turned from them and began to wing its way heavily back towards the hill. It did not get far before it flapped and floundered and finally dropped to the ground.

Gerin and Olwen clung together, shivering with relief. He even kissed her, asking again and again if she were all right.

'Yes . . . yes . . .' she insisted breathlessly. 'And you? We must stop and attend to your neck.' She could feel blood oozing from his wound. He was deathly pale.

Gerin staggered as his feet touched the ground, but Olwen managed to hold him up. She guided him to a stream and bathed his wound. There were four neat holes in his neck, and a smear of blood – both his own red blood, and the creature's disgusting green slime. After she had washed the strange wound thoroughly, she sucked out the venom and then insisted that he lie down and rest for a while.

'We must go back to find the others,' he muttered, trying to rise. But he fell back again immediately. She pillowed his head in her lap and stroked his thick black hair.

'The sooner you sleep, the sooner you'll recover,' she whispered.

His eyes closed, and she began to sing a lullaby she had known as a child:

The Lady is green
who watches the cradle.
The Lady is green
who sings you this song.
The fruit on the table,
the flour in the mill.
The Lady lives long
who lives in the hill.

His breathing became even and she leant down to kiss his forehead. He smiled sleepily, but did not open his eyes.

But it was Neol and his men who found Elined, Cai and Rheged. Alerted by Kicva, they were on their way to raid the farmhouse when they came upon the three toiling up a hill with large blocks of stone. For some mysterious reason of their own, the black winged creatures were nowhere in sight as Neol approached the hill. He halted his men at once and called out to his sister. But she took no notice, and merely continued to try to roll a heavy block up the steep slope. Her hair hung in damp strings around her shoulders, her clothes were in shreds, and her face was very, very pale.

'Elined!' Neol snapped, and gestured for his escort to dismount and seize the two men, who were equally dishevelled, equally absorbed in their work. He himself climbed down and went straight to his sister. Even when he touched her arm she took no notice of him. None of the three seemed to see Neol and his men, but continued mechanically trying to shift their stones even when they were held pinioned. Their eyes were glazed and unseeing.

Neol stared at the strange puncture marks on his sister's cheek, on her bare shoulder and her arm. When the two men were brought over to him he found similar marks on their flesh, too.

His men were now muttering uneasily to each other, terrified by what they saw. It was as though the three were dead yet still moving.

'Here is sorcery,' Neol said to Kicva at his side. 'What do you make of it?'

But even she was silenced by the sight.

Swiftly he turned the party about and commanded that they make all speed for his father's house.

As it happened Olwen, keeping watch beside the sleeping Gerin, saw the party of Neol's horsemen riding by – Cai, Elined and Rheged with them.

When Gerin and Olwen finally reached the Community of the Fish, Viviane flung her arms around Olwen and hugged her close. Then she stood on tiptoe to kiss Gerin on the cheek. Olwen turned quickly away so as not to see his expression.

Hearing the commotion, Caradawc joined them, greeting his old friend with enthusiasm. But Gerin drew back abruptly, eyeing him suspiciously.

'Don't worry,' smiled Viviane. 'This time it really *is* Caradawc!'

Then came the explanations all round, the news, the wild suggestions as to what they should do next. They talked deep into the night. Father Brendan joined them from time to time. He knew enough of their story to understand what they had to do, and he was content that they should use his community as a place to rest and plan.

Idoc, however, represented more of a problem for him. He brooded in the chamber they had assigned to him, hunched in the corner . . . speaking only to himself . . .

'What journey is this they speak of – those who drift by on wings of light? Have I not been on a journey too . . . a journey into darkness?
My heart is lead . . . long has it lost its ability to feel . . . Will her alchemy turn it into gold . . . will her heart carry me away from this dolorous place?
She loves me still . . .
I can see it . . . I can feel it . . .
Fiann, more beautiful than the sunlight through leaves . . . more secret and precious than the white seed in the sacred grove . . .
Fiann who brought me joy and brought me sorrow . . .
Fiann who loved and does not love . . .'

Brendan became so anxious about him that at length he went to Viviane and put his fears into words.

'If you're serious about helping him, you shouldn't leave him so much alone.'

'I hoped that you would talk to him, Father,' she said. 'Your words would surely be a thousand times more effective than any words of mine.'

Brendan shook his head. 'You're wrong. He isn't ready for what I have to say. He hates me and everything I stand for. The only thing that's keeping him here is his love for you – his wanting to be near you. That must be the life-line until he can understand the choices he has to make, and what is at stake if he succeeds or fails.'

'I can't be with him all the time,' Viviane protested impatiently. 'How can I? It would not be fair to Caradawc.'

'I only ask it for now: until Idoc has found again his own reasons for living. He has lost the motive that sustained him for centuries: the desire for vengeance. It had taken him over completely until everything else in him had shrivelled away. Only his love for you, princess, was left – a tenuous thread, but a thread of hope nonetheless. We must build on that.'

''We?' asked Viviane hopefully. 'Are you going to help?'

'Am I not already helping?'

She flushed. 'I'm sorry. I meant . . .'

'I know what you meant. No, I'm not coming with you to search for the emerald, but I'll always be here if you need me.'

Caradawc was furious on hearing Father Brendan's recommendations.

'How can I live with my wife with that . . . that shadow always beside us?' he demanded.

'The wedding vows were taken by Idoc – not by you,' Brendan said quietly.

The four friends looked startled. 'What are you saying?' Caradawc almost shouted, while Viviane turned white.

Brendan continued calmly. 'I am saying that Viviane has undertaken a task, and she must not be hindered in carrying it out. If you love her . . .'

'Of course I love her. I have always loved her! She is *mine*!' yelled Caradawc.

Brendan said nothing more, but turned on his heel and walked from the room.

There followed a long, uncomfortable silence.

It was Viviane who broke it by bursting into floods of tears – sobbing out that the task was far too difficult for her, and that no one could reasonably hold her to it. The men immediately agreed with her.

Olwen alone remained silent. It was not until the tears had stopped flowing and the protestations had played themselves out, that she finally spoke.

'It seems to me,' she suggested, 'though the task is difficult, it's not impossible. We all know in our hearts that we cannot walk away from it. So why don't we just get on with it: the four of us, together?'

Viviane sighed and looked at the others. But they all knew that Olwen was right.

In Huandaw's fortress the strangely inanimate Elined had been put to bed. Several of her women kept watch, with instructions not to leave her alone for a moment. Cai and Rheged had been roughly hurled into a dark cell, and the door bolted on them. They lay where they had landed on the dusty floor, seeming unaware of where they were.

Meanwhile on the hill where Neol had found them, three figures still toiled . . . Then the three became six . . . The tower rose, stone by stone, its dark and malevolent shadow growing longer every hour.

Kicva fretted through the night, knowing her own future rested on whether she could bring Elined back to normality. She tried incantations, infusions of herb smoke, vile liquids for Elined to drink: but nothing worked. She hung the girl with talismans, but still there was no change and she could find no answer.

Huandaw hardly left his daughter's side, watching with impatience Kicva's vain attempts to rouse her from that strange trance-like state. Neol strode in at intervals – his expression growing darker with every visit. Occasionally he took a lamp to inspect Cai and Rheged in their dingy and airless cell – and always found them in the same state. They, too, were breathing husks from which the soul seemed to have departed.

Kicva finally deduced that the weird puncture holes in Elined's flesh must have been caused by some vampire-like creature which had sucked away her soul as well as her blood – and that only by capturing that creature would she have a chance of reversing the baleful influence.

She summoned Neol and urged that an armed party be sent to scour the place where the three had been found, in search of any sign of fiend or goblin. She would accompany them and be ready to act as soon as one was captured.

The search party was being gathered when Father Brendan suddenly arrived. He had come at Viviane's request to inquire about Cai and Rheged, and was shocked when told how the three had been found. He visited Elined first and then was taken to Cai and Rheged. When he saw how the latter were treated, he demanded that they be brought out into the light and properly cared for.

Brendan spent some time in meditation and prayer at the bedside of each of the three in turn. Huandaw and Neol, watching him, gradually grew more and more impatient. They had expected great things because Brendan had a reputation as a miracle-worker and a saint – but nothing seemed to be happening.

Eventually Neol could stand it no longer and beckoned Kicva out of the room. 'I'm going to send out a party of armed men to try to capture one of them as you suggested,' he said. 'Will you ride with them?'

'Of course, my lord.' Kicva was delighted that Neol now seemed to favour her over the priest, and hurried after his striding figure. In the yard men were soon falling in at his command and there was much bustle and confusion as wives and children milled around to find out what was happening. Neol deliberately did not inform them: they would not be happy if they knew that their men were going out after demons.

They were already mounted when Father Brendan joined them, having heard what they intended. Neol grudgingly agreed that he should accompany them, and the party set off, the abbot's ungainly figure almost dwarfing his little mare. Kicva made sure she rode ahead with Neol lest he forget that they had set off on *her* suggestion.

The men began to mutter uneasily when they recognized the route they were taking, and many of them bunched up close to Father Brendan.

Within sight of the fateful hill Neol called a halt. From this distance they could see that a large structure had been raised on the site of the ruin. Above it, what looked like huge black birds were circling, and below it, on the slopes, crowds of human shapes were toiling.

Brendan suggested that the men should stay hidden in a nearby copse, ready to ride out to attack if the creatures came swooping down, while he, Neol and Kicva should continue cautiously on foot, keeping well under cover of the trees and bushes.

When they were near enough to see more clearly, Kicva and Neol gasped. The men and women toiling on that hill were all in the form of Cai, Elined or Rheged: all apparently equally real, and all as dazed and entranced as the ones lying at Huandaw's house.

'Ah,' muttered Brendan. 'I thought as much.'

Neol turned to him sharply. 'What do you mean?'

'I suspected the three at your father's house were not who they appeared to be,' he said quietly. 'I could find no trace of their souls.'

Kicva was shaken that she herself had not suspected this.

'How will we ever be able to tell which one is my sister?' Neol asked helplessly.

'There *is* a way,' Brendan replied thoughtfully. 'But we have very little time.' He moved away from them and stood very still. It was almost as though he too were in a trance.

The other two watched with dismay the doll-like figures struggling up and down the hill: Neol perhaps for the first time in his life recognizing that the physical senses are not necessarily the only judges of whether something is real or not. When he had held Elined in his arms, he could have sworn that it was she – yet it was not. He had always been so sure he understood what was going on. He had even killed because he had been so *sure!*

Kicva was thinking deeply too: wondering how many men and women were walking and working and moving from place to place in the world without any awareness of what they were doing and why they were doing it.

At last Brendan beckoned them to follow him. They crouched down, keeping well out of sight of the uncanny flying creatures, and made their way around the side of the hill until they came upon the entrance to a small cave. There in the womb of the earth they found Elined and Cai and Rheged lying unconscious, trussed in fine web, scarcely breathing.

'If we can wake them, the others will cease to exist,' whispered Brendan.

Neol rushed forward at once and knelt beside his sister. But Brendan put his hand upon his shoulder to restrain him. 'Not so soon,' he cautioned. 'The shock of waking before she is ready may kill her.'

Neol drew back alarmed.

'We have to penetrate their trance somehow,' the abbot mused. 'We have to guide them with our thoughts. We have to lead them so that they wake themselves.'

Neol's instinct was to pick her up, cocoon of web and all, and rush her back home and force her to wake . . . But Brendan was looking at him so sternly he hesitated. Kicva was already squatting on the left side of Elined, while Brendan was standing on the right. The monk indicated that Neol should take up his position at her head. Unwillingly he complied. 'I'll give them a few moments,' he thought, 'but if it doesn't work soon I'll wake her my way and damn the consequences.'

Brendan had said that they must guide her with their thought, and Kicva and he seemed already deep in meditation. Neol was uncomfortable. The rock wall behind him was damp and cold, his legs were cramped, and yet he felt he dare not rearrange himself lest he disturb the concentration of the others. What was he to think? He thought about Elined. He thought about how much he loved her and how he had taught her to ride when she was a very little girl. He remembered how full of life and mischief she was, how prettily she sang and danced. He remembered her once garlanding his armour with daisy-chains before he set off to battle. She had always been so full of tricks – and he had often known her bend the truth when one of her pranks misfired and trouble loomed. He thought about his fury against Cai, though the man's friends so firmly denied that he had raped her. Had she been playing one of her tricks again? This time a dangerous and cruel one.

It seemed to Elined that she was in a room, whose walls consisted almost entirely of glass doors. She was held in a cocoon of web and she was struggling to free herself from it. As she struggled filaments of the web broke loose, some to float away from her, dissolving in the air; others dropping to the floor at her feet. At last she could move freely and release herself from the constricting fibres. Leaping up she ran to a door and gripped the bolt that held it fast. Outside she could see the familiar hills and valleys surrounding her home. Yet she hesitated and drew back her hand.

'Not this one,' she thought. 'Not this.'

She was suddenly afraid. It seemed to her that this door would not lead her where she wanted to be.

She stood before another – but again stayed her hand. She feared to take the step that might change her life.

She started to race about the room from door to door, ever more frantically, like a trapped bird smashing itself needlessly against the glass when all the time there is one window open.

A voice began to whisper in her ear . . . then grew louder . . . sounding strangely hollow as though it came from the end of a long corridor . . .

'Elined, child, listen to me. Open the door . . . any of the doors. You cannot stay here.'

But she could not bring herself to trust, and she returned to the centre of the room, pulling the scattered threads of the web around her again with trembling hands.

'Go away,' she sobbed. 'Go away. You are trying to mislead me. I'm going to stay here . . . safely . . .'

'You will miss so much! Open a door and walk out.'

She curled up like a foetus in the womb.

'No . . . no . . . no!'

She did not trust any of the doors. She did not trust the voice . . . Brendan's voice.

'Only you can release yourself,' he insisted. 'The doors are locked from the inside.'

'But I am in terrible danger if I open the wrong door.'

'Not if all the doors lead to the same place.'

'How do I know that?' she cried. 'How can I know that?'

'You have eyes to see. Use them. At the top of each door is a name. Read each of them.'

Slowly she uncurled, hesitantly took a step . . . then another.

And, indeed, on the glass at the top of every door was a word, so elaborately, so decoratively engraved that she could scarcely decipher it.

'Look at the word behind all the embellishment,' Brendan's voice urged. 'Look at the word behind the word. Do not be fooled by all the trappings and the trimmings.'

She stood on tiptoe and peered. She strained to see, among all the elaborate curls and lines that twisted and turned around each other, the shape of the real word. Slowly she went from door to door – and gradually, painfully, she deciphered every one.

'And what do they say?' Brendan asked quietly.

'They are . . .' She paused, hardly able to accept even now what she had seen. 'They are all different versions . . .' Her voice sank so low that it was less than a whisper. 'They are all different versions of the Name of God.'

As she said it, all the doors seemed to open by themselves – and she found herself walking through the nearest, unafraid.

The others, watching, saw Elined stir and stretch, her eyelids flutter. Brendan leant forward to tug at the web that still held her. Neol instantly went to his aid and together they broke her free.

She gave a great sigh and opened her eyes, looking with pleased surprise into the eyes of her brother. He raised her in his arms and hugged her, and she hugged him back vigorously. Then she turned to look round for Cai, giving a little exclamation of dismay when she saw him. She drew away from Neol at once and stumbled over to Cai's side.

'Is he dead?' she cried in anguish.

'No, but he will be soon – if you don't help us,' Brendan said, and he quietly explained what he wanted her to do.

'Can't you rouse him yourself?' said Neol impatiently. 'My sister has suffered a great deal. I must take her home.'

'I'm not leaving Cai,' Elined said quickly, and the look she gave her brother was the look of a woman who loves, and not of a child who is infatuated.

He stared into her eyes for a long, long moment. Hers did not waver.

'Tell me, my sister,' he said quietly. 'I need to know the truth and I will ask you this once and then never again. Did this man really rape you?'

'No,' she said. 'It was not like that.'

He stood very still and bit his lip, remembering the men who had died for this lie of hers. He might forgive her because he loved her – but he needed time and he needed air. He turned on his heel and left the dank, dark cave, coming out into the sunlight within sight of the hill. The forms of Rheged and Cai were still at work, but there was now no sign of Elined.

He sat on a rock and watched the scene before him . . . no longer thinking about it, or puzzling about it – just watching.

It seemed to Cai that he was in a hall of many-faceted mirrors, and in every facet he saw the reflection of himself and Elined. Eagerly he turned to take her in his arms, but found to his dismay that there was no one there. Puzzled, he looked back to the mirror. Her reflection still smiled and lifted its arms to him. Again he turned. Again he found he was alone. There were a thousand images of her – yet not one of flesh and blood.

At last he stopped responding to the images and retreated to the centre of the hall, as far from the misleading mirrors as he could go. Sitting cross-legged on the floor, he buried his face in his hands.

'Elined,' he whispered. 'Elined!' He believed his heart would break.

It was then she came to him, sinking down beside him in her rustling silken dress. She clasped him in her arms and kissed his eyelids. Joyfully he lifted his head and in that moment he saw her as she truly was – and not as an image in a mirror.

As Noel watched, suddenly the figures of Cai seemed to stumble, and dissolve into fine dust, which hung in the air for just a moment and then dispersed.

Only Rheged toiled now.

It seemed to Rheged that the rest of the world had ceased to exist and that he alone was toiling in the heat of a summer's day, to lift block after block of stone. He strained, he sweated, he groaned – each movement an agony – and all for a prodigious labour to which he saw no end. Why he laboured thus, he had no idea. It was toil without meaning; toil without reward; toil without reason. The eyes looking out of his skull saw only another block to lift. He lifted, he carried, he set down – until, suddenly, he noticed that he was building a dark tower . . . and in that moment he decided not to do it . . .

As the last image dissolved, the monstrous black winged creatures milled around in great confusion. The tower was only half built, and their slaves were gone. For a while they were at a loss what to do, but then they gathered force and swooped down the hill towards the cave.

As he saw them coming, Neol jumped to his feet and yelled a command. At last he understood what had to be done.

Riders came pouring out from under the trees, arrows and spears flying, swords brandishing . . .

The creatures wheeled and tried to flee . . .

Arrow and wing . . . blood green and red . . . all mingled in a fearful slaughter – but Elined and the others rode away at last – unharmed.

On the way back Brendan made a point of riding beside Kicva. He had been impressed with the strength of the concentration and consequent power of her thought-energy. If what he had heard about her was correct, it was sad that this had been so often mis-channelled. He knew that she was popularly consulted as a dispenser of love potions and vengeance spells. But she was a natural healer and *could* be a great force for good. He wondered what held her back, what diverted her from her true vocation. He would have liked her to join his community, and add her psychic strength to theirs in sending out the light to combat the dark forces of the world. But if she couldn't bring herself to become a Christian, he wished she would at least take what was good and positive in her own faith and make something of it.

As though made uneasy by his attention, Kicva broke away and rode ahead of the others. She was disturbed by the pleasure she had experienced in working with Brendan in the cave, and the questions she was now beginning to ask herself.

They reached a little stone bridge spanning a stream, and passed over it in single file. A huge old hawthorn tree grew at the water's edge, its branches pressing against the stone arch. Elined remembered that in spring this tree was a rich cloud of blossom and she had been there once long ago as a child, and, with a friend, had tied a ribbon to it, wishing for a fine and handsome husband. She looked at Cai and smiled secretly. Then she slipped away from the party and slithered down the slope beside the bridge to the banks of the stream. There she gazed up into the branches of the hawthorn to see if she could find her ribbon. Hanging from the branches of the tree, hidden from the riders on the bridge by the summer green, a dozen or more little strips of rag fluttered: some silk, some homespun; all representing a hope, a longing, or a fear.

Elined searched among them and found her ribbon, once blue, now faded almost to white, ragged from the winter storms that had shaken the old tree since she had put it there. Cai clattered down the slope to join her. He said nothing, but smiled as she pointed it out to him, guessing its significance.

'We should give thanks,' Elined whispered. He nodded. For a moment they tried to think of an appropriate way, then Cai drew a ring from his little finger, a ring he had had for as many years as that ribbon had hung upon the tree and which he had almost outgrown. He kissed it, touched it to her lips, and then threw it into the stream that flowed past the tree. For a moment it caught in a root that projected into the water, and then broke free and disappeared behind a tiny island of flowering sedges, emerged again, flowing with the stream, and was lost finally in a flurry of white and silver bubbles.

Neol's shout jolted them out of the precious moment.

They looked up to see that the party had halted and dozens of eyes were staring curiously down on them. Neol was waving impatiently.

When they were on the move again Brendan told Neol he

would not be returning to Huandaw's house with them, but going direct to the community.

'A pity, sir,' Neol said. 'I know my father would want to thank you for what you've done for Elined.'

'I need no thanks,' Brendan smiled. He looked back over his shoulder at Elined riding with Cai, and at Rheged beside them. 'But I think those two young knights deserve an apology.'

'That they'll have,' replied Neol. 'Never fear – they'll be honoured guests.' And then he looked at his sister and his lips tightened.

'And your sister needs forgiveness,' Brendan prompted quietly. But Neol looked as though he was still undecided about that. 'She's learned a lot,' Brendan continued softly. 'We all make mistakes.'

'Even you, Father?' Neol asked with a slight edge to his voice.

Brendan laughed and nodded. 'And even you!' he said with a twinkle.

Neol frowned for a moment, and then grinned. 'Ay, even I!' he muttered ruefully.

13

The quest

But where to start to look for an emerald that was not an emerald?

Father Brendan had left them and gone off in search of their friends, Cai and Rheged, and Viviane knew it was now up to her to make the decisions. The decision she did make was that they should join in a calling-spell to entreat the help of the Green Lady who had such a special interest in the jewel they must find. This instantly agreed, the five of them prepared to form a circle.

Olwen noticed how Caradawc shuddered as he took one of Idoc's icy hands, and was glad that it was Viviane, and not she, who must take the other. Gerin stood close beside her and for a time she could not concentrate on the ritual for the racing of her heart. Gradually, however, she began to lose 'self' and became conscious only of the energy of the circle as a whole. That energy, it seemed to her, was fluctuating alarmingly now between Idoc's dark despair and Viviane's shining hope. One moment Olwen would feel as though she were being dragged down by an unbearably heavy weight. Then she longed to break the circle, yet dared not in case her timidity should cause their quest to fail. At another moment it would seem as though a tremendous force were driving through the circle, and she could feel its vibrations pulse through the arms of Gerin and Caradawc on either side of her. Then she wondered if they felt the same terror she felt. 'This is not good,' she thought. 'This is not a good force!'

She opened her eyes to look across at the princess.

It seemed as though Viviane were being shaken by a giant, invisible hand. Her mouth was formed to utter a scream – though no sound was emitted.

Idoc, beside her, had flared up into a monstrous dark shadow.

Terrified, Olwen tried desperately to break the circle, but found she could not free herself from the grip of the two men on either side. She tried then to cry out a warning to them all, but like Viviane, she could utter no sound. Frantically she prayed that the power that held them would be broken . . . and it seemed that her prayer was soon answered, for the fearful current passing through the circle was wavering and weakening.

Suddenly Viviane opened her eyes and looked around her. Her face lit up with recognition of someone not in the circle – someone beyond them – someone not visible to Olwen.

> *Earth Lady . . . Lady of the sacred groves . . .*
> *Lady of oak and ash and thorn . . .*
> *speak in the language of the river,*
> *sing with the wren's song.*
> *I am listening with my stone ears . . .*
> *but I am hearing with my spirit-heart.*

Olwen could clearly hear the words, though Viviane did not seem to open her mouth. Her face remained transfigured with light. Olwen no longer felt dragged down. Now she was feather light . . . floating. Her arms and the arms of all the others were drifting upwards. Idoc was now standing straight and tall – handsome as the statue of a young god.

> *Look into the eye of the dawn,*
> *child of the emerald quest.*
> *See the fire that burns all darkness*
> *the lake that slakes all thirst.*

'Lady!' cried Viviane aloud as she saw her protectress fading from sight.

But the woman of leaves and flowers, clad in the shimmering cloak of forest-green, with the silver moon-sickle brooch at her shoulder, was no longer with them.

Olwen felt Gerin withdraw his hand from hers, and looked round to see the circle breaking up. For the first time she noticed that they had been encircling the mosaic image of the Fish. She wondered if Viviane had chosen that place deliberately, knowing they would need the potency of the symbol as protection during their invocation.

Viviane was looking so dazed and faint that Caradawc gathered her in his arms.

'I almost gave up . . .' she shuddered. 'But then, just at the darkest moment, things seemed to change.'

'I felt it,' said Caradawc.

Olwen leant forward eagerly. 'You saw her?'

Viviane nodded.

'The Green Lady?' Gerin asked in awe mixed with disbelief.

Viviane nodded again, her eyes shining with the memory.

'She was there,' Olwen affirmed. 'I didn't see her, but I heard her speak – or rather I thought I heard her speak.'

Viviane hesitated. It was plain she would rather keep her own counsel about the whole matter.

'I saw her . . .' she said at last, hesitantly, 'and yet I can't describe her. I heard her voice and yet I can't tell you what she said. I know only that we should set off towards the sunrise point on the horizon – the point where the light comes back to us after the night. There I'm sure we'll find way-guides . . .'

'There was indication of a lake,' Idoc broke in suddenly, his voice strong and clear. They looked at him in astonishment. For the first time Olwen understood why Viviane would not easily abandon him. There had been nobility there once – and it could return. They all could sense the new resolve in him, the determination to make a fresh start. Viviane took his hands.

'Yes,' she said, 'there was mention of a lake . . . and we *will* find the emerald!'

And so the expedition set off: mounted on fresh horses, well clothed and full of hope.

They rode down narrow green lanes where chaffinches sang among the hawthorn branches; they crossed streams; they climbed grassy slopes, wading through tall, white, feathery yarrow flowers and the scarlet of poppies. No one accosted them. No one challenged them. There were times when the nature of their quest seemed totally unreal, and there were times when it seemed perfectly natural. They passed peasants and merchants, even a farmer guiding his cart down a rutted road, singing to his horse. He appeared embarrassed that they had overheard him and replied gruffly when they greeted him.

At midday they were given milk and good warm barley bread by some villagers.

In the late afternoon they reached a ridge of hills. The lower slopes were grassy and easy to climb, but nearer the top a great wall of dark sandstone formed a long barrier. They picked their way carefully along until they found a break in the rock, and then behind the ridge they found a sheltered place where they decided to make camp for the night. Others had used the place before them, for they saw the remnants of hut circles still containing blackened hearthstones and bleached animal bones.

Viviane and Caradawc climbed one of the highest rocks and stood clutching their woollen cloaks against the boisterous evening breeze. They were looking towards the eastern horizon, and below them lay a beautiful green land of field and forest; rivers like silver ribbons, and a small lake in the far distance gleaming like a diamond.

Gerin and Olwen meanwhile set about finding a suitable place for their overnight camp, talking quietly as they unsaddled the horses and rubbed the tired beasts down. Windblown bushes, bent and twisted into extraordinary shapes, provided them with kindling, and the broken wall of a ruined hut would shelter them from the wind.

Idoc had drawn away from the others, and was now perched on top of a rock, looking westwards, in the direction from which they had just come.

'I wonder what he's thinking,' Caradawc murmured, gazing across at him musingly. 'Why does he look back there? Do you think he's still hankering for his tower?'

'The tower is destroyed,' said Viviane confidently. 'He knows he can never go back there.' But as she eyed him thoughtfully, she fancied she saw beside him the faint outline of the figure of the two-way-facing being who had spoken with her in the silver-birch grove. Idoc must understand the past, and let it go, before he could make something different of his future.

Caradawc shivered and turned his back on Idoc. 'I've had enough of him for a while. This is the first time we've been alone . . . don't let's waste time thinking about him.'

He took her arm and helped her down, drawing her after

him into a secluded alcove of rock. There they were out of sight of all their companions, and protected from the wind. Pushing her gently back against the lichen-covered rock, he could feel the whole length of her body against his. The kiss he was seeking came to him easily; she as anxious for his touch as he for hers.

The grass was soft as they slid down the wall to bed on it.

At the end they lay twined around each other like two vines, her shoulder to the rough rock, his head on her bare breasts, his breath so warm upon her nipple that it was as though he were touching it with his fingers.

They might have drifted off to sleep there, naked, in the nest of their discarded clothes, had Gerin not come upon them suddenly.

After attending to the horses and laying the fire, Gerin had gone to explore the sandstone cliffs that surrounded their eyrie. He told himself he was going to watch the sun set, but his heart knew that he was really seeking Viviane. He came upon her more suddenly than he expected, standing high above her and looking down. He stood transfixed, as though turned to stone, knowing that he should not linger yet unable to leave. The alcove they had found was now in shadow but he could still see clearly the two naked figures interlocked.

Lying beneath her lover, Viviane met Gerin's eye, and it seemed they stared at each other for a long, long time before he turned abruptly and disappeared.

Urgently she shook Caradawc, who was on the verge of sleep. 'My love,' she whispered. 'My love!'

He stirred and murmured, and moved his hand from her thigh to her breast, settling down even more comfortably.

'No,' she said firmly, and began to struggle out from under him. 'We will have our future – but now we must join the others.'

'The others can take care of themselves . . .'

'No, they can't. We *must* get up.'

For she had seen Olwen look at Gerin, and she had seen Gerin look at herself. She knew the passions that seethed under the surface of this little group, and how potentially destructive they could prove.

She managed to untangle herself from Caradawc, and quickly pulled on her clothes. It was already chilly and both of them were shivering, which soon persuaded Caradawc to dress. She dusted the grass off their garments and shook and smoothed them; then she drew Caradawc up to the top of the ridge to watch the sun set.

The great dark red orb had already started its descent into the underworld. All was still. The wind that had teased them earlier had dropped. The landscape beneath them seemed to be breathing out a faint blue mist which, mingling with the smoke from villages and farms, rose in the calm air to make a fine blue veil separating earth and sky. Below it the land was shadowy and insubstantial – trees became ghosts, and hills, islands . . . Above it, the sky in the west was a sombre crimson . . . in the east, the colour of old gold . . .

Idoc stood where they had last seen him, staring unblinkingly into the eye of the sun.

When it had finally set Viviane called out to him to come back to the fire with them.

He smiled ironically. 'I feel no cold.'

'Well, come and keep us company,' she persisted, embarrassed that she had forgotten Idoc was no longer flesh and blood. The form he had taken was so lifelike it was difficult to remember that he had no physical substance, or none as dense as theirs.

Olwen was sitting alone by the fire, her cloak pulled close around her. Viviane could see at once that something was wrong.

'Where's Gerin?' she asked quickly, noting with some alarm that his horse was missing.

'He's gone,' Olwen said sadly. 'He leapt on his horse and rode off without a word.'

'Why on earth . . .?' exclaimed Caradawc in puzzlement.

'I called out after him,' Olwen continued sadly, 'but he paid no attention.' She looked at Viviane. 'He seemed very angry.'

Viviane's anxiety was so evident that Caradawc felt alarmed. 'Do you want me to ride out after him?' he asked, looking uneasily at the gathering dark.

'No,' she replied. 'He's free to leave us or come with us as he pleases.'

She could see Olwen was disappointed at this decision and

she tried to put a sympathetic arm around the girl's shoulder, but Olwen pulled away sharply. Viviane pretended she hadn't noticed the resentment in her eyes – and moved away to attend to the fire. Idoc watched every move, but made no comment.

After they had eaten they settled down by the embers of the fire to sleep. But Viviane lay on her back awake, watching the stars, wondering how long they would have to wait for a clue – a way-guide. Olwen was on her side a short distance from her, her cloak drawn right up over her head. Even in the dark Viviane could see her shoulders shaking as she tried to stifle her sobs.

As the moon and the stars wheeled slowly across the sky Viviane sank into a strange state that was not quite sleep, yet not wakefulness either. She gazed around and could not see Idoc. She stood up at once and started to search for him, stumbling over the hilltop in the dark, calling out his name, peering behind rock after rock, a growing sense of panic telling her that he was in danger.

She found him at last in a place she had not noticed in the daylight. It was a kind of funnel of rock, and as they stood at the bottom of it, the sky with all its stars appeared as a small circular hole immensely far above them. No breath of air stirred. She reached for his hand but he slipped from her grasp. His mood had changed, and she could feel the darkness returning to his heart.

'Idoc,' she implored, 'I can't help you if you won't help yourself!'

Though she could not see his eyes, she could sense the bitterness in them.

He spoke at last. 'There's no future for me if you won't leave Caradawc and come with me.'

'You know I can't do that.'

'Then *I* will leave you,' he said. 'There's no point in staying if I can't have you. Gerin was wise to go!'

It seemed to her that he was beginning to shrink, to dissolve, to disappear.

'Idoc!' she cried frantically. 'Gerin is flesh and blood. *I* am flesh and blood. You . . .'

'I am nothing . . . I have ceased to be . . .'

189

His voice was fading.

'No,' she cried, trying to hold his hands, but they slipped like icy mist through her fingers. 'No, you are soul. You are spirit. You are eternal being! Please believe that!'

'I was once . . . but now there is no point.'

She heard the despair in the shadow of his voice.

'You *are* . . . You *can be*! The will to live is all you need . . . We'll find the emerald and we'll give you the strength you need to start the great Journey again. But you have to stay with me . . .'

'Stay with you? Ah – that is the mockery . . .'

She heard an eerie high-pitched sound – a strange music made up of millions of tiny squeaks. She heard the fluttering of wings . . . and pouring down the funnel towards them swooped a million bats. She felt the draught from their wings, but although they came very close, somehow none of them touched her. It seemed they were after Idoc, for he was screaming and beating about his head. It appeared he wanted to live after all! His form grew more distinct with every effort he made to fight his assailants off. Suddenly she felt the ground surge beneath her feet, and looked down with horror to see it was completely covered with rats. These too, rivers of them, were surging around Idoc, biting and tearing.

She remembered the cruel experiments undertaken on such animals in his tower . . .

'Idoc,' she cried, 'think back to your past. Regret what you have done! Ask forgiveness.'

The creatures were all over him, like ants over the carcase of a dead fly.

'Idoc!' She tried to drag him free. 'Ask for help! Ask! Believe! Oh angels from the upper realms *please* help us!' His arm was half eaten away and she could see the bone . . . How human he felt now! Frantically she beat the air around him. 'Leave him alone!' she shrieked. 'He asks your forgiveness!'

But no one being can repent on behalf of another, and the creatures did not let up their savage onslaught for a moment.

At last, groaning, with his head buried in his arms, he pleaded for help, and he believed that help would come even to him, who now acknowledged that he had done so much wrong.

Instantly the rats retreated . . . the bats spiralled up through the funnel and were gone. Viviane fell on the ground beside him and gathered him in her arms to rock him back and forth like a child . . . She loved him again as she had loved him long ago – Idoc, and not Ny-ak. Idoc the young man, her lover – before he had turned his own dreams to nightmares.

When she looked up again the stars shone peacefully down and they lay on an open hillside. There was now no sign of that imprisoning funnel of rock that had held them so fearfully close.

She put her cheek against his.

'I promise I'll not leave you,' she whispered, 'until you yourself tell me that I may go.'

Viviane could never understand how the birds seemed to know the moment just before daylight began to return to the land. They began their song and only then a slow, almost imperceptible, change occurred. She heard a faint, fine trill of birdsong and the darkness seemed almost to take a deep breath and poise, listening. From another direction came another thin run of notes: and then another. The breath was exhaled and with it the light grew stronger, the air becoming cacophonous with bird-song: every type from the busy, domestic chatter of families waking, to the sheer liquid beauty of the dawn hymn of the lark.

Her companions were still fast asleep, but Viviane was restless. She slipped away across the cool, dew-laden grass. And, exhilarated by the dawn chill, she ran barefoot, hair flying and cheeks glowing until she found the vantage point she wanted for viewing the greatest natural wonder of any world: the rising of its sun.

Like the priestess of an ancient religion she felt the urge to raise her arms, to reach out in yearning to the light. The distant landscape shimmered behind its veil of mist, deep white at first, then gradually turning the colour of her rose-crystal sphere. The sky flushed pink, and then deepened and deepened to the colour of ruby – reaching at last a brilliant climax and burnishing the rims of the hills with fiery gold. The misty veil over the low-lying areas drew aside to reveal tree and meadow and stream in exquisite detail . . . clusters of houses and winding paths . . . strip fields and pastures . . .

The sun was now almost too bright to look at, yet Viviane felt impelled to continue gazing. Her eyes ached, yet still she felt that out of the sun her message would come. And out of the sun it did come: at first no more than a tiny speck. And then she saw a giant bird, its powerful wingspan greater than a golden eagle's – every feather numinous with light – leaving its nest of fire and winging its way across the sky.

It circled above her three times, coasting and gliding on the thermals . . . light glancing and shimmering from its feathers. And then it flew away. She called after it. She reached out. She stumbled and might have fallen to the valley far below had Idoc not suddenly appeared beside her and held her back.

'Look,' he said, as he steadied her.

The bird was circling again . . . now a small shape in the vast sky . . . but still so distinctive as not to be mistaken for any other bird. There was a flash of sunlight glancing off it, then one of its feathers began to fall to earth, spiralling slowly, gracefully – holding their attention so completely that they did not notice that the bird itself had disappeared. They noted exactly where the feather finally fell, thinking this must surely be the clue for which they had been waiting.

'What are you pointing at?' Caradawc's voice so close behind startled them. They swung round. Idoc's form was now almost exactly what it had been in those ancient times. He was no longer the shrunken shadow they had found among the ruins of the tower. 'Would it be possible . . .?' Caradawc thought, but, no, their substance was of different realms – there could be no meeting in that sense.

'We have a message at last,' Viviane was saying as Caradawc forced himself to reject the suspicions that crossed his mind on seeing them so close together.

'What message? Where?' He peered at the pale dawn landscape below them. She pointed to where she had seen the feather land.

'In that lake, see . . .' his eyes followed her index finger and he saw a gleam of water – a polished silver coin lying between breasts of green silk. But it was a great distance away, and there was some rough country in between.

'Surely it wouldn't be *so* easy to find?'

'Well,' Viviane laughed, 'we're not there yet. But remember the Green Lady's words? "Look into the eye of the dawn . . . See the fire that burns all darkness . . . the lake that slakes all thirst . . .".'

Caradawc became as excited as she was. But just at that moment Olwen called them. She had prepared breakfast and was impatient for their return.

'I dreamt about a lake,' she told them as soon as they arrived. 'We were all fishing in a lake. It was very strange and beautiful.'

'Did we catch anything?' Viviane asked at once, remembering where the feather had landed.

'I don't remember,' Olwen sighed. 'I just remember casting in the nets and thinking how important it was that we caught something.'

Viviane told her about the feather and how it had landed in a lake. Olwen was delighted.

As soon as they'd eaten, they packed up and prepared to leave.

Viviane was cheerful. The sunshine, the golden bird, the shining silver lake . . . and now Olwen's dream! She was very confident that they would succeed in their quest.

The day became very hot and after several hours they decided to rest. There was still no sign of the lake.

Viviane felt the need to be by herself for a while, and wandered off. She left the well-worn road they had been following and walked through the long grass, glad to be out of the saddle. A lapwing hovered high above her, its attention on some little creature nearby which Viviane couldn't even see. She wished she could hover thus, and see at once so far, and so precisely. The land sloped gently up to a copse of beech trees and she sought their shade. There she rested for a while, cradled in a nest of roots that had been exposed to the air when the heavy rains had leached away the soil. She dozed off, and when she woke she set off, half dazed, to find that she had emerged from the copse on the wrong side. Her companions were nowhere to be seen, and she was facing the steep grass-covered earth walls of what she thought must once have been an old circular hill fort.

Not sure how long she'd slept, she knew she ought to return to the others, but curiosity made her decide to spend at least a few moments exploring. She didn't feel like climbing the steep bank of the earthwork on such a hot day, so she walked around its base. It was not long before she found what must have been the entrance – a great gash in the bank. But beyond it, she could see another wall of earth, a second line of defence. Whatever enemy managed to break through this far would have had to slow down and divert to left or right in search of another entrance.

Viviane passed through the first gap and set off to look for the second, hidden one. The sky seemed very far away and very deeply blue between the two steep-sided banks that towered on either side of her. Suddenly she was startled by a rush of air and the sound of beating wings as a flock of birds swooped low, narrowly missing her head, flying for a moment between the walls of the gully, and then soaring, to disappear over the rim into the sky.

She paused, a little shaken, as though she believed the birds had been sent to warn her off. She knew she should return to her companions – but she was too fascinated by the place to leave it now.

When she found the second gateway, she was still not through to the centre. A third wall blocked her. She hurried on, now determined to find out just how many defences this fort possessed.

The third entrance was different from the two previous ones. There were huge lichen-covered blocks of stone half buried in the grass as though some ancient doorway had once been there.

She peered through, not intending to enter, but found this inner ring so different from the outer, she could not resist exploring it. Here the earth walls seemed once to have been lined with enormous, square blocks of stone – most of them now fallen and cluttering the ground, but some still in place. The latter had been shaped with such great skill that there was not a hair's-breadth of space between them. As the sunlight caught the surface of one block, she thought she could see some carving on it, and went at once to inspect it more closely. Though the surface was weathered and worn, there was no doubt there had once been the carving of a hart on the stone – still faintly visible.

Eagerly she hurried from stone to stone, looking at other carvings. When these walls had been complete there must have been a continuous frieze in low relief. Not many scenes were still intact, but those that were all depicted the natural world – animals and plants.

A fourth entrance led her into a further ring corridor, this one with walls far more complete and in several places still roofed over with slabs of stone. Where the slabs had fallen she had to pick her way carefully over the shattered pieces and she found the walls on either side worn and weathered. Fascinated, she walked further and further, finding that the stonework became less and less ruined. What she had first thought was an accidental crack in the roofing slabs proved to be part of the original design. Exactly down the centre of the roof was a slit through which the sunlight blazed, illuminating the frieze. The carvings were now mostly of human form: the animals featured only as beasts of burden or sacrificially. Flowers only appeared to adorn the human body.

At first, as scene after scene met her eye, she noticed only the skill of the carving and wondered at the people who had left this remarkable record, and then, gradually, she began to notice that all the scenes were of conquest, and slaughter. Whole armies were being massacred, soldiers dismembered. Columns of prisoners with arms bound and chains around their necks were being led by men with whips. The sunlight was now a harsh rod of light burning straight down on her head. She felt increasingly nervous and afraid – but still curiosity led her on.

Another entrance led to yet another corridor. Spears and swords were familiar, as were battle-axes and arrows – but what were these new and terrible weapons – these deadly birds flying over ruined cities? Trembling, she realized that she was looking at scenes so strange, so horrible that she could not imagine humans were the protagonists. No familiar natural living thing was to be seen, only men, clad in disfiguring garments as though trying to deny their true nature . . . contained in boxes as though packaged for death while still living. And still the killing, and the killing, and the killing . . .

She began to hurry, hoping soon she would come to images less gruesome and frightening, almost afraid to go back the way she had come and pass once again those she had already seen. Without her noticing exactly when or how it happened the nature of the corridor began to change. She seemed to be hurrying down a narrow path between towering buildings, each like an ants' nest crawling with people. Harsh, discordant sounds punished her ears . . . blinding lights flashing on and off making her head ache. She was pushed and jostled. She had never seen so much fear or so many ways of trying to hide it.

The corridor ended in a blank wall.

Her heart pounding, she turned and retraced her steps. When she thought she had found the exit she hurried through, only to find herself in an equally bewildering, horrifying chasm between grimy buildings. She was wading up to her ankles in filth, and rats scuttled on every side. Frantically she turned again, trying every gap between the buildings in a desperate attempt to find her way out. Around her she saw people stabbing and killing and dying horribly – narrowly escaping herself as one of the buildings exploded and flying splinters of glass went hurtling past her . . .

Eventually she found herself back at the same blank wall, and leant against it in despair. Then panic seized her and she pounded on it with her fists, screaming at the lifeless stone in a voice as desperate and shrill as any she heard around her.

Suddenly she sensed that someone was watching her – a presence different from the others. Spinning around she saw a young woman standing behind her – gazing at her with eyes that were totally cold and cynical. Viviane had the impression she had seen this woman before. She was extraordinarily familiar, and yet . . . where?

'There's no point in looking for a way out,' the stranger said. 'There is no way out. You have seen Time past, Time present, and Time future. In any of them did you see any comfort?'

'I know you,' Viviane said hesitantly. 'Who *are* you?'

The young woman smiled mockingly – and in that instant disappeared, as though no more than a trick of light. Viviane rushed forward to see if she could find her in the crowds – but to no avail.

Then suddenly her heart stood still. She had seen that same face reflected in still pools and in mirrors. It was her own.

She started to shiver uncontrollably. She had heard of the Double: the shadow that is no shadow. Some called it the 'Fetch' and it usually presaged death. So she was going to die in this horrible place? She collapsed on the ground with her back to the wall, and sobbed. Why, when she needed it most, did Father Brendan's teaching seem so remote? But had he not once told her that in all existence there were no impenetrable walls . . . everything flowed from one to other . . . everything moved . . . everything *changed* . . .?

She twisted round to study the wall behind her. It was already changing – each particle was separating from the rest . . . She put her shoulder to it. She passed through it.

On the other side the scene was very different. The light was gentler, more diffuse. The strange buildings and people had disappeared. This ring, like the first three, was open to the sky. Its walls were not lined with stone carved grotesquely, but composed of earth clothed richly in grass and fern and flower. Underfoot the hard paving stones had given way to soft turf. She began to hope that there would be a way out of this dread place after all.

She noticed that the path twisted and turned back on itself from time to time, but it was always the same path. There were no gates, no diversions. She was treading a maze, one of the kind that is designed to lead one to its centre, and by so doing calm the anxious spirit, very different in purpose from that tortuous labyrinth of buildings which had led her, through fear and confusion, to despair.

Viviane was no longer afraid. She found herself breathing calmly, deeply. Her steps were light and unhurried. Patiently and hopefully she followed the path. She barely noticed that the sunlight was dimming and that evening was approaching. Above her the mighty sky burned deep and darkly blue, and then, like lapis lazuli, blazed with stars.

At the end of the seventh coil she reached the entrance to the centre and stood astonished. Never had she seen such beauty. The full moon had risen above the lip of the high enclosing bank and illuminated the whole of the central area. Around the outside, defining the sacred space, stood a circle of tall stones, menhirs of pure white crystal, glowing in the moonlight. Inside this circle lay a smooth circular pavement of polished stone on which was defined – in contrasting white marble and red porphyry – a spiral path. At the centre was a tree, shimmering with white flowers.

Viviane felt tears come to her eyes, but of a very different kind to the ones that she had shed before. These were healing tears: tears of joy. She stepped on to the white marble path and walked the spiral to the centre. With each turn she learned something new about something she had thought she had known fully before. When she came to the tree she put her arms around it and leant her cheek against its bark. The fragrance of its flowers was more potent than the scent of the finest incense. Among the leaves three birds were singing.

'At the centre of the Soul is the Tree of Life, rooted in the Earth and reaching to Heaven. It is in flower now, but when it seeds, its seeds will be the Spirit.'

Their voices had no sound . . . only light.

She knew that the Green Lady would not be far away.

The soul might return time and again to the Earth – and the future may hold many sorrows for it. But the Spirit . . . Ah! The Spirit soared . . . the Spirit could fly beyond!

Suddenly she remembered the green cord at her waist, and looked down. She had not noticed that it had been unravelling while she was walking. She started to retrace her steps, winding it around her hand as she did so, expecting soon to reach the end of it and return it to her waist. But it seemed to have grown immensely long. And her heart did not falter as she followed it back into the labyrinth of tall buildings.

This time she noticed things she had not noticed before. She saw children playing and laughing in a waterfall from a rainwater gutter; she saw lovers kissing under a broken street-lamp; she saw an old couple sitting at a window, talking quietly. She noticed flowers growing out of the cracks in the walls, and a dandelion shedding its ballerina seeds on to a pile of rubbish.

She half hoped she would meet her double again. This time she would know what to say to her. *'There is a way out,'* she would say. *'Though beings may deny their true nature until almost all is lost, their true nature remains, in spite of their denial, and can at any moment be reclaimed.'*

She reached the final gateway and took a deep breath of relief as she stepped out into the open.

She had been away a long time, and her companions must surely be extremely worried about her. She ran through the little copse like a young doe and burst out breathlessly on the other side, ready to tell her tale. They were calmly saddling up the horses and getting ready to ride on.

Caradawc smiled at her as she appeared. 'Did you have a good walk?' he asked cheerfully. 'We thought we'd move on now.'

She stared at him in surprise. It was clear that time had hardly moved since she had left them.

After a while they came to a fork in the road and were in a quandary as to which path to take. One seemed to wander off towards the south and the other to the north. Neither went to the east. Should they stay on the road in the hope that it would turn east eventually; and if so, which branch of it? Or should they set off across country? They were just debating the question when a rider appeared from the south: a tall, handsome young man in scarlet, fit to be a king's companion. He greeted them cheerfully as he came level with them.

'On the way to the marriage feast?' he asked amiably.

'We know of no marriage feast,' Caradawc said politely, 'but we'd be glad of some advice as to the road we should take if we want to reach the other side of those rocky hills.'

'The road you want lies close to the castle,' the young man replied. 'I'd be glad of your company,' he added with a smile at both the young women, 'if you'd care to ride with me.'

'What do you think?' Caradawc asked, turning to Viviane.

'How far is the castle, sir?' she asked thoughtfully. A diversion might in the long run prove quicker if they could travel on well-made roads the whole way.

'Not far, my lady, not far at all – and I'm sure the good lord will insist that you rest a while and feast with the rest of us on venison and wine before you resume your journey.'

'We haven't time for that, sir, but we'll gladly accompany you until we join the right road.'

Viviane wondered about the young man. He had appeared just at the time when they needed to know the way. Had he been sent to guide them?

Caradawc rode beside him, listening to tales about the bride's father and his vast estates, his riches, his skill in training falcons, his beautiful wife and daughters. Caradawc felt compelled to meet his boasts with boasts of his own, and he was soon enthusiastically exaggerating the merits of Castle Goreu.

Viviane rode with Idoc, while Olwen, still low in spirit, brought up the rear.

To the east of them was high, barren country; to the west the pleasant land that they had ridden across all morning was green and fertile, well ordered and cultivated.

At length they saw the castle, high on a hill, its battlements fluttering with flags. Surrounding it, on the lower slopes of the green hill and in the valley, were the colourful tents of the wedding guests.

Viviane rode up to join Caradawc and the young man in scarlet, who she discovered was called Sir Lionel. The stranger turned his head and smiled at her.

'I urge you to reconsider, lady,' he said earnestly. 'The delay will do no harm, and the rest and refreshment can only be beneficial. Besides,' he added with a naughty look at the two young women, 'my reputation would be greatly enhanced were I to be accompanied there by two such beautiful ladies.'

Caradawc laughed and tried to catch Viviane's eye, but he could see that she seemed irritated. She was frowning thoughtfully. Was this man a way-guide or not? She was beginning to doubt it.

Before she could speak they were joined by a group of riders coming in from a side road; all gaily and richly dressed; all talking and laughing noisily. They greeted the young knight with enthusiasm, slapping him on the back and admiring his clothes, which were indeed extraordinarily elegant. He enlisted their help at once in trying to persuade the travellers to join, however briefly, in the festivities. Viviane tried to resist, but somehow – and she was afterwards never quite clear how it happened – they were swept along and found themselves being jostled through the gateway of the castle by a boisterous crowd.

'Will it matter so much?' Caradawc whispered to her. 'We need not stay long and, who knows, this may well be part of the quest for the emerald. He *did* appear just when we needed him!'

Viviane did not know what to do. She turned to Olwen. 'What do you think?' she asked. From Olwen's expression it was clear that she, like Caradawc, would be glad of a diversion and some good food.

The decision was made for them by a group of girls who danced around them, dragging them laughingly off their horses and garlanding them with flowers. Viviane was soon separated from her companions, and was led into the castle. She looked back over her shoulder to see what was happening to the others and saw that they were undergoing much the same treatment. None of them seemed to mind, and she told herself that she was being over-cautious. It was a pity to delay the finding of the golden feather and, hopefully, then the emerald, but she could not be sure that this whole diversion was not part of the quest. Another thought weighed with her: perhaps a really joyful festival might help to remind Idoc of the good things of life and strengthen his will to live.

The castle was magnificent, far grander than Castle Goreu, and even, she thought grudgingly, grander than her own father's. She had a twinge of homesickness and wondered if she would ever see her childhood home again; the sea washing around the roots of the rocks on which it stood: on summer days wooing it, in winter lashing at it angrily and spitefully like a rejected lover . . . She thought about her father's chair, the throne of the High King of six kingdoms, carved by Celtic craftsmen from oak, the horned god Cernunnos giving his protection. She thought of her mother's little Christian chapel built at the foot of the hill on which the castle stood. There was always the sound of the sea there, and on sunny days the flickering light reflected from water playing on the wall opposite the tiny mullioned window. She wondered why she was thinking of these things now and decided it was because she longed for that time when her parents made the decisions for her. She was suddenly weary of the burden she was carrying for Idoc. Had her father felt the same when he sat in his great chair, his chin in his hand, pondering day after day the problems and petitions his people brought to him?

The girls hurried her along a wide corridor at the end of which was a huge door with elaborately carved panels. She was still gazing with astonishment at its heavy burgeoning of fecund nature – plants and animals twined and intertwined until it was impossible to tell where one ended and the other began – when the door swung open and she was led into a huge, low room, panelled heavily in dark wood and carved all over just as elaborately as the door; but this time the figures were of men and women and animals, all in the act of coupling, in every possible position and with every possible combination – the whole giving an impression of grotesque and obsessive sexuality. A group of young women were clustered in front of a tall mirror in a heavy gilt frame. One – presumably the bride – was being attended by the others.

As soon as she saw Viviane, the bride smiled and reached out her hands to her. 'Welcome,' she said.

Seeing her close by, Viviane realized that she was very young, barely thirteen, her pink and white complexion as virginal as the petals of a newly opened lily.

'I hope you don't find our arrival an intrusion, my lady,' Viviane said nervously. 'My companions and I were intending to pass by, but we met a young man called Sir Lionel, who insisted that we attend your wedding.'

'Of course!' the child laughed. 'Sir Lionel would! But don't worry – you're most welcome. Everyone is welcome!'

Viviane bowed. The bride's sisters continued to weave long ribbons into her hair and fuss around her. All around the paraphernalia of childhood was still evident: the dolls lying on the pillows; a fading nosegay of wild flowers picked with the stems too short; a large play-ball of unspun lamb's wool covered with triangular pieces of different-coloured cloth. And all of this overlooked by those depraved carved figures on the walls and ceiling.

Viviane's sense of unease increased. There was something out of harmony here. She wanted to leave, but she was not sure how to do it politely. At that moment one of the sisters came up to her and suggested she might like to borrow more suitable clothes than the ones she had on, for the wedding. Viviane tried to refuse, but the woman took her arm and propelled her to one side of the room, where gowns of every kind and colour were hanging.

'This one, I think,' she said, taking down one of blue silk and holding it against Viviane.

'I would really prefer to stay in my own clothes,' Viviane protested. But the sisters crowded round, as if to imply that it would be an insult to their parents if she appeared in her travelling clothes.

'You must stay for all the celebrations,' the young bride cried. 'There'll be feasting and dancing and music and juggling and clowns and acrobats ... everything!' Her face glowed with delight at the prospect. 'It should go on for days and days!'

Viviane's protests were ignored and she found herself being stripped, swiftly and efficiently, of everything she had on, including the Green Lady's cord. The whole thing was done with such apparent good humour – the faces around her never ceasing to smile, the voices crooning sweet compliments – that she did not know what to think.

It was only when the hands of the smiling women around her began to touch her body a little more than they need – a casual brush against the breast here, a stroke of the thigh there – that she realized that if she were not careful she would be taking part in a scene that would not be out of place if carved on the wall in this oppressive chamber.

She began to push away their hands, but when she did so, the smiling ceased and their gropings became rougher and more insistent. They were no longer playing games, and she was no longer fooling herself. Sir Lionel was no way-guide, but one of Ny-ak's men. She was now sure of it. The separation of their little party had been deliberate. She began to fight to get away, but they restrained her. She thought she would appeal to the young bride, but she was preening in front of the mirror and seemed neither surprised nor concerned at what her sisters were doing.

There was no mistaking their intentions now and Viviane was revolted at their pawing and their lascivious cries. She fought fiercely and broke away at last, running from the room naked, but clutching her clothes. One last backward glance, to ascertain whether she was being followed or not, revealed the sisters busy with each other, the bride still twisting and turning and admiring herself in the mirror.

She must find the others. Where should she begin? The corridor was deserted but she could hear the hum of voices not far away. She pulled on her clothes hastily, and then paused just long enough for the agitation of her breath to subside before slipping quietly out to join the throng of people making their way noisily towards a chapel where the marriage ceremony was presumably about to take place. The people around her looked ordinary enough and she could not decide whether or not they were involved in Ny-ak's plot. As with her own wedding, the servants and peasants and tenants stayed outside, while the lords and ladies, the companions and relatives of the bride and groom, finely dressed, went into the chapel. She saw no sign of her companions and assumed that they must have already gone into the building. From outside it looked larger than any of its kind she had ever seen, but when she stepped inside she caught her breath. She had never seen anything like it. Tall, slender columns seemed to reach up forever. She looked up and up, and still her eye travelled, to a ceiling . . . no, to a tree canopy made of delicately carved stone. The walls were almost entirely of glass, so brilliant in colour that it would seem some amazing craftsman had sliced through giant gemstones and fitted them piece by piece to form pictures fit for angels. Surely this must have been designed as the most holy place on Earth? Surely here one's heart would soar easily to the Most High with the sheer splendour and magnificence of it all. How different from the lowly stone chapel of the hermit at the Community of the Fish.

Almost dwarfed by the loftiness of the nave, the people crowded in, and, as she was carried along in the stream still pouring down the aisle, she found it very difficult to see if her travelling companions were there. The feeling that they were all in danger would not leave her, and she sent out anxious calling thoughts.

At last she spotted them – just as the trumpets sounded for

the arrival of the bridal procession. They were standing near the front, beside Sir Lionel. Caradawc had turned round, and was straining his neck to peer over the sea of heads. When he saw her his face lit up and he nudged Olwen beside him. She turned at once, but Idoc did not move. She tried to signal them to join her but Caradawc indicated that it was impossible, hemmed in as they were.

Viviane then looked over her shoulder.

The young bride was coming up the aisle, and a shower of white rose petals was falling on her from every direction. The silver sound of the trumpets reverberated in the high, fine vaulted ceiling. Every head was turned to admire her. Behind her walked her five sisters, dressed magnificently, their faces calm and composed, giving no sign of what had occurred in the bride's chamber such a short while before.

As the party neared the space in front of the altar, the groom rose and stepped forward. Curious to see what kind of man would marry such a green child, Viviane stood on tiptoe to catch a glimpse of him. As he turned to face his bride, she saw with horror that it was Gerin.

She looked quickly at Olwen and by her expression knew that she had recognized him too. White-faced, Olwen had lifted her hand to her mouth and was biting into the knuckles.

If Viviane had not already sensed that there was something very wrong with their visit to this castle, she would have had no doubt now. Even if it was conceivable that Gerin should rush off and marry the first woman he saw in order to forget Viviane, these elaborate arrangements could not have been made in the short while since he had ridden so angrily away.

Viviane made a decision. She stood up on the bench and shouted as loudly as she could.

'Gerin! *Gerin!* This is a trap. You mustn't go through with this wedding!'

Startled, he swung round and their eyes met. For a moment she thought he would not even recognize her, but his feelings for her were still so strong that they broke through the spell he lay under. From his suddenly changed expression she could see that he had woken up – that he saw her and he knew who she was.

'Run!' she called urgently. 'Caradawc! Olwen! Idoc! Run!'

She herself leapt down again and pushed her way through the astonished crowd. She hoped that if they moved quickly enough, they might just make it to the door before they were stopped.

But what actually happened she did not expect. Something in her voice, the vibrations of urgency, of sincerity, of love . . . something she might have learned in that ancient life as priestess which she now no longer consciously knew . . . this something must have affected the source of the energy that held the whole elaborate scene together. For suddenly everything seemed to tremble, shimmer, disintegrate . . . The tall windows of jewelled glass disappeared, and there were gaping holes now between fragments of ruined stone walls. The altar crumbled to dust, the shining trumpets vanished. Above them on every jutting piece of stone or broken candlestick perched the voyeurs, crowing with delight.

The bride? Ah, the bride! She was no lily virgin now, but a crone older than the hills.

Viviane, Gerin, Caradawc and Olwen were almost at the door when Viviane realized that Idoc was not with them. She turned immediately. Sickened as she was by the scene before her, she could not abandon Idoc. He was kneeling where the altar rail had been, a huge figure in a cloak of shadows holding a crown above his head. Viviane saw the jewels flash, the gold glimmer. Shafts of light streamed through the broken roof, illuminating the scene, dust motes in the air catching the light and making its rays seem almost solid.

Caradawc put his hand on her arm.

'You can do no more for him,' he said. 'He has chosen. Let him stay.'

'No,' she said. '*He* hasn't chosen. It is Ny-ak who has. See, Idoc is in a trance. He has been tricked like we were. I will not leave him!'

As she began to run back, the voyeurs nearly fell off their perches attempting to get a better view.

Her hair streamed out behind her like fire.

'Idoc!' she called. '*Idoc!*'

The huge figure in front of Idoc put up his hand. She could

not see the face under his hood, but she knew that his eyes could see the end of the world, and that she was of no more moment to him than a mayfly on a summer's day was to a man who lived three score years and ten.

She suddenly felt the force projecting from his hand. She could move no further forward.

She drew herself up to her full height and silently commanded her body to stop trembling.

'Ny-ak,' she cried out fiercely. 'You *cannot* have this being. He has his own destiny.'

It seemed to her that every creature in that vast shell of a building screamed with laughter. The little watchers beat their sides and rolled about, some even falling from their vantage points to be smashed to death on the paving stones far below, unnoticed and unmourned by their fellows. The larger creatures thronging the floor of the ruined church slapped each other on the back with delight.

With a great effort she did not waver. 'Idoc, look at me!'

Slowly he turned. His eyes shone strangely. 'You are wrong, Fiann,' he said. 'He has the emerald. See – in the crown. I will make my vows to him and I'll be saved.'

'Idoc, look again! He offers you nothing. See how all his finery has turned to ugliness and dust. *That* is not the true emerald. Look again!'

The splendour of the building had seduced her too – but now she saw that it had been an illusion hiding the worst evil of all: the misuse of the Name of the Nameless One. Behind Ny-ak were the shadows of the stake, the rack and the gibbet, but he had hidden them well . . . His familiars were dressed in the vestments of the true priests and so were almost indistinguishable to the casual observer . . .

How she wished she had her amethyst with her now so that she could show Idoc by clear-sight just what that crown really was. But she had nothing left of all the gifts she had been given. The rose-crystal sphere had served its purpose. The power of the quartz crystal had sent the black knight's charger fleeing, and broken Idoc's scrying mirror. And without the amethyst the dark tower would still be standing. The crystals had served her well – but she had none left. Even the Lady's green cord, which had given her courage and led her out of the labyrinth, was gone, lost to the bride's grotesque sisters . . . Alone, what could she do?

But Brendan had taught her a great deal in the brief time she had spent with him. She had no power crystals now, no talismans, no spells, no charms . . . but she had her Self – grown slowly to strength through trial and pain. She was no passing shade, but a true being, heir of all the realms . . .

She pointed at the crown, concentrating everything she had ever learned of truth and light in the long centuries of her life.

She held steady till Idoc looked back to where she pointed – and saw Ny-ak's giant form begin to shake with the strain of meeting the accusation of her eyes . . . The shining crown began to lose its lustre, its golden glory – until it was no more than a lopsided ring of rusty iron. The 'gems' oozed from their settings like some disgusting liquid, burning the fingers that still clutched them. Then the fingers themselves began to break away – to fall, knuckle by knuckle, until the mighty hands that had held the crown were no more than dry bones in dust.

Suddenly a wind sprang up – strong and dark and fierce. The creatures of Ny-ak howled as they were torn from their places and hurled across the cavernous building . . . battered against the ruined walls . . . trampled underfoot as they tried to run . . .

Viviane leant against the wind, fighting to keep her place . . . her long hair pulled and tugged and swirled around her . . . but she did not take her eyes off Idoc, nor drop her pointing finger.

She saw the desolation in Idoc's eyes. Once again he had been duped; once again he had chosen the shadow rather than the substance. At last she lowered her hand and reached out her arms to him . . .

The five of them found themselves standing alone at the place where the two roads forked . . .

They looked at each other in awe.

They all remembered quite distinctly and separately what had happened – and yet here they were back where they had started . . . but this time Gerin was with them.

14

Despair

They decided to allow no more diversions, but to head straight across country towards the ridge of hills behind which they hoped to find the lake. Viviane and Idoc rode ahead, keeping very close together, deep in conversation – Caradawc behind them, morose and brooding, wondering if he would ever have Viviane to himself or indeed if they'd ever be free of Idoc. Olwen followed Caradawc silently, busy with her own thoughts. They questioned Gerin about his role as bridegroom. It seemed the bride's father had offered him lands and riches beyond his wildest dreams, and he had accepted without even seeing the bride.

'You'd marry a total stranger?' Olwen asked in astonishment.

Gerin shrugged.

'You'd do better to marry Olwen here,' Viviane suggested quietly, and Olwen had flushed scarlet.

Gerin looked at her then, long and steadily, as though seeing her for the first time. And then he turned, away. 'Olwen deserves better,' he said. 'I could give my wife no love.'

When they reached the ridge their progress was slow, the horses having to pick their way carefully among the loose boulders and rock stacks. Sometimes it seemed as though they would not be able to find a way, but then one of them would notice a break in the rock and they would pass through, only to find that still ridge after ridge confronted them. Though not high, these were difficult to negotiate on horseback, so for a while they walked and led the horses. But even this was slow and tedious work. Viviane was looking very flushed and out of breath. Twice

Olwen asked her if she felt all right, and twice she replied rather sharply that she did.

At last they decided to rest, Idoc's beast having developed a slight limp. Gerin and Caradawc attended to it while Viviane sank thankfully to the ground, resting her back against a rock. Olwen climbed up a little further, to see if they were any nearer their goal. She was just out of sight of the others when she heard a sound to her left and spun round. On a flat platform of rock near by stood the three mysterious young women she had seen in the farmer's barn. Gossamer fine, their silk robes floated out on the breeze, almost transparent with the sunlight shining through them. Their bones seemed like rock crystal, their eyes like amethyst. Their thin hands reached out to her, and it seemed that they were trying to speak but could bring no earth-sounds from their slender throats . . .

'Who *are* you?' she whispered. 'What do you want with me?'

There was now no doubt in her mind that they were be-seeching her for help; but she could not understand what help they expected her to give. 'If only Viviane were here,' she thought. 'She'd know what to do.'

'Wait here,' she then said softly. 'Wait while I call my friend.'

But their agitation only increased and they fell down on their knees before her, arms reaching out in supplication. Olwen trembled. Instinctively she sensed that they were the soul-forms of the three infants whose lives she had saved on the farm. As soon as this thought took hold, she could see the relief on the faces of the three beings before her. They rose and beckoned her to follow them. She took a step towards them, but already they were fading and dissolving like mist at the touch of summer sunlight.

Olwen stood still for a few moments, her heart pounding, wondering what she should do. Was it the wind through the holes in the rocks that made that sound of mournful sobbing?

She scrambled down and hurried back to her companions. It was clear to her now that the three infants were in danger again and she must go to them.

Viviane opened her eyes and looked up at Olwen in surprise

when she announced breathlessly that she must leave the group and return at once to the farm. For some hours now the princess had been feeling ill. Her forehead was burning, and her hair stuck to it damply. If Olwen had not been so agitated herself she would have noticed that her mistress's eyes were shining feverishly.

Viviane had never felt so much in need of Olwen's care and attention, but she said nothing to hold her back when she heard what Olwen had seen.

Caradawc at once suggested that Gerin should accompany Olwen for her protection.

'I think we should stay together,' Gerin replied quickly.

Viviane looked at him impatiently, her face very flushed. 'Go with Olwen,' she said curtly. 'Such visions are not sent lightly.'

She could see that her brusqueness had hurt him, but she felt too tired to try to repair the damage. He turned sulkily away from her and, seizing the reins of his horse, started down the rocky hillside.

Olwen gazed after him sadly. She could sense his reluctance to accompany her, and she herself felt reluctant to leave Viviane.

'For God's sake, go!' Viviane snapped. Another few moments and Olwen might notice how ill she was and refuse to leave her at all. Much as she longed to keep her friend with her, she knew that the sending of the soul-forms must have been a truly desperate measure, and that something very important hung on Olwen's answering their appeal for help.

Olwen gave Viviane one last tormented, apologetic look, then hurried after Gerin.

'Well,' said Caradawc doubtfully as he watched them go, 'I hope we *can* manage without them.'

'We'll have to,' said Viviane.

He looked at her suddenly. Her voice was strained and strange, and he was just in time to catch her in his arms as she fell fainting to the ground. As he touched her, he felt how hot her skin was. 'Viviane!' he gasped.

Idoc moved forward instantly. 'What's the matter?' But he could see at once what the matter was.

Caradawc was now fumbling to wrap his cloak around her, his hands trembling. 'Go and fetch Olwen back,' he cried.

'I'll not leave her,' Idoc replied sharply.

Caradawc gave him a startled look. 'We need Olwen.'

'You fetch her,' Idoc said firmly. 'I'll not leave Viviane's side.'

Caradawc stood up, his face distorted with rage. 'Damn you! Not only will you leave her now, but you'll leave her side for ever!' he shouted. 'You are destroying her!'

But Idoc took no notice, he was crouching beside her, his face lined with suffering. He knew the signs. He knew what ailed her. Had he not himself given this dread disease to countless men and women whom he considered enemies? Her eyes were glazed. She was conscious and yet not conscious. She stared at them both with her fever-bright eyes and did not see them. They could see that she was in agony.

Furiously Caradawc seized Idoc's shoulders. 'What have you done to her, you fiend?'

'Nothing. I've done nothing,' muttered Idoc. 'Once I wanted her to suffer . . . but not now . . . not now . . .'

Caradawc flung him impatiently to the ground and started to run down the hill, calling desperately for Olwen. But Gerin and she were already too far away to hear, and he soon came storming back, out of breath and sweating, furious with himself for leaving Idoc alone with Viviane even for such a short while.

He found Idoc squatting beside her, chanting strange and outlandish words, his face as frantic and despairing as Caradawc's own.

'What if she should die?' Caradawc thought in despair.

Since she had come into his life, he had no thought nor purpose, no dream, no waking moment not intimately bound up with her. His life had not seemed empty before he met her, yet now he realized that it had been. He could barely remember what his thoughts had been then, what his ambitions. It was as though he had passed his life in a kind of daze, and she had awakened him.

A sudden horrifying thought struck him. Idoc was not physically alive in the sense that he and Viviane were alive. What if Idoc was trying to bring about Viviane's death so that she could join him in that other realm?

He rushed suddenly at Idoc and knocked him away from Viviane's side. 'You monster!' he shouted. 'You damned, vicious monster! Leave her alone!'

Idoc reeled for a moment and then bitterly hit out at Caradawc.

Viviane tossed her head from side to side, the shadows closing in, her life ebbing away while the two men who loved her fought each other, filled with hate.

It was Caradawc who first gained the advantage, but it was Idoc who struck the blow that finished the fight. Caradawc staggered back, lost his footing and fell crashing against the rocks, rallied briefly, lost his balance again, and continued to fall down the hill, helplessly grabbing at bushes and boulders until a blow on the side of the head rendered him unconscious.

Idoc watched him go with satisfaction.

Above him Ny-ak stood in the shadows, watching also with satisfaction.

'Go to him. Use his body,' the dark angel whispered. *'For the last time, in the flesh, hold Fiann, hold Viviane . . . then let her die and join us.'*

His whisper was like the sound of wind through dry grass.

Idoc shook his head dazedly and hurried back to Viviane. Her hair was almost black with sweat, her breath rasping.

He crouched beside her, suffering as he did not remember ever having suffered before. He loved her and she was being punished for what he had become. He looked up at the giant shadow of Ny-ak and there was hate in his eyes.

'Let her be!' he hissed. 'Release her!'

'If she dies, Caradawc will not have her.'

Idoc howled like an animal in pain.

'But if she dies now, like this, with nothing resolved between us . . .'

'Hurry,' whispered Ny-ak. *'Both are at your mercy.'*

On every rock the voyeurs perched, breathless and watching. The sun was going down, the darkness growing. Ny-ak's shadow stretched a great distance across the landscape. If he lifted his cloak and swirled it, all would be enveloped, and a darkness darker than the night would lie over the land.

Idoc was aware of his own utter loneliness. Viviane was no

longer there to sustain him with her strength or lead him where he should go. Everything was now up to him.

He took her in his arms, her damp cheek again his own. He yearned to feel her, but he felt nothing – only the agony of indecision . . . the agony of regret.

Ny-ak moved nearer, smiling, confident that all would be as it had been.

But Idoc wanted to give Viviane a gift, and he knew what she wanted more than anything in the world.

He stood up and faced Ny-ak. 'No!' he said resolutely.

The air crackled around him. Lightning flickered like the tongue of a serpent across the sky. Thunder rumbled among the rocks.

But Idoc stood his ground.

Groaning, Caradawc regained consciousness, struggled to his feet and began to climb, pausing from time to time to hold his head as though it gave him considerable pain.

Idoc stood and watched him approach.

Ny-ak had disappeared, but Idoc knew that he would not be far away. Heavy raindrops were beginning to fall like hammer blows on Viviane's head.

'Hurry!' Idoc urged Caradawc silently, watching his slow progress with impatience. Soon it would be pouring a deluge, and there was no shelter for Viviane. He knew that if he leaned over her the rain would pass right through him. But Caradawc was solid. Caradawc would be able to protect her from the rain . . .

Olwen had soon caught up with Gerin. He nodded briefly to acknowledge her presence, and then ignored her. She could tell even by the way he sat his horse that he was still resenting Viviane's words. She followed him in silence, keeping well back, out of his way.

She began wondering what kind of reception they would receive from the farmer. He had made it clear that he was not pleased with her interference before, and would no doubt be even more displeased at any interference now. Perhaps Gerin had been right: they should leave well alone, and keep together on the emerald quest. But then she heard that strange mournful sobbing again. And this time there was no wind.

She rode up close to Gerin and asked if he could hear it too. He shook his head.

'There it is. There!' It seemed to her very distinct now – the wailing of children in fear or pain. The sound was not coming from the direction of the farm, but from a wooded valley in the east. To her it was very real. To Gerin it did not exist.

'Please wait,' she cried. 'Gerin, I think we should find out what is happening there.'

He reined in and sat for a moment with his back to her. His irritation showed in every line of his body. And then he seemed to pull himself together and turned in the saddle.

'Forgive me, Olwen. I've no right to treat you this way.'

She shrugged, smiling awkwardly, not knowing what to reply.

He turned his horse around. 'I'll follow. You lead,' he said, and his voice was much gentler.

They reached the wood at last and rode in under the shadow of its trees. It was not deep, merely a fringe of trees on either side of a river. As soon as they entered it they could hear water lilting musically over rocks. The sound of crying had ceased.

When they emerged from the trees they were astonished to find themselves surrounded by a host of dancing figures. Some had flutes and some had tambourines, but the dominant sound was the rippling of the harp. All were clad in wisps of trailing silk in river-colours – different shades of blue, bound with silver ribbons. The flowers in their hair were predominantly silver-grey and white – and even their skins had a bluish-silver sheen.

Without a word Gerin and Olwen slipped down from their horses and stood entranced.

The lines of dancers dipped and rose, and turned and flowed as a river flows.

'Look,' Olwen whispered, touching Gerin's arm. 'Leading the dance – those three young women. I think they're the ones I saw . . .'

Suddenly they were surrounded by a flow of dancers who garlanded them with flowers and took their hands. Gently but

215

firmly they were pulled away, at first stumbling awkwardly, and then without effort, moving with the dance as though they had always been a part of it. They were passed from hand to hand, dipping and turning and flowing, until they found themselves near the head of the line. Olwen noticed that the touch of the river nymphs was cool and light and sent a bubbling, tingling feeling through her limbs.

At last they were close enough to Olwen's three mysterious ladies to see them clearly. Were they river nymphs too? Their skin was as silvery, their hair as long . . . but there was something about them that was different. Olwen could not decide exactly what . . . They smiled at her and beckoned her on. She followed unquestioningly, with Gerin, now intrigued, close by her side.

After a while the river flowed under an overhang of rock and into the hillside. Without pausing, the dancers flowed in with it – and Olwen and Gerin with them. At the entrance they noticed that those around them were removing their coronets of flowers and throwing them into the water. Olwen and Gerin found themselves doing the same. The flowers floated along, swirling in spirals and circles as the water carried them into the darkness.

At first Olwen and Gerin found themselves half blind as the dimness of the cavern contrasted with the brilliance of the sunlight outside. But soon lights appeared, bobbing about on the water, and the whole place became gently illuminated. Each flower was now a lamp. Some were carried strongly forward by the current; while others, caught in side eddies, accumulated in little pools around the edges, their light reflected off the low rock ceiling in a thousand shimmering ways.

As they progressed deeper into the hillside, the river fell down in a series of steps. The flower lamps, swirling wildly on the brink of each, fell down at last with the water, momentarily disappearing and then re-emerging undimmed in the pool beneath.

It became increasingly difficult for them to dance as the rock floor at the side of the river became more and more uneven. At last they were no longer dancing at all, but picking their way carefully behind the three young women. The music had ceased without their noticing it, and the other dancers had fallen back and disappeared. The cavern was now very silent apart from the swish of the water, and Gerin and Olwen found that they were treading carefully, trying to make no sound themselves, occasionally whispering to each other to avoid this hazard or that.

At length they came to a place where the path narrowed to a tunnel and they had to pass through it on their hands and knees. On the other side they were almost blinded by daylight. They had emerged on the other side of the hill and beside them the river leapt joyously off a ledge of rock and fell, singing and shining, to a small lake far below.

In the centre of the lake was a forested island and the towers of a castle, apparently built entirely of transparent crystal, were showing above the trees. The three young women led them down a rough set of steps covered in fern and moss, to the water's edge, where a boat was drawn up waiting for them. Gerin took Olwen's arm to help her into the boat and sat with his arm around her as they were rowed to the island. Her heart was beating very fast now, but she questioned nothing. The young women did not speak.

The lake on the lee of the island was very still, and very deep. The boat glided in among the images and shadows of a water forest, hardly disturbing the fishes that swam among the reflections of the trees . . .

As they stepped on to the island they looked up and saw a vaulted roof of dazzling leaves carried high above them on ribs and arches of living wood. Their feet sank into the soft, deep pile of leaves that had fallen and lain undisturbed for centuries. They followed in silence, and were led through the forest to the castle. There it seemed to them that they were at the heart of a crystal looking outwards, the forest's intricate splendour of green and gold light glimmering through the walls and passing through the bodies both of the young women and of themselves. Olwen stood close against Gerin, her back to his chest, his arms around her from behind. It seemed to her, now that she was so close to them, that the three were more human than the river nymphs, and yet not as human as she was. She had heard legends of mortals marrying faeries, and had wondered how this could be . . .

They were led into a crystal chamber as richly furnished with plants as the forest outside the walls, and were shown a couch of polished hazelwood, strewn with silken cushions. Above it vines, reaching to the sunlight, hung in leafy strands to form a canopy.

Then she heard whispering . . .

It seemed to come from all around her . . . three voices whispering together . . .

> *'We are of no world and of two . . .*
> *lost between worlds . . .*
> *Ai . . . ai . . . i . . .*
> *Waiting for a birth that will bind us*
> *to one or to the other . . .*
> *Ai . . . ai . . . i . . .*
> *Three from the ancient times . . .*
> *Three daughters of the Green Lady . . .*
> *The Lady of the Emerald . . .'*

Olwen started, and Gerin's arms tightened around her.

'Your father . . .?' breathed Olwen – for the first time too curious to remain silent.

She couldn't understand the answer at first. The light had dimmed as though a cloud had crossed the sun.

Gerin asked the same question, more boldly.

This time they heard the answer . . . sharply . . . clearly . . . bitterly.

'Idoc!' they heard, and the word was almost spat out.

> *'Idoc, the vehicle of Ny-ak . . . presumed . . . dared . . . to*
> *touch the Faer Lady, the Lady of Leaves . . . Ny-ak and*
> *he together . . . took by force . . . ai . . . ai . . . ai . . . held*
> *and ravaged . . . held and ravaged . . .'*

The lament faded away . . . the echoes very faint yet taking a long time to die.

Olwen held her breath. How closely they were all linked! How complex the drama that they were playing out.

'Long . . . long . . . long ago,' breathed the air around them. *'Long ago . . .'*

There was so much pain in the sound – so much regret. Was

it the Green Lady herself who moved through the island forest, listening to her daughters? They thought they saw a figure shimmering with green light stepping from behind a tree . . . but it disappeared again almost at once.

Within the chamber the crystal light returned and the three young women stood close beside Gerin and Olwen.

'Why me?' Olwen asked. 'What do you want of me?'

> *'We have tried many births and they have failed . . .*
> *in one coffin now lie three small bodies . . .*
> *man rejoicing . . .*
> *woman weeping . . .*
> *But you were sent to us and you will understand us . . .*
> *You will give us life in your world . . .'*

Olwen was silent, remembering Kicva's curse. She was to bear no children. What did they mean?

'Perhaps,' she thought, 'perhaps because they would not be children quite like other children.' She stood very still, becoming increasingly aware of the physical presence of the man she loved. Had the three soul-forms disappeared – or was it that she no longer noticed them? Gerin was kissing her hair. Gerin was kissing the nape of her neck. She turned in his arms and he touched her lips with his. She reached up to him and he lowered her on to the couch . . . Close and closer . . . within and without . . . deeply loving . . .

She had not thought even in her dreams that there could be a feeling as potent and as precious as this. She was poised on a breaking wave, yet for that moment it felt like eternity . . .

When at last Olwen opened her eyes, Gerin was up on his elbow looking down wonderingly at her. They were back on the grass of the riverbank where they had first climbed down from their horses. There was no sign of the crystal chamber, the forested island; nor of the three young women.

'I'm sorry,' he muttered. 'I shouldn't have done that.' There was a touch of bewilderment in his expression. It had been good with Olwen – as good as if he loved her.

'It's all right,' she whispered. 'We were sent for.'

'What do you mean?'

'Don't you remember anything? The dance . . . the river running into the hill . . . the lake and the island on the other side?'

He shook his head, puzzled, but she could tell that he remembered something. He looked down at her in a way that he had never looked at her before. Her hair, blue-black, was spread out around her head, small twigs and leaves of grass caught up in it. He had never noticed before how deeply tranquil her eyes were. He leant down and kissed her very tenderly but very lightly on her forehead.

With no more words said, they stood up. Gerin paused a moment before he mounted his horse, looking back over the saddle at Olwen, long and soberly. She had pinned up her hair again and was as quiet and calm a figure as she usually was. Never as magically beautiful as Viviane, but as she had lain under him on the grass, she had blossomed into a beauty that he would not easily forget.

She knew that he was looking at her and she flushed, fiddling nervously with the stirrup strap on her own steed. Would he resent her for having received what he would rather have given Viviane? Would he return to his old indifference now that there was no supernatural influence drawing him to her? She used to think that if he would only make love to her once, she could live the rest of her life on the memory of it – but she knew now that making love once was not enough. She would never cease to long for him – and abstinence now would be far more painful than it had ever been before.

'What are you thinking?' she asked shyly, her mouth very dry.

He smiled. 'I was thinking,' he said, 'that Viviane was probably right. I should marry you.'

Her heart gave a lurch. She longed to cry out 'And will you?' but she held herself back. She stooped down to look at her mare's hoof so that he would not see her face.

When she stood up he was beside her.

'And will you have me?' he asked, his brown eyes smiling into hers.

She was flushed and speechless – but she managed to nod.

He laughed and lifted her up. He swung her round, then put her on her horse. He did not kiss her.

'I can't promise to forget Viviane,' he said, a shadow of seriousness crossing his face.

'I wouldn't expect it,' Olwen said.

'Do you think it is possible to love two people at the same time?'

'Yes,' she said. Did not Viviane love both Caradawc and Idoc – and possibly Gerin too?

'Is it possible to love three daughters equally?' her own heart inquired. Yes. For she already loved the three conceived in her womb that day. 'And Kicva may curse all she likes,' she thought. 'No human curse can carry against a true destiny.'

The night seemed very long. Caradawc held a shivering Viviane in his arms, trying to keep her warm; while Idoc sat beside them, brooding. He was already regretting his histrionic rejection of Ny-ak the afternoon before. He had done it for Viviane's sake, but she was not even aware of it. He was no longer sure that he wanted to make the effort to change direction. Ny-ak promised him immediate and effortless power. Was that not what he wanted above all else?

But he was no longer sure even of that. There had been a moment, as he rejected Ny-ak, when he had felt a surge of energy and excitement far superior to any he had ever felt before. But it had passed, and now, in the darkness – listening to the grating of Viviane's breath as her body struggled to hold on to the physical world – he suffered. He had begun to glimpse what love truly was and he was frightened. In love he might have to surrender *himself*; in loving he might no longer be the master . . .

Just before dawn he made his decision and left.

He did not have to search long for Ny-ak. One call – and he was there.

By first light Viviane and Caradawc were alone.

The sunlight woke Viviane first, and she found herself almost suffocated under the weight of three cloaks and Caradawc himself. She struggled free and, in doing so, woke him. He looked at her in astonishment. Her eyes were clear and, although she was very pale and there were dark rings under her eyes, she seemed miraculously recovered.

Their delight at this gave way to alarm on Viviane's part when she discovered that Idoc was missing.

'We must find him,' she said at once, struggling to her feet. But she was still weak, and Caradawc had to hold her upright.

'You're in no state to find anyone,' he protested. 'You need rest.'

'There's no time for rest . . .'

'There'll be no time for anything if you *don't* rest! Don't worry about him. He'll come back.'

'No,' she said. 'I can feel it. He has left us completely.'

'Then let him go.

'No!'

'We have our own lives to live.'

'But don't you see – we can't go forward until we've undone the harm we did in that other life. We're fighting for our own freedom here as much as for his.'

'We've done all we can. We've really tried. Surely that's enough?'

'We've not tried everything yet. We've not found the emerald!'

He shrugged. 'Well, if you believe we'll ever find that!'

'I do believe it. And I *will* find it! You may come with me if you want to, or you may go back home. If I have to do it alone, I will do it alone!'

He looked at her. Her face seemed feverish again, but this time with anger. She was gathering up her belongings and straightening out her clothes from the discomforts of the night. Only Idoc's cloak, which had been laid over the others, was still wet from the rain, and she pushed it aside.

'Are you coming?'

'Are you going to search for Idoc – or are you going to look for the emerald?'

'First the emerald. I believe that with the one I will find the other.'

Caradawc watched her as she prepared to leave. He was exhausted: he had passed through the worst night of his life for physical discomfort and emotional distress. He had thought that she was dying and he had been prepared to give up his life to be with her.

And here they were quarrelling.

'Viviane,' he said quietly.

'What?' she snapped.

'I love you.'

She looked at him, startled.

'If you go on, I will go on. But I would rather return home.'

She stared at him in dismay. She was ashamed of her impatience and anger. 'I'm sorry,' she said in quite a different tone of voice. 'But I must go on.'

'In that case I'll come with you.'

She looked relieved. She held out her arms to him. 'I love you too, Caradawc, and when this is all over . . .'

'Ay,' thought Caradawc, holding her close, 'when this is all over . . .'

At last Viviane and Caradawc reached the most eastern of the ridges and stood looking down on the landscape beyond. Eagerly they scanned it for the lake – but there was no sign of it.

Viviane felt close to despair. The last few hours of their climb had been gruelling, feeling as weak as she did, but she had been sustained by the thought that if they could only climb the last ridge the worst would be over and the emerald would soon be within their reach. Caradawc, knowing her disappointment, put his hand sympathetically on her waist. He was not expecting to find the gem, and indeed had never really believed that it existed – but for her sake he had hoped somehow . . .

She did not remember a forest beside the lake. It had seemed to her that the feather landed in open country, and that the lake was a shining sheet of water that must be in clear view from any high place. What was wrong? Why could she not see it? She sat down with her head on her knees and wept. She was so tired, so very tired . . . She could sense that Caradawc no longer believed in what she was doing, and was impatient to go home. Idoc had escaped, and Brendan had said it was important that they kept him with them until by his own choice he started on the upward journey through the Realms. Perhaps she had failed already and there was no hope for Idoc. Perhaps that was why she could not see the lake. Would it be so terrible if they gave up now and went home? They had done their best, as Caradawc had said. She really felt that she could not bear any more travelling, any more seeking, any more strange and difficult adventures.

She tried praying for guidance, but she was too tired to pray, and her thoughts went round and round in circles.

'Caradawc,' she sighed, 'I'm beaten. Let's go home.'

He was delighted and decided at once they would not go back the way they'd come but look for an alternative route. The countryside ahead of them was criss-crossed with lanes and he could see an occasional farm cart trundling along. Nearer the villages, people were working the fields. Everything seemed very peaceful and normal. He foresaw no difficulty in finding someone to give them directions.

He looked back at Viviane and was shocked at her expression. She had always seemed stronger than he, full of courage and resourcefulness. Now she was sitting on the ground with her knees drawn up in front of her and her head down on her knees, defeat and despair in every line of her body.

He had wanted to give up and he had wanted to return home, but he realized that for her to give up meant much more. He hated to see her so low. She reminded him suddenly of Idoc as he had been when they had found him at the foot of the hill after the tower was destroyed. Both had been driven by a purpose larger than themselves; both had lost that purpose, and with the loss had believed that they had lost everything. Like Idoc, she had 'given up on life'. He knew that he could not let that happen to her, just as she had known that she could not let it happen to Idoc. They must go on.

He would find the lake and the emerald for Viviane. It would be his marriage gift to her.

Ny-ak had taken Idoc back to his tower in triumph. It had been completely rebuilt, though Idoc, looking at once for the old familiar things, found that it was not quite the same.

Ny-ak, sensing his dissatisfaction, promised him that everything he required would be instantly provided.

'Just say the word,' his voice resounded in Idoc's mind.

Idoc paced about the octagonal chamber. There was a mirror: but it was not his mirror. There was a table: but it was not *his* table. He felt out of place where he had felt so totally at home before. He was glad to be back and yet . . . and yet . . .

'What is the matter?' Ny-ak asked sharply.

'I don't know,' Idoc muttered. 'Something . . . something . . .'

'We need to be together again,' Ny-ak coaxed smoothly, ingratiatingly. *'You were nothing without me – and you will be nothing again if . . .'*

Idoc frowned. He remembered how his powers had multiplied the last time he had taken Ny-ak into himself. But did he want to go the whole way this time? He would like to see how he could manage on his own . . . He was now suspicious of Ny-ak's claim that he was nothing without him. Fiann had loved him long before Ny-ak took him over. He was then in line for High-Priest: honoured, respected for his knowledge and his skills. And had he not become 'nothing' *after* . . .?

Ny-ak's visage contorted with rage. It was that mere mortal woman! She had done more damage to his vehicle than he had thought. She must be destroyed. At once a hundred ways of destroying her came to mind, each more horrible than the last. Then he hesitated. If he destroyed her while Idoc still loved her, Idoc might turn against him and shut him out forever. No, he must be more cunning. Idoc himself must destroy her.

He led Idoc to the mirror.

'Look!' the demon urged.

The dark surface became milky. Ny-ak laid his hand on it and drew it across. As he withdrew his hand, Idoc was presented with a scene so real in every detail he could have believed he was looking through a window at something happening only a few yards away. Caradawc and Viviane were making passionate love, and Ny-ak spared Idoc no detail.

He tried to turn away, but Ny-ak forced him back.

'Wait. There is more.'

Idoc endured it all: every desire he had ever felt for Fiann was violated. She cried out Caradawc's name as she had once cried out his own – and at the end they lay talking about what a good life they would have now that Idoc was gone.

'I *never* loved him,' she was saying. 'At first I feared him . . . then I felt sorry for him.'

225

'Yet you told me you once promised you would never desert him unless he consented,' argued Caradawc.

'That was just a trick – I never meant it. If he hadn't left us I would have found some other way out of that promise, never fear.'

She sounded so callous, so cynical . . . and jealousy clouded Idoc's reason.

Ny-ak smiled, pleased with his deception.

A tormented Idoc swung round. 'I believed in her! I trusted her!' he wept.

'Look again. Hear what she says now.'

'No,' snapped Idoc. 'I have heard enough. She will *never* break that promise to me! And I will *never* let her go!'

'Better still,' thought Ny-ak, 'two vehicles instead of one! Let him bring her back to the tower. Let him bind her to him until he breaks her spirit. That would be a revenge far more satisfying than merely the destruction of her physical body.'

He stood back and watched Idoc pace the room with rage.

'Leave me!' snapped Idoc. 'This is something I must do myself'

Ny-ak bowed and, with a last backward glance of satisfaction at his handiwork, he left.

'Viviane,' said Caradawc at last, afraid to let her brood longer. 'Come. We can't stay here. We must go on.'

She lifted her head slowly and looked at him with sad, inquiring eyes.

'I think we should go on, not back,' he said firmly. 'We've come so far.' He held out his hand to help her to her feet. Gratefully she accepted it and rose to stand beside him. She looked helplessly at the landscape below them.

'But there is no lake,' she said.

'Just because we can't see it from here, doesn't mean it doesn't exist,' he said. 'It must be down there somewhere. We'll ask the local people. We'll find it, the lake at least, though I can't promise the emerald,' he added wryly.

Her body seemed to straighten like a drooping plant that had been given water.

'Do you feel well enough to go on?' he asked. She was still very pale and drawn.

'Yes. O yes!' she said joyfully, something of her old spark returning. 'You're right. We can't give up now.'

The change in her was beautiful to see, and Caradawc had never felt so close to her.

Hand in hand, leading the horses, they started down the rocky slope to the wide valley floor.

Meanwhile, Gerin and Olwen were on their way to rejoin them: each with his or her own anxieties about the meeting. Gerin felt growing affection for Olwen now, and did not want to hurt her, yet he could not be sure how he would react when he saw Viviane again. Olwen had her own fears. Once she nearly suggested that they set off and seek a new life for themselves somewhere far from Viviane and Caradawc and all the problems of Castle Goreu. And once this had crossed Gerin's mind, too. But both had hesitated and the right moment for saying such a thing had passed.

As they drew nearer to where they expected to find their friends, the silence between them grew more tense.

15

Lucifer's Emerald

Once on low ground Viviane and Caradawc were shocked to find all was not as pleasant, green and flourishing as it had appeared from the safe distance of the rocky ridge. Bushes and trees all seemed deformed and diseased. Their leaves were twisted and curled and darkened, their stems livid with mould. Not a single trunk grew straight and true. Even the birds seemed dispirited. One hopped across their path on a single leg, its wings ragged, almost featherless.

When they reached the edge of the cultivated fields they could see that the wheat crop was equally affected. The whole crop was blighted and brown, not an ear worth saving. The peasants themselves were skeletal-thin. Most of them didn't even look up when the strangers passed, and those who did gave such an impression of surliness that Caradawc could not bring himself to ask them directions. Instead they made for the village they could see in the distance. But there it seemed things were no better: ragged people stood about idly and listlessly, singly and in groups, as if aimlessly waiting for time to pass. But, sensing a diversion at last as the two strangers appeared, everyone gathered round them, staring.

'Let's get away from here,' Viviane whispered. They reminded her of the voyeurs. There was something horrible in the way they were all closing in, peering, watching, as though she and Caradawc were some kind of freak-show sent to entertain them. As Caradawc cleared his throat and began to ask about the lake, Viviane could see he was equally disturbed by the attention they were receiving but was trying not to show it. The villagers ignored his question and continued to stare, jostling each other for better viewing positions, several reaching up to touch and tug at their clothes. Caradawc tried to turn Osla around, realizing that they would get no help here, but the bridle was held tight and the crowd surged forward threateningly. When Viviane and Caradawc instinctively drew back, they were pulled off their horses, then pushed and prodded and poked and passed from one foul-smelling villager to the other.

Viviane was terrified. She could sense that open violence was not far away. The mob was bored and here were outsiders to torment! The touching and prodding were becoming rougher and she and Caradawc had now been separated. More and more people seemed to be arriving, and with each addition the atmosphere grew more charged, more dangerous.

'Foreigners!' the crowd began to hiss.

'What ya come here for?'

'There's no place here . . .'

'Go back where ya come from . . .'

Blows were beginning to fall. Stones were being flung.

Oh God, thought Viviane, would they ever get out of this nightmare? Their horses had been led away and were nowhere in sight.

Suddenly the mob gave way and, like a miracle, Gerin and Olwen came riding through, hooves thundering and scattering their tormentors left and right. Frantically they grabbed at the saddles and hauled themselves up while the horses were still moving.

Only when they were well clear did they dare stop to clean up – and then discuss what they should do next. They were quite a distance away from the ridges of rock they had so painfully negotiated earlier, and now deep in the countryside they had observed from above. The sun was setting and a noxious-smelling fog seemed to emanate from the ground, spreading across the fields towards them. It hung close to the earth, no higher than their stirrups, but still it meant they could not easily see where the horses were stepping.

'Should we try to go back to the ridge?' Caradawc asked finally.

'We would have to go back past the village,' Olwen pointed out.

'Never!' said Viviane, shuddering.

They felt very vulnerable, for this was like no countryside they had ever seen. A feeling of tremendous evil hung over it, increasing with every lengthening shadow.

'The best we can do is find a reasonably high spot away from this stinking fog,' Gerin suggested. 'Then keep close together and take it in turns to stand guard all night.'

They were beginning now to suspect that the vision of the golden bird, the feather and the lake had been sent to mislead them – just as had Sir Lionel. As soon as the dawn came, they decided, they would get as far away from this place as they could.

But it was still a long time until dawn.

They settled eventually on a mound that rose like an island above the level of the fog. The horses were hitched near by – stamping, snorting, pulling at their tethers nervously. Sleep was not going to come easily this night.

Viviane and Olwen lay together for warmth under the two remaining cloaks, for Caradawc and Viviane had lost theirs to the mob. Gerin and Caradawc sat together at the highest point, ostensibly to keep watch, but the two young women could hear the low murmur of their voices for a long time. Occasionally they rose, stamping around in an effort to keep warm.

Viviane brooded about Idoc – remembering her promise never to leave him unless he should tell her that she might. She had started to regret that promise as soon as it was uttered, but she knew she could not go back on it. She was ashamed now that she had so nearly given up on her quest, and frightened too, for her only chance of ever being free of Idoc was for him to choose to be free of her – and without the help of the emerald she felt they did not stand a chance of that. Caradawc seemed to assume that Idoc had left her already, but she knew that he had not; and she knew also that as soon as she found what they were seeking, she would have to find Idoc whether he wanted to be found or not.

What would this mysterious jewel be like, she wondered, and what were their chances of finding it? She tried to sleep, knowing that she needed the strength of body and clarity of mind that sleep would give her, but it would not come. The events since she had followed that hart in the forest to the blind stone circle on the hill now passed and re-passed through her mind, and throughout she traced the slow unfolding of her understanding about the realms and levels of being through which we make our long life's journey.

'Are you asleep?' Olwen whispered, knowing well that she was not.

'No,' Viviane confessed sadly.

'Do you mind if I tell you something?'

'Of course not.' She was glad of a rest from her thoughts. 'What is it?'

Having initiated the conversation, Olwen was now at a loss for words.

'Is it about Gerin?' prompted Viviane. She had already noted the subtle change in their relationship. When it had come time to take their positions for the night, she had noticed the secret look that passed between them. She hugged Olwen. 'I'm glad,' she whispered.

'Is it so obvious?'

'Couldn't be more so!'

Olwen flushed and laughed. 'I'm so happy,' she said.

'I know.'

'I shouldn't be, when we're in such danger, but I just can't help thinking how happy I am.'

'What happened about the three soul-forms?' Viviane asked. Olwen told her, knowing that she could tell Viviane anything and everything, and there would be no misunderstandings.

At midnight Olwen was sleeping soundly but Viviane still lay awake. Glancing up, she suddenly realized that they were surrounded by a circle of tall, silent, hooded figures, darker than the moonless night itself. Terrified, she looked over at Caradawc and Gerin, who were supposed to be on guard; but they too were sleeping. She summoned the courage to call out, but found her throat was too constricted with fear to utter a sound. If she lay very still and pretended that she were asleep, might they leave her alone? But that was a forlorn hope. She had the feeling that those eyes – if eyes there were under those dark cowls

– could not so easily be deceived. It was a wonder the hammering of her heart did not wake Olwen.

Time passed, and still the figures did not move. The uncertainty of their intentions began to drive her crazy. Anything – anything was better than this waiting!

Gradually anger began to take the place of fear and Viviane decided to act. Carefully she rose to her knees, then stood up. She was trembling, but determined to give a good account of herself. She did not even try to use her vocal cords, but demanded in thought who they were and why they stood there.

She waited for a reply, but none came.

Angrily she repeated the mental question, growing bolder.

Still no reply. She was surrounded by silent hooded darkness, and brooding malevolent presence.

On the third questioning she shouted aloud. 'Who are you? Answer me!'

Caradawc jerked awake and hurried to her side, dagger drawn.

'What's the matter? Who are you shouting at?'

She pointed, anger giving way to terror again. Why would they not reply?

'Where?'

'There,' she said. 'All around us. Can't you see them?'

Caradawc stared where she was pointing; stared all around them. He saw nothing – no one.

'Can't you see them?' she shrieked, clutching his arm. 'There! There! There!'

'There's no one there,' he repeated firmly.

Gerin had joined them now, and Olwen was stirring.

'She says she can see people surrounding us,' Caradawc explained.

'Where?' said Gerin. He too could see no one.

Finally Viviane could bear it no longer. She rushed forward to beat at the dark figures with her fists, cursing them furiously. Startled, her companions watched, and could see nothing but a frantic woman beating and shouting at empty air. Then, suddenly, she disappeared.

At first they thought she must have fallen over the edge, and confidently expected to find her lying bruised and shaken in the slimy, creeping fog at the foot of the mound. The two men went at once to look for her, leaving Olwen still half asleep. She heard them calling out to Viviane, lightly at first, then in growing alarm. There was no sign of her at all.

As Viviane's fist had lunged at the first dark, hooded figure it passed right through, and she experienced a cold so intense she would never have believed it possible. Even if she had been on a dead world cut off from its sun, so distant from any source of heat or light that it had never known warmth of any kind, it could still not have been as cold as she now felt this. It was the cold of the ultimate negative, the cold of the void.

Too late, she tried to draw back. But she could not – and fell headlong into that cold and the darkness, and all feeling, all thought ceased.

How long she remained in that state there was no means of her knowing. The World of Changes, where time could be measured before and after and during, had ceased to exist for her. And then scenes and events from her long spiritual life began to reappear to her, but she could not tell if they were from the past or from the future – and she did not care. The tower often appeared in these scenes. Strangers stood where Idoc had stood. Some called their work 'sorcery' and others called it 'Science', but all had one thing in common – they did not understand the truth of what they were and what they were doing. Spears became heat-seeking missiles; and though the language of those who ordered their use might change, the same motives drove them and by the same justice they were ultimately destroyed.

Suddenly Idoc was beside her. She could clearly see his face, cold and hard. Behind him stood the same dark, hooded figures whose faces she could not discern at all.

'You left me,' he reproached. 'You broke your promise.'

'No,' she said. 'You left me. I am still seeking the emerald for you.'

'You seek it for Caradawc and yourself.'

'No!' she protested.

'You cannot lie to me. I listened to you when you were not aware of it.'

'Then you would know that what you say isn't true.'

His eyes flashed darkly. 'Once you bound me,' he said, ignoring her last remark.

'I also released you,' she said hastily.

He ignored, this too. 'It is now your turn to be bound.'

She looked in horror at the dark figures behind him. Was she to have to pay in full: to suffer what he had suffered; to be limited to one place and one time – never to journey through the realms and regions of that mighty scheme which even the archangels did not fully comprehend?

As though he read her thoughts, he answered her question. 'No,' he said. 'I'll not do to you what you did to me. The binding of which I speak is between you and me.'

She looked at him quickly, questioningly.

'Step forward,' he commanded and held out his hands to her.

She hesitated. Was there any way she could escape? The sinister figures had not moved, yet now they formed a tight circle around them.

'Idoc,' she pleaded. 'We are bound and have always been bound by our destinies. There is no need for this.'

He was close to her now, looking down into her eyes. He was as handsome and as tall as when he had been her lover in that other life; and she trembled with something of her old desire. But his eyes were dark and full of bitterness. 'You tried to leave me.'

'No!'

He gripped her suddenly by the wrists and she cried out with the pain. He nodded at the figures ranged around them. 'Begin!' he commanded.

Slowly the hooded figures moved, gliding in a circle. At first she thought she heard a strong wind arising, but then realized it was them, the swish of their robes and the sinister whispering chant of the binding spell. She tugged and pulled desperately, but could not release herself.

'Idoc,' she cried. 'I gave you my word. There's no need for this.'

'You will never leave me!'

'Unless you say I may!' she sobbed.

'I will never release you!' he declared fiercely. 'There's no end to your tricks – and I will not fall victim to them again. *You will never leave me.*'

It seemed to her that as the fell figures moved, invisible bands of amazing strength were being wound around Idoc's body and her own, pulling them closer and closer together . . .

In the morning sunlight the landscape revealed to Caradawc, Gerin and Olwen was very different from the sombre, grotesque landscape of the previous evening. Before first light the fog dispersed, and they found themselves on a green mound full of buttercups, shimmering green woods stretching off to the north, meadows of sweet grass and flowers to the south; and to the east, catching the gold of the sun, a vast and shining lake.

They stared at it in astonishment. Viviane's lake. But there was no Viviane to view it with them.

They searched for her frantically, scarcely noticing now the beauty of the scene. Even Olwen, who had been so happy, could not enjoy her own happiness any longer.

At last, after hours of fruitless effort, they gave up in despair, and sadly talked of going home. But none of them wanted to leave the place without her.

It was Olwen who took the initiative finally. 'We should continue looking for the emerald,' she said firmly.

'Without Viviane the whole thing is pointless,' Caradawc said gloomily.

'I don't believe so,' Olwen said. 'We know her disappearance must have something to do with Idoc. The emerald was to help us free him from Ny-ak's influence. If we achieved that – surely Viviane, too, would be released.'

'*If* we found it! And *if* we could find Idoc . . .'

'We *will* find it,' Olwen said confidently. 'We *will* find Idoc!'

Caradawc shrugged, unconvinced and totally despondent.

'It's worth trying,' Gerin broke in. And after more hesitation Caradawc reluctantly agreed.

But where to begin? Olwen wished she felt as confident as she sounded.

'We were directed to this lake,' she murmured thoughtfully, 'so surely it is here that we'll find it.'

The three of them stared out over the lake. Its placid waters seemed to extend forever, silver-grey with hardly a ripple. A heron flew over effortlessly, its reflection swimming beneath it.

'It's no ordinary lake,' Olwen sighed, 'but it's no ordinary gem that we're looking for. There will be a way of finding it, but it won't be the way we expect. I suggest we *let* it happen rather than try to *make* it happen.'

The shoreline was edged with fine dove-grey pebbles and pure white crystal sand. Near by, the water rolling the pebbles had excavated small tunnels and caves under the roots of a huge old oak tree that leaned over the lake. In some places the roots had grown round the pebbles, enclosing them, so that rock and tree seemed to be of one substance – as they had appeared to Viviane in the Green Lady's chapel.

It was Gerin who first noticed a boat drawn up on the beach, and they ran towards it. But it proved to be only a small canoe: far too small to carry the three of them.

'It was probably intended for Viviane,' Olwen commented, 'but I think one of us should use it.'

'I'll go,' said Gerin at once.

'No, I will,' Caradawc argued.

But Caradawc was too heavy for it – and so was Gerin. They turned to look at Olwen. Without a word she climbed into it, and they pushed her out on to the cool, clear waters. Looking down she could see tiny fish darting over the white sand, weaving in and out of the golden ripples. As she glided further from the shore, the water became deeper and the fish larger. A great salmon leapt out into the air with a marvellous curving movement – glinting silver briefly in the sunlight before it returned to its own medium with a sound as musical as the plucking of a harp.

'I wish, dear God,' Olwen whispered, 'that Viviane were here. But as she isn't, please let me find the emerald . . . and with it Viviane.'

She discovered that she did not need to use the paddle at all, because the canoe seemed to slide through the water by itself, the wake silver behind, a path of gold ahead. Surely she had already travelled further than the distance to the furthest shore?

Looking back, she could no longer see either Gerin or

Caradawc. She thought she should be frightened, but in fact felt no fear. Instead she felt amazingly peaceful and happy. The canoe stopped suddenly, and she sat there in the warmth of the sunlight, smiling at the beauty of it all – almost forgetting why she was there. Leaning over the side she gazed down into the water. It was so clear that she could see to the white crystal sand of the lake-bed.

On it lay, in full view, a huge emerald, its many facets catching the light from different angles as the water stirred and rippled gently over it. She held her breath in awe and delight.

'Ah, poor Lucifer,' she thought, 'to lose such a gem!'

As she slipped into the water, the canoe rocked wildly, and the disturbance to the water caused the rays of light from the jewel to break up and scatter as though a million emeralds had been at that moment flung into the lake. Twice she dived, and twice she missed the true gem by seizing only its reflection – but the third time her hand closed on the real one, and she drew it up to the surface with her.

She had to struggle to get back into the boat, but then set off at once for the shore. By contrast, returning, she had to paddle very hard, the huge emerald resting in her lap.

Suddenly a shadow passed over her and she looked up in alarm. High, high above her a gigantic bird circled, coasting on the thermal currents of air, watching her keenly. Even from this distance she could make out a wing-span wider than the greatest eagle, the beak hooked and sharp, the talons deadly dangerous. But its feathers were the purest gold and she realized that this must be the fearsome, beautiful bird that Viviane had witnessed.

Olwen folded her skirt over the emerald protectively. Had the mighty creature merely been waiting for her to retrieve the jewel – and now intended to snatch it away before they even had a chance to use it?

She heard a shout, and to her joy saw Gerin wading into the water to greet her. He put his hand on the edge of the boat and leant forward to kiss her, before even asking if she had been successful.

'You disappeared across the water,' he said. 'I thought I'd lost you forever.'

Her happiness knew no bounds. Triumphantly she held up the gem. As the sunlight caught it, a blaze of green light almost blinded them all. Then words seem to flow from her unbidden as she stood on the lake-shore clasping the extraordinary jewel – strange words and strange names that meant nothing to her. A sudden mist began to roll in from the shining lake, and it billowed like smoke along the shore. For a moment her companions could not see her, and then just as suddenly it lifted, revealing everything as it had been before – except for one extra figure.

'Idoc!' yelled Caradawc, rushing forward. 'Where is Viviane?' he demanded angrily.

'She is here.'

'Where?'

'With me. She is mine now and you will never touch her again.'

Then they saw her: a grey, submissive form a step or two behind him – her shoulders hunched, all life and strength drained out of her, hardly recognizable.

'What have you done to her?' screamed Caradawc. Furiously he tried to seize him, but found he could not. Idoc's figure looked solid enough, but when Caradawc reached for him, there was nothing there.

'Idoc,' Olwen cried out, 'forget the images of your dark mirror. We have found the emerald. See!'

'I see no emerald,' Idoc said coldly, deliberately not looking at what she held in her hand.

'Here!' she persisted. She could sense that he was struggling to resist the temptation to gaze at the amazing jewel.

'Viviane!' commanded Olwen. 'Look at the emerald.'

Idoc raised his hand as Viviane started to take a step forward. 'No!' he said; and she retreated at once, her chin sunk on her breast, her long grey hair half covering her face.

'Look up, Viviane. Look up!' urged Olwen.

'I cannot.' Viviane's voice was faint and expressionless. 'I belong to Idoc . . . I owe him . . .'

'No! You owe him *nothing!*' cried Olwen. 'All has been paid. You have given him another chance – and you yourself are given another chance.'

She brandished the jewel in the air, and the air swirled and shimmered with green light – brilliant shafts of it probing deep into their hearts . . .

Idoc and Viviane looked up, startled.

Inside the gem they saw the image of themselves – and what they had become.

'Idoc,' pleaded Viviane. 'Release me. Let me go!'

He turned to look at her, a terrible suffering in his face. As he hesitated, it was as though everything in existence was waiting and listening for his answer. There was no sound. No movement. The emerald light itself took on a different quality. It was now still and steady. It cast no shadow; it hid nothing.

Everything was clear and in sharp focus, from the tiniest ant in the grass to the mightiest tree, from the darkest thought to the brightest. Idoc understood at last that he could never possess the woman he loved, because, in possessing her, everything that he loved about her ceased to exist.

He spoke at last, and they could sense how painful it was for him to say these words.

'Go,' he said. 'You are free. One day I will look for you again; and on that day I will be worthy of you.'

Viviane stepped forward joyfully, colour flooding back . . . a life and a will of her own returning. She raised her arms and spun around, delighting in the feel of the air on her skin again.

And then she paused to look back at Idoc. He was already beginning to fade from sight.

The joy in her face died. She reached after him, calling his name . . .

'Let him go,' Olwen urged quickly. 'He has chosen a new start . . . Is that not what you wanted?'

Viviane dropped her arms. Yes, that was what she wanted – but something of herself was being torn away as she watched him go. She looked back at Caradawc – and he could see what she was going through. Would he ever be sure of her? Would she ever love him as she had loved Idoc – through everything . . . in spite of everything?

Olwen touched his arm. 'She loves both of you,' she said quietly. 'But no two loves are ever the same. You will lose her if you demand it.'

Caradawc looked down at her. Her strength had supported

them when they wanted to give up the quest. Her eyes were steady. He trusted her. Gerin stepped forward and put his hand on his friend's shoulder.

'It's true,' he said in his deep voice. 'Olwen knows.'

None of them noticed the bird until it swooped. The huge wings flapped as the creature hovered for a moment, golden light rippling from its feathers, the air churning so violently that they had to cling to each other to prevent themselves being blown over. Olwen screamed as its beak lunged towards her hand. And then the mighty being rose to the sky, taking the emerald with it.

Viviane ran forward, shaking her fist at the sky.

'Bring it back!' she cried. 'Bring it back! The Green Lady needs it . . .'

But the bird was already no more than a distant golden speck in the azure.

They had barely taken the mystical jewel into their possession – and it was already gone. Shocked and stunned, they stood staring into the sky – Olwen sobbing to think how nearly she had lost her hand.

A sound made them return their attention to earth. Standing at the edge of the lake, with the silver water lapping about her feet, stood the Green Lady, tall as a young rowan tree, her robe of leaves rustling around her, cornflowers and the magical five-pointed periwinkle in her hair. She was reaching out her hand to them in greeting, and as her sleeve fell aside, they could see the fine silver-green of her arm. Then she began to sing, her voice hauntingly sad.

She sang of a love she had once had long ago . . . of how they had lived in peace and harmony . . . of how each and every being had enjoyed a place to be and purpose to pursue . . . how each and every being had flourished in harmony with each and every other . . . Then – and her tune grew more measured, more sombre – her lover had cut down the forests and drained the lakes; had ripped open the hills and covered the fields so that no living thing could grow there . . . He had wanted control. He had wanted power. Eventually he had power over all things . . . but it gave him no joy . . . For what he had power over had been changed out of all recognition . . .

Angrily he had left her . . .

Now she was going to call him back . . .

The notes of her song flew out over the lake like silver birds. The hills gave back an echo as fine as harp music. They could hear the yearning in her heart. They could hear the name she called . . .

Ny-ak appeared, tall and gaunt, his eyes hollow, his limbs like the charred branches of a tree that has been struck by lightning.

'Why do you call, woman?' he asked coldly. 'We have nothing to say to each other.' His voice rumbled across the lake like thunder, and they could see dark clouds gathering on the horizon. A wind sprang up and the reeds at the water's edge were shaken like spears before a battle.

'If only we still had the emerald,' whispered Viviane, moving close to Caradawc. They could feel it – the coming conflict.

So the two great angels confronted each other. How could he resist her, Viviane thought: she was as beautiful as a summer's day in a green and temperate land. But he was angry. His human vehicle had deserted him; he had been crossed and thwarted at every turn. He was in no mood for overtures of peace. He raised his finger and pointed at the sun. A black cloud covered it instantly, and from that cloud poured down a thousand demons of darkness – tearing, biting, snapping, screaming, shrieking . . . while the four humans clung desperately to the oak tree at the water's edge to prevent themselves being swept away.

But the Green Lady turned her shoulder to the onslaught and summoned up her own forces. The sun was cleared of cloud again, and from the horizon of the dawn came a host of beings as clear as crystal, as refreshing as rain, spreading a net over the earth which, where it was touched, sprang into leafy growth – and the demons caught in it were turned to stone.

Ny-ak watched the blessed transformation with bitter anger.

He raised his arms on high and a whirlwind of foul air lifted up the grains of sand, the rocks, the twigs, the leaves, hurling them higher and higher until a solid tower of darkness stood beside them on the shore.

Caradawc held Viviane close.

There were no windows in the tower. Only a door.

The Green Lady stooped and cast a small object at the tower's base. They could not discern it, but it must have been a seed – for the foundations began to crack and a green shoot began pushing through the rock. Fissures spread rapidly, and from every one a growing leaf-bud emerged, until the tower had become a living tree . . .

Ny-ak scowled darkly and drew the sword from the scabbard at his side. No lightning flash was ever as livid as the light that burned from that blade. The tree was felled . . . the tower with it . . . the earth shuddering to receive the debris.

She lifted the lake in her long hands as though it were a cloak of silver silk. She threw it upwards – and as it floated in the air, it rained down a myriad fishes of diamond and amethyst. Then it fell on the flashing sword and clung to it, entangling Ny-ak's arm and impeding his movements.

Cursing, he shook himself free, the sword clattering to the ground wrapped in the embracing silk.

'Ny-ak,' she cried. 'Why do you fight me? We could be lovers and all the world would benefit.'

'Woman . . . I need power. How could I accept an equal?'

'Then you will never know love at all,' she answered sadly.

She turned away from him and took a step on to the dry bed of the lake.

Watching, Viviane and the others saw her pause and then, before their eyes, take root and turn into a tree.

Astonished, they looked back at Ny-ak. Where he had been, another blind tower had risen on the ruins of the old.

Weary as they were, Caradawc, Viviane, Olwen and Gerin all agreed at once to set off for home, and this time, the route seemed direct and uncomplicated. Viviane felt that a load had been lifted from her and, no matter how heavy and tired her limbs were, her heart was light.

On all the journey they said not a word to each other: each deep in his or her own thoughts – turning over the events of the past days . . . wondering about the future.

At the great gates of Castle Goreu, Cai and Elined came forward cheerfully to greet them, for all the world as though they had been a happily married couple for years. Behind them Rheged was grinning. He alone of the friends was not paired off, but he did not seem to mind. For the first time now Viviane felt that her husband's home was her own home, and their future together would be a happy one. As though sensing this, Caradawc put his arm around her waist and led her proudly forward.

Behind them Gerin lifted Olwen from her horse, and, to seal the decision he had made, held her close and kissed her long and deeply, in front of witnesses.

Then there was feasting!

Then there was celebration!

Not one doubted that the dark days were over and all would now be well . . .

APPENDIX

The traditional legend of Lucifer's Lost Emerald

Story, comment and sources from *Crystal Legends* by Moyra Caldecott, also available from Bladud Books.

There was once an archangel called Lucifer, Light Bringer, Star of the Morning. He walked in the City of Heaven as a prince, a favourite of the King of Kings, God of Gods. He was the fairest of the archangels, his raiment fine and rich, the diadem around his forehead studded with precious gems. In the centre was an emerald of the same substance as the emerald rainbow that spanned the sky above the throne of the King of Kings and reflected in the sea of crystal beneath the throne.

It was through this emerald, as through a window in the mind, that Lucifer saw the full glory of God, and we, many regions and realms below the Heavenly City, catching the faint glimmer of it, were in those days encouraged to seek such a glory.

The City of Heaven is beyond our imagining, but it has been said that it is built of gold as transparent as crystal, that its walls are of fine jasper, that it has twelve foundations, each of a different precious stone. From the first to the last they are as follows: jasper, sapphire, chalcedony, emerald, sardonyx, sardius, chrysolyte, beryl, topaz, chrysoprase, jacinth, and amethyst. The city's twelve gates are each of a separate pearl from the Ocean of Consciousness that has been since before the Word was first spoken.

Beside a river as clear as crystal, flowing with the Waters of Life from the throne of the Most High, the Tree of Life grows, bearing twelve different fruits for the healing of all the realms of Heaven and Hell.

In this city are many different orders of being, among them nine different orders of angels, the highest being the Seraphim who draw the hearts of mortals towards the Divine Love, the Kerubim, who pour forth wisdom, and the highest order of all, nameless ones, all-seeing, who occupy thrones close to the Throne of the Most High, Mary herself being one of these.

Below these are other orders of angels, each created for a specific purpose, each with a fixed role to play and a fixed relationship with the Most High.

All were satisfied with this rigid hierarchy, until the Lord of All Himself decided to introduce an interesting maverick into the situation. He created Man in his own image, different from the angels, independent, free.

Pleased with his new creation and knowing that the very freedom he had given Man enabled him, potentially, to rise as high as the greatest angels – though at the same time it was possible for him to sink lower than the lowest – God demanded that the angels should bow down before Man. Some say it was Lucifer led the rebellion of those who, from jealousy of the freedom Man had, refused to bow down to him. Some say it was not, but, in the confusion and the fighting that followed among them – the loyal angels and the disloyal ones – many fell from the Heavenly City to earth and there made mischief among men, determined that they, the new created would never, no matter how hard they tried, aspire to Heaven to sit on the angelic thrones. In the Fall damage was done to Lucifer's diadem, and the Great Emerald was loosened and fell like a green meteor in a shower of light to earth.

Ever since that time Man has sought it, for with its recovery it is believed will come the power to see the Glory of God, and, by seeing, to reach towards it beyond the influence of the fallen angels.

Comment

A legend is often like a kind of cosmic rumour.

There is an image, or an idea, mentioned either in the ancient oral tradition or in work of literature, and because it resonates so appropriately with our experience and expresses so felicitously something of importance to us that we have found frustratingly difficult to express, it takes hold and grows generation by generation into something of greater potency than it originally appeared to be, yet never far from what it potentially was. Other elements accrete to it, giving and taking power to and from the central stem.

Such an image, an idea, is the war in heaven and Lucifer's lost emerald.

It appears first, to my knowledge, in the Bible, in the Old Testament:

How art thou fallen from heaven, O Lucifer, son of the morning! . . . For thou hast said in thine heart, I will ascend into heaven. I will exalt my throne above the stars of God . . . I will be like the most High. (Isaiah 14:12–14)

And then in the New Testament:

For if God spared not the angels that sinned . . . (2 Peter 2:4)

And the angels that kept not their first estate, but left their own habitation . . . (Jude 6)

It appears in the Middle Ages. Lucifer's crown had been given to him by 60,000 angels. One stone fell to earth, and from it was carved a vessel of great beauty which came after many ages into the hands of Joseph of Arimathea. He offered it to the Saviour, who made use of it in the Last Supper. Later it became known as the Holy Grail.

In *c.*1200 Wolfram von Eschenbach claimed that his story *Parzival* came from a Provençal singer named Kyot, who in turn had it from an Arab poet in Toldeo named Flegitanis. It describes the Grail as a miraculous stone that fell from heaven, the 'lapsit exillis':

*Those who took neither side when Lucifer and the
Trinity fought – these angels, noble and worthy, were
compelled to descend to earth, to this same stone . . .
Since then the stone has always been in the care of those
God called to this task and to whom He sent His angel.
Sir, such is the nature of the Grail.*

*By the power of the stone called 'lapsit exillis' the
phoenix burns to ashes, but the ashes give him life again
. . .There never was a human so ill but that if he one day
sees that stone, he cannot die within the week that
follows. And in looks he will not fade. His appearance
will stay the same as when the best years of his life
began, and though he should see the stone for two
hundred years, it will never change, save that his hair
might perhaps turn grey. Such power does the stone give
a man that flesh and bones are at once made young
again.*

(Parzival, Book IX, pp. 251–3)

In Milton's *Paradise Lost* the war in Heaven is described in
great detail:

*He it was whose pride
Had cast him out from heav'n, with all his host
Of rebel Angels, by whose aid aspiring
To set himself in glory above his peers,
He trusted to have equalled the Most High,
If he opposed; and with ambitious aim
Against the throne and monarchy of God
Raised impious war in heav'n, and battle proud,
With vain attempt. Him the almighty Power
Hurled headlong flaming from th' ethereal sky,
With hideous ruin and combustion, down
To bottomless perdition, there to dwell
In adamantine chains and penal fire,
Who durst defy th' Omnipotent to arms.*

(Book 1, lines 36 – 49)

his hand was known

> *In heav'n by many a towered structure high,*
> *Where sceptred angels held their residence,*
> *And sat as princes, whom the supreme King*
> *Exalted to such power, and gave to rule*
> *Each in his hierarchy, the orders bright.*
> *Nor was his name unheard or unadored*
> *In ancient Greece; and in Ausonian land*
> *Men called him Mulciber; and how he fell*
> *From heav'n they fabled, thrown by angry Jove*
> *Sheer o'er the crystal battlements; from morn*
> *To noon he fell, from noon to dewy eve,*
> *A summer's day; and with the setting sun*
> *Dropt from the zenith like a falling star*

(Book I lines 732-45)

The references to the story are so numerous that I cannot quote them all, but I will give one more, this time from *The Secret Teachings of All Ages* by Manly P. Hall (p. xcix) because he has gone into the ancient mystery teachings more than most:

> *The Lapis Exilis, crown jewel of the Archangel Lucifer,*
> *fell from heaven. Michael, archangel of the sun and the*
> *Hidden God of Israel, at the head of the angelic hosts*
> *swooped down upon Lucifer and his legions of*
> *rebellious spirits. During the conflict, Michael with his*
> *flaming sword struck the flashing Lapis Exilis from the*
> *coronet of his adversary, and the green stone fell*
> *through all the celestial rings into the dark and*
> *immeasurable Abyss. Out of Lucifer's radiant gem was*
> *fashioned the Sangreal, or Holy Grail, from which*
> *Christ is said to have drunk at the Last Supper.*

The Grail group of legends is one of the most powerful in the Western tradition and draws for its strength, as all good myths do, on our deepest human experiences and for its symbols on our earliest cultural memories.

The Quest is our most universal and enduring human experience. The quest for meaning and purpose in our lives; the quest for reassurance that there is some kind of permanence or afterlife; the quest for love and satisfaction, both physical and spiritual; the quest for knowledge and wisdom and maturity. We symbolize it in our myths and legends constantly, often linking it with that haunting feeling that we have once had the very wisdom and knowledge and sense of purpose we seek, but that somehow we have lost it . . . Shambhala . . . Shangri-la . . . Eden . . . Atlantis.

The Grail legends rise from this need to seek for something higher and better in our lives, and for the symbolism in them we draw on cultural memories from both pagan and Christian sources.

It is almost impossible to say what the Grail is other than that it is what we seek and the finding of it will transform us into a higher state of being. Paradoxically, however, we have no chance of finding it unless we are already in a higher state of being.

In the Middle Ages a series of stories seemed to bubble to the surface of our Western consciousness around a single theme, the search for the mysterious Grail, and they were written down from the rich and ancient oral tradition in Wales, in France, in Germany, evolving and changing but always linked to the same characters and the same quest.

In Britain they first appeared among the stories we now call the *Mabinogion*. Peredur, the son of Evrawc, becomes Parzival in the great work of Wolfram von Eschenbach in early thirteenth century Germany, Percival in *The Story of the Grail* by Chrétien de Troyes in France, Percival in Sir Thomas Malory's *Le Morte d'Arthur*. Most of them suggest that the Grail is the chalice that Christ used at the Last Supper; some, Wolfram in particular, that it was a stone fallen from heaven, Lucifer's lost emerald. Some combine the two ideas. The chalice Christ used to institute the first Eucharist was carved out of the Sacred Emerald that fell from heaven.

My theory is that Lucifer's mysterious and powerful emerald glimmers in the mythic imagination throughout history and throughout the world, appearing in ancient Egypt in the possession of Horus ('Horus, Lord of the Green Stone': *Pyramid Texts*, Utterance 301), and as the Wisdom Book of the God Djehuti (Thoth) that glowed in the dark, was lost and sought as fervently as any Grail, and reappeared at last in the form of an inferior copy about 300 BC as the Emerald Tablet of Hermes Trismegistus – the tablet on which was inscribed in raised letters the tenets of the philosophy that became so influential as Hermeticism.

There is mention of an emerald tablet originally inscribed by Cham, one of the sons of Noah. And there is a link with Melchizadek, king of Salem, who instructed Abraham in esoteric lore, and in whose order Jesus was said to be a high priest. It appears in the legends of Chartres Cathedral, brought by the nine Templars who lived for nine years on the ruined site of Solomon's Temple in Jerusalem imbibing the arcane knowledge of Solomon and Sheba. The name Chartres itself comes from words indicating 'guardians of the stone', and Frédéric Lionel, the eminent French esotericist, in his *Legends and Symbols of the Cathedral of Chartres* (Golden Way Foundation), claims that the magnificent statue of Melchizadek in the central bay of the north porch, is holding an emerald – *the* emerald!

Another intriguing echo comes from Cairo in the ninth century. Caliph al Mamoun, son of the man to whom Scheherezade told her thousand and one stories, made the first incursion into the Great Pyramid in search of a gigantic emerald that was supposed to be buried at the centre. It is through his tunnel that we now enter the pyramid as tourists.

Another branch of the story takes us to India with Alexander the Great who used the power of the emerald to conquer the whole world – but was ultimately lost because he had not learned to conquer himself.

Lucifer's lost emerald presages the loss of Eden by Adam and Eve. It has to be symbolic of the most important quest through all the realms. In the search, we find ourselves. In the finding, we find God.

Sources

The Bible: Isaiah 14:12 and the Book of Revelation.

John Milton, *Paradise Lost*, Book I.

Wolfram von Eschenbach, *Parzival: A Romance of the Middle Ages*, translated by H. M. Mustard and C. E. Passage (Vintage Books, New York, 1961), Book IX, pp. 251-3.

Wolfram von Eschenbach, *Parzival* translated by A. T. Hatto (Penguin Books, 1980).

Peter Lamborn Wilson, *Angels* (Thames & Hudson, 1980).

Gustav Davidson, *A Dictionary of Angels* (The Free Press, New York, 1967).

Emma Jung and Marie-Louise Von Franz, *The Grail Legend* (Hodder & Stoughton, 1971).

Caitlin and John Matthews, *The Western Way* (Arkana, 1986).

Manly P. Hall, *The Secret Teachings of All Ages* (1901; The Philosophical Research Society Inc., Los Angeles, 1977), p. xcix.

John Matthews, *The Grail: Quest for the Eternal* (Thames & Hudson, 1981).

John Matthews, *At the Table of the Grail* (Routledge, 1984).

T. W. Rolleston, *Myths and Legends of the Celtic Race* (Harrap & Co., 1911), p. 407.

Frédéric Lionel, *Legends and Symbols of the Cathedral of Chartres* (Golden Way Foundation).

S. A. B. Mercer, *Pyramid Texts* Vol. 1 (Longmans, 1952), utterance 301, paragraph 457c.

About Moyra Caldecott

Moyra Caldecott was born in Pretoria, South Africa in 1927, and moved to London in 1951. She married Oliver Caldecott and raised three children. She has degrees in English and Philosophy and an M.A. in English Literature.

Moyra Caldecott has earned a reputation as a novelist who writes as vividly about the adventures and experiences to be encountered in the inner realms of the human consciousness as she does about those in the outer physical world. To Moyra, reality is multidimensional.

www.ingramcontent.com/pod-product-compliance
Lightning Source LLC
Chambersburg PA
CBHW020549020726
47494CB00006B/1988